GOLDEN POPPIES

ALSO BY LAILA IBRAHIM

Yellow Crocus
Living Right
Mustard Seed
Paper Wife

GOLDEN POPPIES

LAILA IBRAHIM

To my beloved Julie.
You are a treasure
in my life—always.
♡ & ✧

LAKE UNION
PUBLISHING

Published by Lake Union Publishing, Seattle

www.apub.com

Amazon, the Amazon logo, and Lake Union are trademarks of Amazon.com, Inc., or its affiliates.

ISBN-13: 9781542006446
ISBN-10: 1542006449

Cover design by Shasti O'Leary Soudant

Printed in the United States of America

For the founders who created a living constitution
that could someday apply to me.
For the justice makers who had the vision and determination to make it so.
And for the people who are still waiting for the foundational promise of
this nation: life, liberty, and the pursuit of happiness.

The right of citizens of the United States to vote shall not be denied or abridged by the United States or by any State on account of race, color, or previous condition of servitude.

Fifteenth Amendment to the Constitution of the United States

Ratified in 1870

To the wrongs that need resistance,

To the right that needs assistance,

To the future in the distance,

Give yourselves.

Carrie Chapman Catt

PROLOGUE

JORDAN

I thought my education would protect us—like forged armor too strong for the evils of hatred to penetrate. But I was wrong. Maybe every generation needs to believe they will end the trampling, as if it had not been thought of before. Without that certain and foolish hope, I don't believe we could go on.

CHAPTER ONE

JORDAN

Chicago, Illinois
April 1894

"Well, I guess I ain't never gonna see them beautiful poppies . . . or look on Lisbeth's face again," Mama declared, looking straight at Jordan.

Her dark-brown eyes were glossy. She didn't bother to blink away her tears. Jordan's eyes matched her mother's. She stifled a protest, forcing down the urge to tell Mama she was wrong, that her appetite would come back along with her strength. But there was no point in fighting for a lie. Mama was dying and leaving Jordan forever.

Invisible hands choked Jordan's throat tight. She sat on the bed by her mother, so close she felt a bony hip against her thigh. Her daughter, Naomi, stood near. For weeks they'd searched in vain for something, anything, that would stay in Mama's stomach. The devastating truth, hiding in plain sight, had finally been spoken.

Mama took Jordan's hand, her shriveled thumb stroking the back of it. "I had a good life . . . a ver' good life. The Lord has blessed me more than I have a right to. I ain't afraid to go home." She sighed. "I jus' wish I could see how it all turns out." Mama let out a weak laugh. "Ain't I a foolish ol' woman!"

"Grammy, no one would ever call you a fool," Naomi countered. "You deserve everything you have . . . and more. After working so hard for all of us your whole life, you get to just rest. I'll be back with a tonic to ease your pains."

Jordan was struck by Naomi's calm confidence. Her reserved daughter had somehow turned into this poised young woman.

Naomi left her grandmother's bedroom. The click of the door echoed in the chamber. Dim light filtered through the lone window. It faced a narrow light well, a small gap between row houses that were built right next to one another.

Mama's body had shrunk under her faded quilt. Jordan's gaze traveled across the various fabrics that kept her mother warm—disjointed parts of their lives stitched into a whole. The dress Mama had escaped in was at the center, the homespun plantation cotton still strong and whole, though many of the other fabrics had worn through over the years. Surrounding the rough, enduring material were blocks made from the remnants of Samuel's trousers, Jordan's dresses, and Pops's shirts.

Jordan stroked some of the colorful patches that skipped across the top of the quilt. Whenever a hole wore through, Mama cut a square from the best part of a grandchild's worn-out shirt so "they can warm my spirit whiles I sleep too." Jordan rubbed the pieces of her children's clothes, reflecting on the days when they were young. She ached for the feel of Naomi and Malcolm's precious little bodies in her arms.

Jordan ran her finger over an embroidered red shoe. It was all that remained of the baby blanket Lisbeth Johnson had made for her more than four decades ago—a little girl trying to stitch her way into their family. As a child, Jordan used to imagine herself with a real pair of those bright-red shoes, dazzling the sanctuary on Sunday morning.

The maroon dress Jordan had been married in had become the new binding for Mama's quilt fifteen years ago.

Mama had rejected every offer to make her a new quilt, saying she was going to sleep the rest of her days under the one that kept her warm for so long. Too soon she'd get her wish. Mama would take her last breath underneath the same comforter that covered Pops when he died ten years earlier in this same room.

Jordan picked up the treasured family Bible and rubbed the worn leather cover. Its thin pages were the first words she had ever read. The Lord's messages of hope and faith had been a reliable source of comfort throughout her life, but in the months since her husband's sudden death, the words rang hollow. She'd recite them to soothe her mama, but she didn't expect them to penetrate the pile of pain that covered her own soul.

"Would you like me to read to you, Mama?" Jordan asked.

"Oh, yes." Mama nodded with a satisfied smile. "You know jus' what I need."

Jordan opened to the bookmark, swallowed hard, and continued where they'd last left off: Matthew 5.

"No," Mama interrupted. "Not that. My heart wants to hear Matthew 13."

Jordan sighed quietly. Mama was preaching to her through the good book. She turned the silky pages until she found the passage. Jordan took a sip of water and read in a hushed voice. Mama closed her eyes, a soft smile on her face, as she listened to the parable of the Sower.

13:3 And he spake many things unto
them in parables, saying,

Behold, a sower went forth to sow;

13:4 And when he sowed, some seeds
fell by the way side,

and the fowls came and devoured
them up:

13:5 Some fell upon stony places,
where they had not much earth:

and forthwith they sprung up, because they had no deepness of
earth:

13:6 And when the sun was up, they
were scorched;

and because they had no root, they
withered away.

13:7 And some fell among thorns;

and the thorns sprung up, and choked
them:

13:8 But other fell into good ground,
and brought forth fruit,

some an hundredfold, some sixtyfold,
some thirtyfold.

13:9 Who hath ears to hear, let him
hear.

Jordan continued, knowing that Mama had chosen this

passage to remind Jordan to be good soil for the word of God. Her voice choked up, but she kept going through the assertion that faith was like a mustard seed: small but mighty. Mama patted her hand, comforting the comforter.

Jordan's faith had vanished into the August night with her husband's last breath. They'd been preparing for bed when Booker called for her. She'd found him splayed on the ground against his wardrobe; his brown eyes, round and panicked, conveyed in an instant he was leaving this earth. She knelt by him, straightened his body, and took his hand. She did her best to provide comfort in his last moments. Tears streaming from her eyes, she kissed his cheek and whispered *thank you* into his ear. She rubbed his forehead and patted his chest as he struggled to breathe.

She hadn't called for Naomi or Mama—out of kindness or selfishness, she didn't know. It had just seemed right to be alone with her husband as he passed over. She stayed by him until the warmth left his beautiful brown skin, and her own heart was left cold.

Now Mama was being taken from her. God was testing Jordan and, unlike Job, she was failing.

★★★

When Mama was snoring softly, Jordan crept away from her bedside. Naomi pounced with a demand before Jordan could sit on their worn but comforting couch.

"Ma, write to Lisbeth; ask her to come before Grammy passes over," Naomi urged.

Jordan smiled at her daughter. At nineteen years old, Naomi had stepped past childhood, but the echo of it was still on her face. Her training as a nurse was a blessing in this painful time.

Naomi had finished school just before the turn of the year

from 1893 to 1894, but hadn't secured a full-time position because they'd agreed to move to Oakland. A transition that would be delayed now that Mama's stomach couldn't keep in any food.

Malcolm, Jordan's twenty-three-year-old son, had studied to be a lawyer, but worked as a Pullman porter like his father before him. Last fall he'd been assigned to the Chicago-to-Oakland route. Soon after, he'd begun making the case for them to move west, asserting that a fresh start at life would be good for Jordan's spirits. The bleak February had caused her to agree.

Resistance must have shown on Jordan's face, because Naomi argued, "You heard her. *Poppies and Lisbeth.* Grammy wants to see Lisbeth before she passes. The least you can do is ask. Malcolm leaves for Oakland in the morning—he can deliver a letter. She lives near the place he stays, right?"

Jordan nodded. She felt Naomi's eyes on her, waiting for a reply.

"I'll consider your suggestion," Jordan responded. That was all she could agree to at the moment, though she had to decide quickly. Malcolm would leave for work before sunrise the next day. She'd need to write that letter tonight if he would be the bearer of their sad news. Her chest clenched as she imagined the words she would have to put to paper:

> *Your Mattie, my mother, is dying. Please come. Her deepest sadness is that she will not be with you one last time before she leaves this earth. I understand it is a great inconvenience to travel two thousand miles to visit with an old woman you haven't seen in decades, but it would mean so much to her, and to me, if you can manage it.*
>
> *If you cannot come, will you please write a*

note of farewell?

Tears were streaming down Jordan's face when she sat at her oak desk to write to Lisbeth Johnson. Naomi was correct. She would push aside her own desires to make this appeal for Mama, but either response from Lisbeth was fraught. Rejecting the request would feel an insult, but a visit from Lisbeth would be an imposition. Jordan didn't relish the idea of sharing this time with a White woman she hadn't seen in more than twenty years. But for Mama she would face one or the other.

CHAPTER TWO

SADIE

Oakland, California
May 1894

A well-dressed Negro stood on the front porch of their modern Victorian home. Sadie hoped her expression did not come across as rude. She rarely saw a Colored person in Oakland.

"May I help you?" she asked the dark-skinned young man.

"How do you do, ma'am?" He nodded and smiled. "I'm Malcolm Wallace. Does Mrs. Lisbeth Johnson live here?"

Sadie nodded. "She's my mother." A flicker of familiarity danced in her. "You're Miss Jordan's son?"

"Yes, ma'am," he replied. "Mattie Freedman's grandson."

"Oh my!" Sadie beamed at the handsome young man. "Momma will be delighted to meet you. And I am too, of course. Your mother remains larger than life in my heart and mind. She was my favorite teacher of all time. Please come in."

Jordan had been only nineteen—barely out of childhood herself—when she became Sadie's first teacher. Sadie had felt Miss Jordan was perhaps the wisest and kindest person in the world. Miss Jordan's enthusiasm and sparkle remained dear in Sadie's memory, though they had not seen one another in decades. The history and affection that connected their mothers must have added to her regard.

Miss Jordan's mother, Mattie, had been Momma's beloved wet nurse and caregiver at the Fair Oaks plantation in Charles City, Virginia. Mattie had escaped to Oberlin, Ohio, when Momma was about twelve. Sadie didn't know if it was entirely a coincidence that Momma had moved there after she and Poppa married. Some of Sadie's fondest childhood memories included Miss Jordan and Mrs. Freedman. They'd been kith to one another, family by circumstance, until Sadie's family moved to Oakland in 1873.

Though they had not lived in the same place, nor visited with one another, in the intervening years, Momma shared a regular correspondence with Mattie. Jordan acted as scribe since Mattie was illiterate. They kept up with the biggest changes in one another's lives, celebrating stories of marriages and births and mourning news of deaths. Momma spoke of Mattie so often that her spirit lived in Sadie's mind and soul.

Sadie showed Malcolm to their living room—modern with gaslights and a coal fireplace—and pointed to the couch upholstered in an elegant French fabric. "Please have a seat while I find my mother."

She disappeared into the kitchen, put the kettle on for tea, and went into the backyard. Her mother knelt in the garden, transplanting tomato seedlings into the soil. Momma's gray hair was pulled into a loose bun. Only the veins popping out on the back of her hands revealed her fifty-seven years. She'd been pampered and privileged as a child, never working in dirt. But after she left the plantation, she farmed right alongside her husband and children: planting, harvesting, and collecting most of the food they ate until 1890, when Poppa died from a weak heart.

Sadie's life was the reverse of her mother's. She'd tended to the land and the animals on their farm before her memories began. Dirt was a constant in her childhood. She'd been determined to keep up with her older brother, and by the time she was fifteen, she drove the plow team as fast and straight as Sam, though he outweighed her by forty pounds.

Now her husband, Heinrich, discouraged her from soiling her hands. He wanted Sadie's nails and fingers to look and feel like a lady's. He suggested they get a palm tree for their new yard rather than have a kitchen garden. Sadie had nodded in agreement at his proposal but did not take any action. If she did nothing about it, he would most likely forget his idea—Heinrich was too focused on his business to pay attention to the household.

In contrast Momma preferred to grow much of their own food and had ambitious plans for the garden—kale, tomatoes, lettuce, and peas. She assumed Sadie would be a part of bringing it to fruition. With gloves Sadie was able to satisfy both her husband and her mother.

"This clay soil is impossible!" Momma declared. "We're going to need to mix in sand to give the roots room to grow."

"Momma, we have a visitor." Sadie corrected, "*You* have a visitor."

Her mother's eyebrows came together in a furrow.

"Miss Jordan's son is here," Sadie explained.

"Malcolm?" Momma grinned.

Before Sadie could reply, Momma leaped up. Wiping her hands on her skirt, she abandoned her project, leaving plants and tools scattered on the ground. Sadie followed her into the living room.

Momma beamed as she declared, "Malcolm, it is a real pleasure to meet you at last."

The young man stood to shake. Momma showed her dirty palm.

"I'm sorry. I was working in the garden and then rushed to see you before washing up," she explained.

"I'm not afraid of a little grime." Despite the soil he took her light hand in his, then they all sat down.

"I feel as if I know you from Mattie's letters," Momma said, her voice high and energetic.

"And I you, ma'am," he replied. "From my mother's and grandmother's stories."

"What brings you to Oakland?" Momma asked.

"I live here part time, ma'am," he replied. "Working for the Pullman Company as a porter."

"I understand those are excellent jobs for . . . a good job for young men."

"Yes'm."

"You do not need to call me ma'am," Momma told the polite young man.

"Yes, ma'am. Sorry." He laughed. "It's just my way."

Momma laughed too. "You may call me whatever you like," she said. "Thank you for coming to see us. Though many miles and years separate us, your family is important to me." Momma smiled, her eyes moist. "Very dear indeed."

It was striking to see Momma so animated, and so overtly emotional. It was a side that Sadie saw only when Momma was with her grandchildren.

"I come with a letter from my Ma," he explained, "bearing sad news."

Momma's hand flew to her heart; pain filled her eyes, and tears threatened to spill over. Compassion welled up in Sadie.

"Has Mattie . . . ?" Momma asked, fear riddling her words.

"Not yet, ma'am. But we believe it will be soon." He

held out a letter with his well-manicured hands.

Momma's hand shook as she took the envelope. She placed it on her lap and sighed. They sat in a bittersweet silence. Sadie could hear the tick of the clock on the oak mantel. Sadness for Momma, and for Miss Jordan, welled up in her. The prospect of facing life without a mother struck a painful chord.

"Would you like me to read the letter to you, Momma?" Sadie broke the uncomfortable silence.

The older woman nodded. Sadie took the note and read aloud:

> *Dear Lisbeth,*
>
> *I hope this letter finds you and your family well. I have sad news that I must share. Mama has been unable to eat for several weeks; we believe she has a growth that is preventing digestion. Naomi and I are caring for her, keeping her comfortable as best as we can. Before her illness we had decided to move to Oakland to join Malcolm, whom you have just met. He is quite enamored of your city and has convinced us we will enjoy the climate as well as the citizens.*
>
> *Mama agreed to the move, excited to see the bright poppies and, more important, your dear face. I cannot do anything about the poppies, but I can ask you to come to bring more joy and ease to her passing. Is it possible for you to make the trip to Chicago? It would mean so much to Mama, your Mattie, and to me as well.*
>
> *I understand that it may not be possible for you to make such a journey. If that is the case, will you pen a note for Malcolm to bring when he*

returns to Chicago?

Fondly,

Jordan

Sadie finished reading the painful news with a sigh. She looked at her mother, expecting tears, but instead her jaw was set with focused determination.

"Is it too late for me to purchase a ticket on tomorrow's train?" Momma asked Malcolm.

A sweet smile tugged up his lips. "Thank you, ma'am. It will mean so much to everyone."

Momma swallowed. "I owe you thanks for the invitation. Mattie cared for me from the day I was born. The best of me comes from her. I can never fully repay all she did"—Momma's voice cracked—"but I can show her my devotion and gratitude by coming now."

Momma's loyalty to Mattie Freedman wasn't a surprise. The elderly woman had been more like a mother to her, caring for Momma from the day she was born. However, Momma's intention to travel to Chicago placed Sadie in a familiar, and uncomfortable, bind. She did not want her elderly mother to journey so far alone, but her husband would not approve of her taking a long, expensive trip.

"About that ticket." Momma's tone shifted again.

"Yes, ma'am," Malcolm replied. "I can arrange everything for you. I'll send a porter for your bag at eight o'clock tomorrow morning. I'll put a ticket on hold at the counter where you can pay. Arrive by nine if you do not want to be rushed."

"Will there be room for two?" Sadie interjected, despite her reservations. "I'd like to accompany my mother."

Momma nodded with a small smile, satisfaction in her

eyes.

"Thank you, Sadie. It will be nice to have your companionship," Momma said, "if you believe Heinrich won't mind your absence too terribly."

Sadie's heart quickened at the sound of her husband's name. She expected Heinrich to balk at her decision to accompany her mother, though she did not know how much he would protest. He was a man of routines and showed his displeasure when they were disrupted. If she arranged for his care while she was gone, he might be more forgiving.

"I will manage Heinrich," Sadie declared, sounding more confident than she felt. Over the ten years of marriage she'd slowly learned how to be a good wife. Before their wedding she'd been naïve enough to think that most marriages were like her parents' with an equal partnership between husband and wife. She had entirely underestimated the differences between her and Heinrich, an immigrant from Germany. He had many assumptions about the role of a wife that Sadie did not bring to their union.

Heinrich did not understand Sadie's attachment to her family. Many of their earliest disagreements centered on her desire for both of them to be close to Momma, Poppa, Sam, and his wife, Diana. He reported that his mother had few opinions and she kept to herself. She had no friends or family that took her away from the house. Heinrich had not visited with any extended family during his childhood.

They had come to a fragile peace that allowed Sadie to continue her familial relationships while giving him the freedom to stay clear of them. Sadie wished it were otherwise, but she was resigned to his attitude.

She often reminded herself that the situation could be more painful. He might need to move back to Germany or elsewhere. Momma and Poppa had resettled from Virginia to

Ohio and then to California. Heinrich had moved to a new continent for financial opportunity.

Sadie was grateful her husband was utterly devoted to his employer, Mr. Spreckels, a fellow German who had become the sugar king of the West. Spreckels had made a fortune exporting beet sugar, fruit, and vegetables from the lush fields of California to the East. Heinrich's work provided them a comfortable life with the income for modern luxuries like gaslights *and* allowed her to live near her family in Oakland.

After a nice visit with Malcolm, Momma and Sadie said farewell and walked for twenty minutes through downtown to her brother's home. He lived with his family on the other side of the produce district. Married for a dozen years, Sam and Diana ran a successful wholesale business together. Their three children, Tina, Elena, and Alex, showed her Greek roots in their nearly black hair and dark-brown eyes.

Diana's parents had refused to attend Sam and Diana's wedding, disapproving of her marriage to an American. But after Tina was born, they forgot their objections and showered the young family with food and attention. Diana welcomed them back into their lives, never speaking of the disrespect they showed to Sam. The early struggles in her brother's marriage had taught Sadie that compromise and strife were part of being husband and wife.

On the way to Sam and Diana's, Momma stopped for lemon drops, a treat for her beloved grandchildren. She bought a large stash for Sam and Diana to dole out over the many days they would be away. Sadie pushed down her envy, reminding herself that Momma would dote on her children too, if God gave her any.

Sam and Diana lived on the bottom floor of an older duplex nestled between the estuary and Lake Merritt. A few times a year, when the breeze shifted in the wrong direction, the stench of sewage from the lake would drift into their five-room home. But most of the time it was an ideal location, close to their produce store and the amenities of city life. Both Diana and Sam had been raised on farms, and neither one missed the constant work with unpredictable outcomes.

Instead of farming, they bought produce from the farmers in San Leandro and then paid peddlers to sell fruit and vegetables directly to customers in Oakland and the neighboring towns of Alameda and San Antonio.

Momma walked up the clean-swept wooden porch and opened the painted wooden door on the right without knocking.

"Hello!" she called out.

"Come, come," Diana yelled from the back of the house.

They walked through the living room and dining room to get to the large kitchen.

The delicious smell of garlic cooking in olive oil welcomed Sadie. The children swarmed around their Nana, giving big hugs and receiving the sour candy. Tina, nearly eight, had lost all of her baby softness but had yet to show any of the changes that would transform her into a young woman.

Elena tugged Sadie's hand. "Come with me to pick lemons. We're making lemonade for supper!"

Sadie scooped up little Alex. Despite her own lack of children, or perhaps because of her childless status, she felt joy radiate from her chest as she held him. She kissed the top of his head, his dark hair silky and smooth. He pointed at his sister, and they followed Elena into the backyard.

Diana and Sam's gardening skills were on display. Rows of plant starts were beginning to take hold, delicate green leaves poking through the brown soil. A torrent of pink bougainvillea contrasted with bright golden poppies and white Shasta daisies. Tight buds of purple flowers were about to blossom on a vine. Thin leaves of crocuses made Sadie smile; the blooms had come and gone in a flash in February. These special crocuses were split from bulbs that Momma had carried from Oberlin when they moved in 1873.

Even as a girl, only eleven years old, Sadie had felt the tradition of them when she and Momma dug them up in Oberlin, wrapped them in cheesecloth, and nestled them into wood shavings for protection on the journey. Momma had learned to hunt for crocuses from Mattie, yet another tradition that came from Mattie to their family.

Each year they were the first sign of spring. In Ohio they bloomed in April or May. In Oakland they showed their bright-purple and yellow blossoms in January or February. They'd been split and moved many times. Descendants of those ten bulbs from Ohio were planted in every yard any of them had ever lived in.

The lemon tree was heavy with juicy yellow fruit. Sadie put Alex on the ground and held out her skirt as a basket. Elena pulled off fruit and handed it to Alex. One at a time he set them on the outstretched cloth, the yellow of the fruit popping out from the blue cotton.

"Mama said to get eight for the lemonade," Elena explained. "Do you want any to take home?"

"Yes. Thank you," Sadie replied, impressed at her niece's thoughtfulness. "How about four for us?"

Elena walked over with four more in her hands. She counted, double-checking to make sure she'd finished the job. Satisfied at the number, she walked back into the house. Sadie admired the young girl's confidence.

In the kitchen, Diana was stirring the onion and garlic. Her black hair curled around her head, making a halo, with a few gray hairs adding a lovely contrast. Sam was finishing up

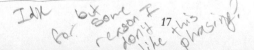

17

the workday at their market.

"Will you stay for supper?" Diana asked.

Sadie shook her head as Momma nodded.

"One more, then," Diana declared to no one in particular.

"Momma told you we are leaving tomorrow?" Sadie asked.

"Yes," Diana replied. "You need help for Heinrich?"

Sadie nodded.

"I've sent Tina to check with cousin Lexi," Diana said. "She's looking for housekeeping jobs right now; the family she was working for moved away."

"That would be wonderful," Sadie replied. "Thank you."

Diana was like that. She learned what needed to be done and just did it. After Sadie had lost her babies, Diana was the one person with whom she could fully share her sorrow. She listened and soothed without being either dismissive or too emotional. Diana understood Sadie's pain because she'd lost a pregnancy between Tina and Elena. Sadie's foreign sister-in-law was her dearest friend.

Momma asked, "Diana, do you know of a means for transporting poppies for many days? Mattie had so hoped to see them. I would love to bring her some of their colorful petals."

Diana scrunched her face, considering possibilities. Unlike most flowers, poppies died soon after being plucked, even when placed in a water vase.

"I have two ideas," Diana said. "Dig up the whole root with the dirt and place it in a pot that you can water. It might make it through the journey. And take some petals pressed in a book; they won't be the same as live ones, but can give the feel if the plant doesn't survive the journey. In fact I have a book for you to take on the train: *Iola Leroy*, by Frances Harper. You haven't read it yet, have you?"

Sadie shook her head. Momma did too.

"You know of it?" Diana asked.

Momma shook her head while Sadie nodded.

"It's written by a Colored woman. The heroine of the story is mixed—Colored and White—before the Civil War. It has love, history, intrigue. You will love it!" Looking right at Momma, Diana said, "It will remind you of your childhood."

She left the room and returned soon with the book in her hand. Grabbing a cup, a paring knife, and a large spoon, she gestured for them to follow her into the back garden.

Diana passed the book to Sadie and knelt on the ground in front of the riot of poppies.

Sadie opened the book to the title page. The right page said:

Iola Leroy

Shadows Uplifted

By Frances E. W. Harper

The left page had a full-size image of Miss Harper standing with her hands on a chair. She looked straight at the camera, almost in a challenge, but also confident, calm. This book's existence was an affirmation of how far race relations had progressed since the end of the war. Sadie had never held a book written by a Colored woman.

Diana dug deep into the moist clay soil until she loosened the long orange root of a poppy flower. She placed it into the tall glass cup and packed in soil around it. Two bright-orange blossoms waved over the lacy green leaves.

"Not too much water, I think," Diana cautioned as she handed it over to Momma's care.

Then she sliced three poppy flowers from their stems, took the book from Sadie's hand, and marched back inside.

Diana opened the book to the middle and smoothed the flowers against the pages, giving thought to the arrangement: one flower was wide open and the others on their sides. She closed the book and tied it shut with twine.

"You can read it when you are there," she declared.

"Thank you, Diana," Momma said. "I'm certain your efforts will bring a smile to Mattie's face."

Satisfaction shone from Diana's eyes. They heard the click of the front door.

Tina returned, alone and panting from the half-mile run there and back.

"She can't come now, but cousin Lexi says she can work as your housekeeper for as long as you like," the girl reported.

"That is wonderful news. Thank you, Tina," Sadie replied. "I'd best head out to break the news to my husband." She wanted to sound humorous, but her voice betrayed her concern. Had she known more of Heinrich's personality at the time, perhaps she might have had a different answer to his proposal. But as it was, they were husband and wife, so she had to work around him.

Sadie gave each child a hug long and hard enough to last for the two weeks they would be apart. She'd never gone so long without seeing them and was surprised at the powerful emotion it brought up. She walked away from her boisterous family and returned to her quiet and orderly home.

★★★

"A nigger knocks on our door, makes a demand of your mother, and now you are traipsing off to Chicago?!" Heinrich practically shouted at her.

"Negro." She corrected him in a calm voice. "The polite term is *Negro*. I repeat my request that you use that word when you are speaking to me."

Sadie sat across from Heinrich over dinner at their mahogany Chippendale table. It could open to seat twelve but none of the leaves were in it. She was glad Momma had stayed for dinner at Sam and Diana's and was not home to see Heinrich's reaction.

Sadie rubbed the leaf carved into the arm of her chair. Those leaves had sold her on this set. They had ordered it all the way from Ireland, and it took months for delivery.

"*Negro, nigger,*" Heinrich's tone was measured, but his face was still bright red. "It does not matter to me what they are called. I do not understand how you are leaving for Chicago tomorrow."

"I have told you about Mattie and my mother's fondness for her," she reminded him.

"If my very own mother were dying, I would not return to Germany to her bedside," he declared. "The old woman does not need you to be there to die. Death will come with or without you."

"My mother is making the trip, and I cannot dictate her movements. I wish to accompany her," she answered, hoping she sounded resolute and calm. "We will not be gone for so long. Four days' travel to Chicago. I expect we will return a few days later."

Heinrich clicked his tongue against his teeth, wordlessly expressing his objection to Sadie's plan.

"How will I eat? Who will take care of the house?" he challenged.

"Diana's cousin works as a housekeeper; she is available to take care of you," Sadie explained.

"Diana," he growled, not bothering to hide his contempt. He found Diana to be overbearing and mannish. "You expect me to pay for a foreign maid? For two weeks?"

Sadie's confidence melted and her eyes welled up.

Heinrich tsked his disapproval. "I am not meaning to be cruel," her husband said. "I am a rational man. We Germans are a sensible people."

Traveling to Chicago to see Mattie wasn't practical, but not all of life could be decided by reason; some things were a matter of love. Heinrich didn't agree or even understand that sentiment. The differences between them formed a persistent crack in the foundation of their marriage. She'd learned to keep hidden the fracture by keeping her family and her deepest beliefs away from her husband, but this situation brought their differences into the open. She could not hide this situation from him. It was impossible to simultaneously fulfill her obligations as a daughter and as a wife.

Sadie would not change Heinrich's mind before the morning, so she did not argue. She hoped this would be like the palm tree in which he would make a strong statement but not follow through on his demand. She expected that as long as Lexi put food on the table at the right time and kept the house running, he would be assuaged.

Heinrich did not have the same devotion to family she did. After her father died, Heinrich repeatedly rejected her suggestions that Momma move in with them—even though they had only two people living in an eight-room house. In contrast, Sam and Diana welcomed Momma to join their larger family in a much smaller residence.

Heinrich was finally won over to the idea by the assertion that Momma would be a great help with their children. But in the intervening years, there were no living children to be cared for. Sadie was failing to do what other women did so easily.

Sadie's hand touched her belly. Her monthly bleeding hadn't come since January. A tentative and wary hope filled her, but she had little faith that this time would be any different than the others. Too many times she missed her bleeding, dreamed of holding a baby in her arms, only to be devastated a few days, weeks, or even months later, when bright red signaled the death of her deepest longing. Twice she'd kept hope alive long enough to see the beginning of a face in her failure.

She no longer informed either her mother or husband of her cycles. It was too painful to disappoint them as well as herself. Diana was the one other person who knew how often her body had let them down.

Sadie understood Heinrich's resentment for her failure to bear him children. She shared it. Would he be able to accept her choice to leave him so that she could be with her mother? If he understood the possibility of her condition, he would absolutely forbid her from going to Chicago. Tonight she would be attentive to him to atone for adding the complication of her absence to his already stressful work life. In the morning she would leave with her mother even if he was displeased.

And while she was gone, she'd pray for his understanding, or at least acceptance.

CHAPTER THREE

JORDAN

Chicago
May 1894

Mama stared right at Jordan. Her clear caramel-brown eyes shone with wisdom and certainty. If Jordan looked only at Mama's eyes, she wouldn't believe she was lying in her deathbed. Jordan inhaled the warm and stuffy air. Mama's comfort won out over Jordan's desire for an open window.

"You been tryin' to hide it from me, but I can tell you stopped talkin' to God. Your spirit ain't been the same since your Booker left us last summer."

Jordan exhaled. She didn't want to think about her husband's death. She didn't want to talk to Mama about faith. After all the hurt, she just couldn't believe that God cared about her, so why have a conversation with Him?

"Maybe since before, when Margaret and the baby died." Almost too quiet to hear, Mama stirred up that pain. Jordan's heart twisted at the mention of her daughter and grandbaby, taken by yellow fever on April 5 and April 8 in 1892. Margaret had only been twenty-one, baby Grace not yet one.

"I'm fine," Jordan lied, and they both knew it. "Don't

you worry about me. Just rest."

"A mama always worries about her babies. No matter how old they get," Mama declared, looking intensely at Jordan.

Jordan gave her mother a bittersweet smile.

"You know that, don' you?" Mama challenged. "Or no matter where a mama is."

Jordan nodded.

"Even if they gone from this earth," Mama said.

Jordan took in a shaky breath. She had no response.

"I'm going to get you a cup of tea." Jordan rose to leave.

Mama's gnarled fingers grabbed Jordan's hand. "Talk to the Holy Spirit, Jesus, God. You pick . . . but you gotta find your faith, Jordan, to get you through the hard times."

"Mama, I don't know what I believe in anymore," Jordan confessed.

"You don' have to know how or why faith work, you just got to find someone when you feeling lost," Mama insisted.

Jordan swallowed. "How?"

"Start by counting your blessings, Jordan," Mama whispered. "Never forget to count the treasures God gave you."

Jordan stared at the small woman in the bed. Skepticism must have poured from her eyes; she didn't feel blessed.

Mama scolded, "You ate the fruit of freedom from a tree you ain't planted. You know that, don' you?"

Mama was referring to one of her favorite sayings: "You eat from trees you did not plant and are obliged to plant trees you will not eat from."

Jordan nodded.

Mama continued, "I ain't saying you don' have reason to be blue. You los' a lot—more than most—way too young and too many times. But you gonna see the ocean! Imagine that.

The ocean, baby." Wonder filled the older woman's voice.

Jordan jerked her shoulders up and down.

"It ain't nothing to shrug at!" Mama scolded. "You the first woman to see the ocean in our family since . . . well, prob'y since Africa. They was all bound up and taken to a strange land. They had enough faith in a better tomorrow to get us here. It ain't the promised land, but you know you got it easy—so easy—compared to them. Don' you forget it!"

A tear slipped out of Jordan's eye and slid down her cheek. She wiped it away.

"You think I don't know that, Mama?" Jordan pushed out through a tight throat. "Every morning and every night I tell myself that I'm blessed, but I can't get my soul to unfurl again." She took a shaky breath. "I have asked God to bring me peace so many times, but He's not listening. Instead, He's bringing me additional pain by taking you from me."

"God listening. He always listening. And He always loving. But He don' always have the power to make our prayers come true. If He did, justice would be flowin' like water. Our Lord is jus' like a mama. He wanting what's best for His children but not always able to make it so." Mama patted Jordan's hand and said in a raspy voice, "The Lord gave me a long life, a good life. I don' need more. I can go in peace."

"You may be ready, Mama, but I'm not." Jordan didn't try to keep the bitterness out of her voice. Four deaths in three years. She could not forgive God. She didn't even want to.

"Jordan, when you first born, you cry and the folks around you have smiles on they faces. If you live you life right, when you die you have a smile on you face and the folks surroundin' you have tears in they eyes."

Mama continued, "We been blessed to have each other on this earth. I gonna die with a smile on my face. You tears are gonna bless me on my way home. I gonna see Pops, my mama, Margaret, and baby Grace. They all gonna be welcomin' me to heaven. And now I get to watch over you and yours—like they been watchin' over us."

Jordan took her mama's hand in hers. Filled with sorrow, her heart hurt so much that it felt ready to burst. She brought Mama's warm, bony fingers to her cheek and kissed them tenderly. She swallowed hard.

"I love you, Mama. And I'm gonna miss you." Her voice cracked. "So much. Every day. Thanks for being my mama."

Mama patted Jordan's cheek. "I love you, baby. Always have. Always will. In this life and the next."

★★★

Later that evening Jordan paused outside the door of her mother's death chamber as Naomi sat with Mama. The tone of their voices gave Jordan pause. She hovered by the wall, just before the open doorway, to overhear the conversation between her daughter and her mother.

"This is gonna hit her hard," Mama whispered. "You know that, right?"

"I agree, Grammy," Naomi replied. "But how can I help her?"

Jordan was the *her* they were speaking about. Her throat swelled up.

"She need hope again," Mama said. "In the future."

Naomi spoke, but Jordan could not make out the words.

"Like a new granbaby or gettin' back to teachin'. Somethin' to help her have faith in what's to come," Mama said. "That girl has always expected more from life than is right and then gets too disappointed by the natural course of events."

Anger flared in Jordan. Mama shouldn't be telling Naomi

her business. She rushed through the door.

The two women startled, Naomi looking as if she had been caught in a lie, and Mama holding that self-righteous *I know better than you* expression.

"You need to get some sleep," Jordan barked out. "Naomi, let Grammy rest."

Naomi nodded, squeezed Mama's hand, and exchanged a conspiratorial look with her grandmother.

"Don' blame the girl. I brought up my worry 'bout you," Mama explained.

"Naomi and Malcolm aren't anywhere near ready to have babies," Jordan reprimanded. "Don't encourage them in that direction. They aren't even married."

Mama shook her head from side to side with a small smile. As far as she was concerned the birth of a baby *was* the wedding.

"How 'bout teaching again . . . when you get to Californi'?" Mama suggested. "I think that gonna revive your spirits. It always gave you hope, planting seeds of knowledge in the little chil'ren."

I'm too tired, Mama, Jordan thought but didn't say out loud. It was such a selfish sentiment, *too tired.* Jordan didn't need to add disappointment and distress to her mama's passing. Instead she smiled with a nod and lied, "That's a good idea."

After the war, when she was still young, idealistic, Jordan had taught in a freedmen's school in Richmond, Virginia. She poured her life into the students, working for a better tomorrow for her people. Before true equality was established, the government had abandoned its commitment to the freedmen. Jordan's devotion kept a Colored school open, but it had been a constant strain. Abandoning the school and students when her family fled to Illinois was a festering wound to her soul.

In Chicago she had applied to be a teacher for three years before she finally secured one of the few positions for a Colored woman in the Chicago Public Schools, but that had been taken from her as well. In 1892, she was fired in the middle of the year with no explanation. But she knew why she had been dismissed. She organized for Negro representation at the Columbian Exposition and was labeled a rabble-rouser.

She did not want to hand over her reputation and well-being to a government that had no regard for her. She'd rather clean houses than devote herself to causes that could never be won. Mama would be deeply disappointed in her if she knew the truth. But she just didn't have her mama's faith, or strength.

"More?" Jordan asked, pointing to the Bible, grateful for a distraction that would be a comfort to Mama.

Mama nodded, patted her arm, and closed her eyes, but before Jordan could start reading, Mama interrupted. "Promise me something, Jordan." Her voice was quiet and firm.

Jordan raised her eyebrows in a question, wanting to know the request before she committed to it.

"Dig up some crocuses to bring with you across this land, okay?"

Relieved, Jordan sighed and smiled. She replied, "Yes, Mama, I can *promise* you that."

Mama smiled. "Then you gonna know that spring is gonna come. A better day always comes after the col' of winter . . ."

Jordan was glad she could offer her mother this promise. She didn't ruin Mama's victory by reminding her that there was no winter in Oakland.

CHAPTER FOUR

SADIE

Train to Chicago
May 1894

Heinrich went to his office rather than seeing them to the train. His farewell was warmer than Sadie had expected, but still held the message: *I am not pleased with your choice.* She left an affectionate note under his pillow and hoped he would soften when he found it.

The station at Broadway and Seventh bustled with activity. Mounds of bright lemons, red cabbage, and green broccoli were waiting to be loaded. Eastern markets for California produce had led to the wave of westward migration. Oakland had grown from ten thousand people to fifty thousand residents in the twenty years Sadie had lived in California. It was small compared to the three hundred thousand occupants of San Francisco, but Oakland was a real city by any measure.

In most of the nation, these types of vegetables and fruits would not be ripe for months, or grow at all. Through the modern technology of the railroads, this produce would travel thousands of miles, across the desert and lands recently covered with snow, to family tables in urban centers such as New York City and Boston. Sadie knew more than most women about the complex and fragile produce-export business because it was Heinrich's work.

His employer, Mr. Spreckels, had made his fortune from the sale of California goods in the East. In turns Heinrich vented or boasted about the difficulties of his industry. Try as they might, no one could accurately predict when a product would be ripe. Heinrich's job coordinating between the farmers, the railroads, and the produce markets in Chicago, Boston, and New York was immensely stressful. Intent on dominating all markets, not only sugar, Mr. Spreckels was continually expanding his reach and used Heinrich to do so.

Canning the produce at its peak and then sending it east in scheduled allotments was more labor intensive, but it was an increasing part of their business. Very little produce was wasted if it was canned, and profits could be made year round. However, it meant Heinrich had to oversee a growing number of demanding enterprises and their employees.

Sadie and Momma walked alongside the train, past the freight cars, the second-class cars, the dining and lounge cars, until they came to the second Pullman sleeping car. A short queue had formed at the door. The conductor taking tickets looked familiar, but Sadie only got a quick glance at his face before it was blocked by other passengers. By the time they got to the front of the line and he reached out for their tickets, her suspicion was confirmed.

"Cousin Willie?" she asked.

The man's light-brown eyebrows furrowed in confusion; then a huge grin tugged his lips up as he recognized the pair.

His eyes shimmered when he replied, "Is that my cousin Sadie? Aunt Lisbeth?!"

Sadie nodded at the handsome young man she hadn't seen in a few years.

"Oh my!" he exclaimed. Then he opened his arms wide, embracing each one in turn.

"What a pleasant surprise," Momma declared.

"How far are you traveling?" Willie asked.

"Chicago," Momma explained. Then her voice got soft. "To see Mattie one last time."

"Oh." His face fell in sorrow. A loud sigh escaped from his body.

Sadie heard a loud throat clear from behind her. Getting the unspoken message, she said, "We must let the others board the train and allow you to do your job."

"I'll find you when I can so we can catch up," he said.

"I hope to visit with your mother while we're in Chicago," Momma said. "We came in such a rush I didn't have time to write to Emily to inform her that we're coming."

Momma rarely referred to Emily as a sister, though they'd been fathered by the same man and had grown up on the same plantation. Emily had been a house slave at Fair Oaks with no acknowledgment of her lineage, while Momma had had all the privileges that went with being the daughter of a planter in Virginia. It was hard for Sadie to reconcile the mother who raised her with the knowledge of Lisbeth's childhood with Mattie and then Emily as her servants, her slaves.

Momma doled out information about her childhood in measured doses if at all. She answered most questions about that time by saying, "It was a long time ago; I hardly remember."

Aunt Emily, Uncle William, and Cousin Willie had been extended family to Sadie from the time they moved to Ohio when she was five until she moved to California when she was eleven.

In the intervening twenty years, they had not once seen

Aunt Emily or Uncle William, though Momma and Emily traded letters on occasion. Cousin Willie had called on them a while back when he had been temporarily assigned to the Oakland route for one trip.

Willie's eyes widened; he looked concerned.

"Is Aunt Emily unwell?" Sadie asked.

He shook his head almost imperceptibly. "Mother is fine." He put a smile on his face, but his eyes were flat. "She will be glad to see you as well."

Sadie felt dismissed and left with the suspicion that he was withholding information from them, but this wasn't the time or place to press her cousin for answers.

Malcolm was waiting for them in the car. He was dressed in porter attire: dark pants, dark vest, and the signature round cap with a small brim and stiff sides.

Sadie opened her arms, ready to hug him, but when she saw him pull back, she dropped them. She had a deep affection for him because he was Miss Jordan's son, but apparently he did not share the sentiment.

"Welcome aboard!" Malcolm greeted them.

"Thank you," they chorused in unison.

"Have you ever ridden in a Pullman car?"

They both shook their heads.

"You will be amazed to find it as comfortable as the finest hotel in Europe."

He gestured with a tilt of his head for them to follow him. They walked down the right side of the wood-trimmed car, passing three pairs of seats on the left. Malcolm stopped and waved toward two wide chairs covered in a rich-green brocade that faced one another next to a large window— their home for the journey.

"This will be your living room, dressing room, and bedroom," he explained. He gestured to gold velvet curtains hanging by the windows. "These are for privacy, should you desire it day or night."

He pulled up a board nestled behind the seat. "When you are ready to sleep, this comes up to make a partition between you and your neighbors."

He patted the cushions and said, "This folds into the lower bunk. The upper bunk is here." He tapped a rounded wooden cabinet that bulged in the elegant ceiling. "The water closets are at each end. The smoking car for the men is this way, and the lounge is down here."

Malcolm explained the route of the train, details about stops, and the etiquette for the dining car.

"Where do you recommend we keep this?" Momma showed him the glass that held a plant with three bright poppy flowers.

His eyebrows raised up in a question.

"For your grandmother," Sadie explained.

Malcolm broke into a wide grin. "She is going to be delighted. I wish I'd thought of it myself."

He took the glass and set it on the armrest by the window. "Will that work? I can bring twine to attach it so it won't fall."

"That is perfect," Momma replied. "Thank you."

"Thank you," Malcolm replied in earnest. "Please don't hesitate to let me know if you need anything else. I'm your guide and at your service."

It was nice to see him with a genuine smile on his face. Sadie smiled back.

She looked around the Pullman sleeper. Indeed this was as fine as the newspaper advertisements proclaimed. The pair of wide seats seemed to be a private living room. And the wood paneling gleamed like a library in a fine home.

Their belongings were tucked away yet able to be

accessed when needed. It was as luxurious as the hotel Sadie had stayed in during her honeymoon in San Francisco.

Out of the window Sadie studied the scene. The crew bustled around, preparing the train for departure. Well-dressed passengers waited to board. Down the row she saw peddlers selling food to second- and third-class passengers. They would sleep sitting up for the journey. Sadie was grateful to have means to be in a sleeping car. Heinrich's work was stressful, but it provided them all she could ask for financially.

Malcolm returned with the twine and then assisted other passengers. They kept him busy running for beverages and blankets and making reservations in the dining car. Most were polite or indifferent; a few were rude or downright cruel.

Sadie bristled when she saw a man with angry eyes pull out a ten-dollar bill and wave it at Malcolm.

"George, if I like the way you treat me on this trip, this is yours in Chicago," the man with sandy brown hair declared. "If not, then, well . . . I'll be taking my wife out to a nice dinner when I get there. Understand me?" the man challenged, a smirk on his lips and arrogance shining from his eyes.

"Yes, sir. Of course, sir." Malcolm grinned at the man. "My job is to make you happy."

Sadie's stomach turned watching the interaction. She did not understand how Malcolm could be so calm or why he did not correct the man for using the wrong name.

Sadie leaned in and whispered to her mother, "Did you see that?"

Momma nodded without expression.

"Aren't you outraged?" she questioned.

"Malcolm knows his job, Sadie," Momma lectured.

"People are cruel, very cruel, to servants."

"But . . ."

"Do not make it worse for Malcolm by asking him to reassure you that he is fine," Momma scolded.

Sadie was stunned. Had her mother lost her moral bearing? Her face must have shown her dismay.

"Sadie, I know you are not accustomed to seeing racial cruelty, but you read the newspaper enough to understand the ways of this nation. Each community has its own code. On the train we will see *all* of them." Momma went on, "You cannot change that man, but you can learn the truth about the world and decide what kind of person you want to be."

Momma patted Sadie's leg and then looked out the window, signaling an end to their conversation. Sadie felt like a child.

Soon the train jerked and slowly rolled away from the depot. People of all ages, mostly White, but a few Negroes and Chinese, waved from the platform. Sadie didn't know them, but she was touched by their farewell and enthusiastically returned the gesture.

The tracks pointed toward the bay and then turned a sharp right, running past Emeryville and then Berkeley. The Marin hills stood to the west, like a sentry across the sparkling water. The scene was mesmerizing, the land both familiar and yet new from this angle.

In Berkeley, rolling hills rose to the east while the bay glistened to the west. A riot of brilliant-orange poppies covered the hills, contrasting with the dark-green canopy of oaks and the grass—still bright green from rain. It was a beautiful time of year.

They turned inland to their first stop, Martinez, a small community Sadie had never visited before. Many farmers shipped their produce from this station. She opened her window to get fresh air but was disappointed. The wind blew the soot from the engine through the opening, making the stuffy air preferable to the smoke.

They resumed their journey, crossing the Carquinez Strait and leaving the bay behind. Fields surrounded the train on both sides. People with hoes in their hands bent over the land. Most wore the wide woven caps that marked them as laborers from China.

Malcolm stopped in front of their seats, offering two metal cups filled with water.

"Would you care for anything else?" he asked.

Sadie shook her head. "No, thank you. This is lovely."

She smiled at him, wanting to say more, longing to have the right words, but her thoughts were muddled. Momma was right. What could she do to make it better? This was Malcolm's life, and she was only a short-term guest in it.

The next stop was at the capital of the state: Sacramento. Sadie had imagined it would be imposing, larger than San Francisco, but it looked less developed than even Oakland. Only the capitol building marked it as special. Soon they pulled out, heading for the Sierra and then out of the state.

Sadie had only a vague memory of their travel from Ohio to California when she was eleven. Her father had loved the scenery and spoke of their journey often in the years after. She had pictures of it in her mind but wasn't certain whether they were recollections or pictures her imagination made from his stories.

A large granite boulder suddenly flew by only feet from the train. She jumped back and then laughed at herself. She leaned in close to the window. The train rushed past tall evergreen trees that towered over the window of the car. Some were so close together that they blurred into one mass, and others were far enough to register as separate trees. Most were so close she feared they would strike the glass. It was dizzying, but quickly she adjusted to the motion.

They were in the Sierra mountains. She thought she would have noticed the ascent, but she hadn't felt the train climbing higher. Only the landscape out the window told her they'd changed elevations.

The view suddenly opened to a gorge with a mighty river tumbling below, churning across huge rocks. Though it was light out, a quarter moon chased them as they rushed along the riverbank. The sight was nothing short of majestic.

"Your father teared up at this beauty." Momma sighed. Sadie took her hand. They both missed him.

"I can see why," Sadie replied with moist eyes of her own.

Their tender moment was interrupted by the shouting of a pinch-faced woman.

"Are you testing my patience on purpose?"

The rude matron glared at Malcolm as she poured the liquid from the cup onto the floor of the train. Sadie saw him take a deep breath.

"I'm sorry, ma'am. What did you wish me to bring to you?" he asked.

"Lemonade! I asked for lemonade. And you brought me iced tea!" she exclaimed.

Sadie wanted to correct the woman; she had asked for iced tea. Sadie had heard her. The whole car had heard her. She started to rise, but Momma restrained her.

"Let him do his job without interference."

Sadie signaled to Malcolm as he walked toward them. He stopped with his head cocked, ready to listen.

"She asked for iced tea," Sadie said. "I heard her. Would you like me to correct her?"

Malcolm shook his head and implored, "Please, ma'am. Just let it be. If you chastise her publicly, she will complain to Mr. Smith, my conductor, which never goes well for me."

"You cannot mean that Willie Smith will not treat you fairly," Momma asked.

Malcolm's head jerked back, and his face pulled inward in confusion. "You are acquainted with Mr. Smith?"

"He's my nephew," Momma explained. "I haven't been in regular contact for many, many years, but we were close when he was a child. In fact, your uncle and grandmother assisted in his family's move from Richmond, Virginia, to Oberlin, Ohio. Emily and William Smith?"

Malcolm looked more confused.

"You do know the story of our families?" Momma asked.

"Yes, ma'am, I just . . ." He shook his head and pasted a smile on his face. "I'm glad that you believe Mr. Smith will be a friend to me. He's new to this route; we haven't worked together before."

"I can't imagine he will show any race prejudice when he—"

"Thank you, ma'am," Malcolm interrupted. "I best be getting on with my duties."

He tipped his cap politely and left them. Now Sadie was confused by Malcolm's attitude. He appeared to be hiding information from them. Perhaps it was none of her business, as Momma kept telling her, but she was curious about the mystery.

★★★

Once they crossed into Nevada, the scenery out the window was dramatic in an entirely different way. The desert spread out before them, long past where the eye could see. Stunted shrubs gave it texture. The temperature rose until it was uncomfortable even to be seated and gazing out at the land. Sadie held an entirely new level of respect for the settlers who crossed this territory by wagon and the workers who laid the tracks for the railroad.

"Your table is ready." Malcolm interrupted Sadie's thoughts.

"Thank you," Sadie replied with a smile, and they followed him to the elegant dining room.

If anything, it was more ornate than the sleeping car. The two carved seats on each side of the tables were upholstered with damask cushions. White cotton tablecloths covered the surface laid with silver utensils, glassware, and a vase with flowers. Each window had rich velvet curtains. Glass and electrical bulbs shone from above. Most striking were the great number of Colored men dressed in long white tunics, ready to serve. It was as sophisticated as the Palace Hotel in San Francisco.

Malcolm ushered them to a table where two people were already seated. The well-dressed gentleman rose. He was older than Sadie but younger than Momma. The woman next to him was closer to Sadie's age.

"I'm Mr. Davis of Chicago." He did not reach out his hand. "My wife"—he gestured toward the petite woman next to him.

"It's a pleasure to meet you," Momma said. "I'm Mrs. Johnson and this is my daughter, Mrs. Wagner."

They sat down. Sadie picked up the elegant menu waiting on the table.

PULLMAN DINING CAR LAFAYETTE

DINNER

—

Chicken with Rice
Consommé, Clear

—

Celery

—

Baked Whitefish, Tartar Sauce
Saratoga Potatoes

—

Boiled Beef Tongue, Tomato Sauce

—

Chicken Croquettes, Mushrooms
Pineapple Fritters, Wine Sauce

—

Prime Roast Beef
Roast Turkey, Cranberry Sauce
Boiled Potatoes
String Beans
June Peas
Cauliflower

—

Lobster Salad

—

Apple Tapioca Pudding, Cream Sauce

—

Neapolitan Ice Cream
Preserved Fruits
Assorted Cake
Marmalade
Dry Canton Ginger

English, Graham and Oatmeal Wafers

—

Fruit

—

Roquefort, Canadian and Edam Cheese
Bent's Biscuits

—

Cafe Noir

———

★ MEALS, ONE DOLLAR ★

—

Hygeia Water Used on Table.

—

En Route

The offerings were extensive. Sadie looked at Momma studying the menu.

Mr. Davis asked, "Is this your first journey by train?"

Momma replied, "Our second, but the last journey was nearly twenty years ago. Trains have changed in the intervening years."

"Indeed!" he proclaimed.

"And you?" Sadie asked, looking at Mrs. Davis.

"We took the train to San Francisco last month," she said. Then she added, a coy smile lighting up her face, "For our honeymoon."

"Congratulations!" Momma said, matching the woman's excitement.

Not every marriage should be celebrated, but all weddings seemed to be.

"Where are you headed to?" Mrs. Davis asked.

"Chicago," Momma replied, "to visit an old friend."

"Our hometown," Mr. Davis said.

"We will be traveling together for a few days, then," Momma said.

They both nodded.

"The menu changes each night. I cannot understand how they do it, but the food is delicious," he proclaimed.

The right side of the menu listed French wines and champagne, cordials, California wines, whiskey, beer, and sodas. Momma pointed at the prices. Some of the beverages were four dollars a bottle—four times the cost of the entire meal. The financial crisis caused by the crash of 1893 hadn't been equally hard on everyone. The beer included Heinrich's favorite—Bartholomay's Bohemian. Sadie thought of her husband hundreds of miles away, being served by Lexi. She hoped he was satisfied with his supper.

Sadie settled on the chicken croquettes, and Momma ordered the roast beef. The waiter was so friendly she wondered if Cousin Willie had requested special treatment for them. But then she noticed that the all-Negro serving staff were equally kind and jovial to the surrounding tables.

The food arrived on beautiful china plates with a floral pattern and the word Pullman embossed in blue letters. Mr. Davis was correct. It was as delicious as any meal Sadie had ever eaten.

Mr. Davis declared, "Mr. Pullman began his career in New York, but he wisely moved to Chicago to make his fortune. He is most inventive and deserves every penny he earns.

"Do you know how he made his name?" the man asked.

Before they had a chance to reply to his question he launched into an explanation. "Mr. Pullman used his patented method to raise an entire block of stores in downtown Chicago—without disrupting their business. They'd been built so close to Lake Michigan that a seasonal swamp flooded them. He used hundreds of laborers and six thousand jackscrews to lift the buildings. At the sound of a whistle, the workers simultaneously gave the screws a quarter turn. Each movement was so slight that they did not break a single pane of glass nor disturb the shoppers. Can you imagine that? Sipping tea in a restaurant or buying a coat while the building you're in is being raised?"

Like Heinrich, Mr. Davis clearly admired a self-made man. Heinrich believed that Mr. Spreckels was a similarly admirable and astute businessman. Some men considered such men greedy and overly ambitious, but the fact that Spreckels and Pullman were attempting to drive out all competition did not bother Heinrich in the least. He thought Spreckels was wise to take full advantage of the opportunities that industrialization and urbanization were offering in the moment.

Mr. Davis paused in the midst of his lecture with a dramatic scowl. He shook his head. Sadie turned around to see what was disturbing him. A well-dressed Negro family was being seated.

Mr. Davis hissed, "I do not see how they can consider these first-class accommodations if they are serving Negroes."

Sadie's stomach clenched. She wanted to challenge his assertion but did not want to ruin their meal by being argumentative. And she was at a loss for the right words.

Momma replied, "Surely income is the measure of class, Mr. Davis. Not complexion."

"Oh, I see," Mr. Davis responded, his eyebrows raised. "I have no race prejudice, but I am not so naïve as to believe that standards are not lowered by racial mixing."

He continued speaking about Mr. Pullman, though Sadie suspected there was less enthusiasm in his story. Without a break he talked about his construction business and the difficulties of finding good American-born labor that would work for a fair wage.

Sadie found the conversation tiresome as well as offensive. She didn't want a direct confrontation but wished to change the topic. Mr. Davis didn't leave her any room to steer the conversation in a different direction.

Looking at Mrs. Davis, she started another topic: "Do you have recommendations for sightseeing while we are in Chicago?"

The woman smiled and declared, "The Field Columbian Museum. Do not miss it. There is a wing devoted to the new science of anthropology."

Mr. Davis agreed. "There is nothing else like it in the United States. Our friend Marshall Field was the primary benefactor, but I made a donation as well."

Willie came to the table, their desserts on a tray in his hands.

"May I join you?" he asked.

"Of course," Momma said. "Mr. and Mrs. Davis, this is my nephew Willie Smith. He's the conductor."

Sitting up tall, Mr. Davis belted out, "I knew by your uniform."

Willie brought a chair, blocking the narrow walkway, but none of the staff denied him that right.

Mr. Davis leaned in. "So now they are making you let niggers go where they will."

Sadie sucked in her breath. Her stomach rose, and she had to swallow back bile. She studied Willie's reaction. He took a deep breath.

"There are no standard regulations," he replied, his voice measured and calm. "Each conductor makes the rules of his own train."

"Unless that Negress newspaperwoman has her way," Mr.

Davis said. "Then no man will have the freedom to decide his own lifestyle."

Sadie asked, "Ida B. Wells?"

The man nodded. He looked between the three of them.

Sadie's mind raced, searching for the right words to signal her admiration for the Negro newspaperwoman who was shedding light on the rising practice of lynching Negro men in the South.

Mr. Davis seemed to make a social calculation and said, "Perhaps you are forward-thinking. Negroes in the West are a different caliber. If they have the means, who am I . . ." He left his sentence incomplete. A large grin on his face, Mr. Davis changed tactics and asked Willie, "Can I buy you a whiskey in exchange for tales from the rails?"

Her cousin smiled and nodded, gracious after such insulting words. Like Malcolm, he seemed accustomed to racial disparagements. Willie disappeared and returned with two glasses of amber whiskey.

"I understand conductors get tipped in more than cash," Mr. Davis declared.

Willie nodded.

"Your best tip?"

Willie grinned. "Tickets to a baseball game."

"A fan?" Mr. Davis exclaimed.

"Ever since my cousin Sam gave me a mitt when I was six," Willie said.

Momma and Willie exchanged smiles at the memory.

"Your son?" Mrs. Davis asked.

Momma confirmed.

"Have you ever gotten a special tip from a lonely lady?" Mr. Davis asked with a conspiratorial leer.

Sadie flushed. She glanced at the new Mrs. Davis, embarrassed for the young woman. The new bride did not look up, but her shoulders showed defeat.

"I'd best get back to my duties." Willie stood, ending the gauche conversation, leaving the uncomfortable question unanswered. Sadie wished she could also leave this unpleasant man, but she had no excuse for a polite departure.

When their bills arrived for signatures, Sadie glanced at Mr. Davis's check. Only one drink was on the tab. Willie had rejected the man's gift. They exchanged pleasantries with the Davises as they left the table, but Sadie made a note to ask Momma if they could request different companions at their meals for the duration of their journey.

Walking back to the Pullman car was easier than the journey to the dining car. Either the train route had smoothed or Sadie had learned how to better navigate the bumpy ride. She had no way of telling.

Several of the "living rooms" in the Pullman car had already been transformed into "bedrooms." Two sections were partitioned off with their curtains closed. Malcolm was in the process of converting the one next to theirs.

He pulled the lower seats together and turned down the back cushions to make a flat bed that ran parallel to the window. Reaching up high, he unhooked a latch and suddenly the curved ceiling became the bottom of a top bunk. The already made-up mattress was narrow but would accommodate Sadie. Malcolm grasped the wooden partitions behind the left seat back, and tugged upward. He repeated on the right side. The open living room transformed into a private bedchamber. He prepared the lower bed with sheets, a pillow, and a blanket. Remarkably, the whole process took less than five minutes.

"Ready?" Malcolm turned to them.

Momma nodded. Sadie watched the process again, and in short order they were in the privacy of their own bedroom.

They could hear their neighbors past the green curtain, but no one could see them change out of their gowns into their sleep clothes. It was awkward, but quite manageable.

"Would you like to stay down here and gaze out the window for a bit?" Momma asked.

"That would be nice," Sadie replied.

Momma climbed under the covers and slid over. Sadie sat opposite her, on top of the covers with her legs stretched out. Momma patted her through the cotton fabric of her skirt. Sadie took her hand. They smiled at each other, and grace opened Sadie's spirit. She couldn't remember the last time she'd had a quiet moment like this with her mother. Perhaps never since she'd been married. She considered telling Momma that her bleeding was late, but decided it was still too soon.

They gazed out at the clear sky with no hint of cloud or fog. The Milky Way, a bright smear against the black, was breathtaking. Sadie felt small in the midst of the great heaven.

"We don't see skies like this in Oakland," Momma said. "I miss it."

They traveled in a pleasant silence. Sadie felt her shoulders loosen. She hadn't realized she was holding them up.

"Thank you for taking this journey with me," Momma said.

Sadie nodded. "I'm very glad to be here. This is spectacular."

"Yes," Momma agreed. "It is amazing indeed."

★★★

Sadie fell asleep immediately despite the strange circumstances in her tiny upper bunk. Sharp side-to-side jerks woke her up from time to time, but she drifted right back to sleep. The rhythmic clicking of the wheels against the track was her lullaby.

She woke to the sound of voices on the other side of the green curtain. Peering over the edge of the bunk in the half-light, she saw Momma curled up, her eyes closed. Rather than disturb her rest, Sadie lay in the dark space, so cramped it could seem a coffin if she let herself think that way. She forced herself to avoid that thought.

Sadie started to roll to her stomach, but her breasts were too tender to allow it. She smiled, grateful for a pain that might be a sign of success.

She opened the curtain to the car just a bit. Bright sunlight hit her eyes. It was full morning outside of their cocoon.

"Good morning," Momma croaked up to her.

"Sorry to wake you," Sadie said.

She heard a rustling of covers. "Come on down. It's beautiful!" Momma said, awe in her voice.

Sadie slid over the side, hoping no one saw her bare leg when it slipped through the curtain. She sat across from Momma, sharing a blanket to keep warm.

The poppies were still bright and perky. So far they were withstanding this journey. Behind them, through the window, was a glorious scene.

In the night they had traveled into Nevada. The arid landscape was so different from home, yet beautiful in its starkness. Dry land was dotted with flat meadows. Cows grazed in the bright grass while gnarled trees stood guard in the background. Far ahead the Rocky Mountains appeared only as small bumps on the horizon

"Do you remember any of this?" Momma asked.

Sadie shook her head. "Has it changed?"

"The land is the same, but I think there are more homes. More farms."

They passed a lone chimney marking a spot where the hopes of settlers had sprung up and burned away.

"So sad to see the remnants of a family," Sadie said.

Momma nodded.

The Truckee River ran between the train tracks and craggy hills. Lush green trees grew on the banks, contrasting with the low golden hills too dry to support any life other than little tufts of brown scrub.

"On the other side of the Rockies there were buffalo before, in some places as far as the eye could see," Momma said. "I understand we won't see any this time."

"That must have been amazing," Sadie replied.

"It was. The railroad has changed our nation. New opportunities opened for our family, but it came at a cost," Momma said.

Sadie looked at Momma.

"The buffalo; the Indians; families separated forever." Momma shrugged. "I try not to dwell on it."

Sadie squeezed her momma's hand. They rarely spoke of the family and friends they had never seen again once they moved to California. Granny and Poppy Johnson had visited them in Ohio before they headed west. Sadie might have hugged them longer had she realized it would be the last time they would touch or speak. Every letter was a treasure, but it wasn't the same as being with each other. Her grandparents had died in turn, first Poppy and then Granny. Their youngest son, Mitch, had been their sole caretaker. And now he lived alone on their family farm in Virginia.

Sadie and Momma traveled on, speeding through the vast and varied land that made up their nation, in a comfortable silence.

CHAPTER FIVE

JORDAN

Chicago
May 1894

Jordan heard voices in the living room. Naomi must be back from the train station with Lisbeth and Sadie. She smiled, excited that they had managed this surprise for Mama while she was still aware and in good spirits. Whatever was ailing Mama was not taking her quickly from this earth. Jordan patted her mother's leg and rose from the bedside.

"Mama, I'll be back in a moment," Jordan explained, "with a special surprise for you."

"I don' need anythin' extra from you, my dear. You and Naomi been takin' such good care of me."

"Thank you, Mama, but you're getting this treat . . . I'm certain you will be pleased."

She opened the door and closed it quickly to prevent her mother from getting a glimpse of their guests. Lisbeth Johnson, her bright-blue eyes peering out of a notably older face framed by white hair, was in her living room.

"Thank you for coming," Jordan whispered as they hugged hello.

"It's my honor. I'm touched and grateful to be invited to

this tender time," Lisbeth said; her eyes showed her emotion.

Jordan took in a deep breath. It was too soon to start the tears. But then she looked at Sadie. Her breath caught, and powerful emotion swelled in her. Sadie was transformed into a lovely woman, but those eyes. They were the same. This was the little White girl that Jordan had taught, and adored, so long ago.

Sadie held back, looking nervous. Jordan smiled and opened her arms. Sadie beamed and came in for an embrace.

"Miss Jordan, it is so sweet to see you again," the young woman said.

Jordan nodded. "You too, Sadie." It had been a long time since anyone had called her Miss Jordan. She'd been Miss Freedman and then Mrs. Wallace for most of her career. Only in Oberlin had her students called her Miss Jordan. It transported her back to being nineteen, Naomi's age.

Jordan took Lisbeth's warm hand. "Come."

She opened the door to the bedroom, stepped through, and then paused when Lisbeth was framed in the doorway. Jordan's heart beat hard in anticipation.

Mama looked at her from the bed, then at the doorway. Her eyes squinted as she tried to make out who was there. Gray eyebrows pulled inward, showing confusion.

She didn't recognize Lisbeth. Or her eyesight was too poor to see her features. Then it came.

"Oh my!" Tears sprang to Mama's eyes, and her left hand covered her heart. She reached a wrinkled and bony right hand out toward Lisbeth. It shook up and down. From age or excitement? Most likely both.

Beaming and teary, Lisbeth rushed to Mama.

Mama shook her head slowly from side to side, a sweet smile on her face. "Look at you! I thought I ain't never gonna see you again in this life. My, my, my." Mama gently cupped

Lisbeth's wet cheeks. "You came all this way for me?" she asked.

Lisbeth nodded. "Nothing could keep me away, Mattie."

Mama looked at Jordan, her eyes sparkling. "Thank you. This a special su'prise, all right. A very welcome su'prise."

Jordan swirled in joy.

"These are for you, Mrs. Freedman." Sadie held out a pot of golden flowers. "California poppies."

"All right, all right," Mama proclaimed. "Those some of the most beautiful I ev'r seen. Malcolm spoke the truth. They a sight to see. That Oakland mus' be a sight indeed. Think we can grow them here in Chicago?"

"Perhaps, if they go to seed," Lisbeth replied. "They are annuals. You have to plant the seeds after the snow has melted. They don't like the cold."

"Me neither," Mama said with a raspy laugh. "Maybe I did belong in California." A faraway look covered her face. She shook her head. "Ain't it somethin'. All the places you get to visit that I ain't never gonna see." Mama patted her quilt. "Sit right here. Tell me about your travels. What you see in this wondrous land that God made for us."

Lisbeth smiled and sat. She took Mama's fingers. They hadn't seen each other in years, but they looked so right, so comfortable together with Mama's dark hand sandwiched in Lisbeth's white palms.

Jordan didn't really understand their connection. She couldn't imagine that kind of devotion to and trust with a White woman. But the glow in Mama's eyes confirmed that it had been right to invite Lisbeth Johnson. The love that formed between them five decades ago was still palpable.

"I'll leave you two to your visiting," Jordan said. "Mama's Bible is right there if you want to read to her. We'll just be in the kitchen making supper if you need us."

"Thank you, Jordan." Lisbeth looked straight at Jordan, her hand over her heart. She nodded and smiled. "Thank you."

Jordan nodded back and let them be.

★★★

"You can put your belongings in Malcolm's room." Jordan showed Sadie the other bedroom.

"Are you certain?" Sadie asked. "We do not want to put him out."

"He's on a turnaround. He'll be fortunate to squeeze in a two-hour visit with Mama between the time he sets up for the next passengers and welcomes them on the train."

"The porters' work is exhausting," Sadie said. "I don't know how he manages so many hours in a row."

"Four hundred hours a month," Jordan said.

Sadie's eyes grew large. "That does not give him much time for family . . . or sleep."

Jordan nodded. Most people were not aware of the sacrifices the train men, and their families, made.

She and Booker had decided the pain would be worth it to give their children the boost they needed for a better life. But their expectation that the shackles of oppression could only loosen was foolhardy. Even in Chicago, Jordan, Malcolm, and Naomi's education was no guarantee of work or a stable life.

Jordan did not share Malcolm's confidence that the race prejudices in California were less confining and more malleable, but the prospect of life without snow was enough.

"Malcolm won't be back for nine days," Jordan said. "And then only for one night. You may not even see him."

Sadie nodded.

Jordan continued her orientation. "The outhouse on

the left is ours. The washstand is behind the kitchen, on the laundry porch. The pump brings clean water directly into the kitchen; it's very convenient."

Sadie smiled. "You are kind to let us stay here. Please let us know if it becomes too much, and how we can be helpful."

Naomi replied, "We're grateful to you for the joy you brought to Grammy by coming. The expression on her face was priceless."

"It was. I hardly remember her," Sadie said, "but you'd think she lives next door with the way my momma always talks about her."

Jordan swallowed hard. She *was* glad to bring Mama the comfort of Lisbeth during her transition, but it was complicated to share her own precious time with her mama with Lisbeth Johnson.

"Shall we work on supper?" Jordan walked into the kitchen without waiting for a reply.

Naomi led Sadie outside to fetch wood for the cookstove. Jordan pulled out barley, beans, and bacon grease.

"Your husband still works with food distribution?" Jordan asked. It was unlikely that his employment had changed since Lisbeth's last letter, but the financial depression had altered many situations.

Sadie nodded. Jordan sighed. She didn't want to work hard to keep up their conversation. There was a memory of being close, but perhaps they had nothing to speak about.

"How did you meet your husband?" Naomi asked.

Sadie's face pulled into a wistful smile. "My cousin Emma," she replied. "Her husband worked with him. He was lonely, a new immigrant in a strange land—Heinrich, not my cousin's husband. He came for Easter supper and . . ."

Naomi asked, "Did you know at once?"

"Naomi!" Jordan bristled at the personal question.

Sadie laughed. "I am happy to speak of it." She thought for a moment and then replied, "It feels so long ago. Almost like it happened to another woman, but I remember being swept away by his passionate devotion. It was almost immediate, like he knew we were meant for one another. His certainty carried me through. And I thought him so handsome."

Sadie looked at Jordan, a question in her eyes. Jordan didn't know what she was asking, but nodded anyway, encouraging her to continue.

"I was of the age to be married. He had good work with good prospects. I thought he'd be devoted to family." She laughed again, this time with a wry edge. "I made that part up in my own mind: his devotion to family."

Jordan was surprised that Sadie would speak so freely. It gave her hope that their visit would not be too constrained.

"Where is he from?" Naomi asked.

"Germany. Bavaria," Sadie said.

"Does he enjoy living in California?" Naomi asked.

Sadie thought again. "He can be like an overly eager boy. His great disappointment is that he missed the Gold Rush, and he dreams that he would have struck big were he born during that time." She smiled. "He is slowly coming to accept that he will be a manager, not an industrialist. He works closely with Mr. Spreckels, the sugar king. We have been very fortunate.

"What about you?" Sadie asked Naomi with a conspiratorial smile. "Do you have a beau?"

Jordan studied her daughter's face. Naomi shook her head and pulled in her lips. Naomi had been focused on school, rejecting every suitor who had come her way. Jordan was mostly relieved that her child had waited to find a husband—especially now that they were moving to Oakland. But, like most mothers, she wanted her daughter to find a good man.

"And Malcolm?" Sadie asked.

Jordan shook her head and shrugged. "He argues he cannot afford a family until he is in the California bar. He says he will settle down after he starts his own law practice."

"I understand it is a difficult test," Sadie replied, empathy on her face.

"He is convinced he passed the exam in California, but was not admitted to the bar," Naomi inserted.

"Why not?" Sadie asked.

"The judge who examined him openly stated his prejudice against Colored lawyers," Jordan explained, trying to sound even, and not as bitter as she felt.

Sadie's eyebrows furrowed in disbelief, maybe outrage. "That's not fair!" she replied.

"No, it's not," Jordan agreed. "He paid an enormous amount of his earnings to take it. He's appealing his case, and we strive to remain hopeful that he will find justice from the courts. If he doesn't win his appeal, he will pay to take it again, hoping the next time he will go before an unbiased judge for his examination."

★★★

"Do you have everything you need?" Jordan asked Mama at the end of the day.

The house was dark and quiet—everyone else had turned in for the night. Jordan and Mama were alone. Jordan had taken to sleeping in Mama's room in case she needed anything.

"Yes, I do," her mother said. "And then some." Mama took Jordan's hand and smiled. "That was very kind of you. To sen' for Lisbeth."

Jordan nodded.

"I hope you gonna keep takin' care of each other when you get to Oakland," Mama said. "I don' know why God keep puttin' us in each other's lives but He do."

A chill tingled through Jordan. She didn't understand their connection to this family, but she couldn't deny the truth of it. Having Sadie and Lisbeth in the house during this passage was right.

"I'm glad they're here too," Jordan reassured her mother.

"I been thinkin'," Mama said.

Jordan chuckled. Even on her deathbed Mama was planning.

Mama said, "Don' bury my shell with me."

Tears filled Jordan's eyes. She bit her lip and took a shaky breath.

Mama put her hand to her neck, touching the shell on a string that was always tied there. Jordan had one just like it stored away. Lisbeth too.

According to Mama the cowrie shells had come from Africa—long ago, likely in the early 1700s as far as Jordan could account. They traveled across the Atlantic Ocean on the neck of a terrified woman in the hold of a crowded boat. Generation after generation, Jordan's maternal grandmothers passed the shells down to subsequent daughters—whispering words of protection, strength, and freedom along with the gift from Africa.

Mama had worn one around her neck for as long as Jordan could remember, the rest squirreled away in a treasure box. When she ran before the war, Mama left one for Lisbeth. Jordan was given hers when she stayed in Richmond. They'd yet to give one to Naomi. She didn't know how many were left in the box. They'd be part of her inheritance soon. Too soon.

Mama continued, "I wan' you to take my shell with

you to California—throw it in the Pacific Ocean to let the ancestors know we free now. You understan'?"

Mama's yellowing eyes stared at Jordan. There was no denying what was coming.

"I will, Mama," Jordan forced out through a tight throat. Mama patted her arm.

"Thank you, Jordan," Mama said. "That jus' feel like the right thing to do."

Mama closed her eyes. Her breathing grew longer.

Half asleep she spoke again, "Bury me in my red dress. I wanna look bright when I meet Jesus."

Jordan smiled and took a deep breath. "All right, Mama."

"And see ever'body else," Mama added. "Don' tell, but I'm most excited to see my mama. Only 'cause it been the longest since I seen her. An' I have so many questions."

A sweet smile filled Mama's face as she planned her family reunion in heaven. Tears streamed down Jordan's face as she watched her mother drift away.

CHAPTER SIX

SADIE

Chicago
May 1894

"You Momma wrote to me about you angels that never made it from heaven," Mattie said in a sweet, raspy voice.

Sadie's throat choked up. She looked at Momma, an unspoken request for help filling her eyes.

"We continue to pray for a little one to join our family." Momma patted Sadie's hand.

Mattie gave Sadie that look of pity she hated so much. "Losin' an angel is hard on a spirit, ain't it, Jordan."

Miss Jordan looked at Sadie, her jaw set hard, though her voice was kind. "I'm sorry, Sadie. It's a pain that never really leaves you."

Sadie bit her lip and nodded.

"We have not given up hope we'll have the joy of a baby one day soon," Momma said.

Sadie nodded in agreement, as if she fully shared her mother's faith that God wanted her to be a mother. She touched her belly. It felt more rounded, but that might simply be her hard desire bulging out.

Mattie smiled and waved Sadie over. Sadie came close

to the wise woman. Mattie reached out her dark hand, the joints of her fingers swollen, and placed it on Sadie's belly. Tears pushed at the edges of Sadie's eyes.

"God gonna bless you with a baby soon. I feel it in my bones."

"Thank you, ma'am. I sure hope so," Sadie said. Then she smiled. In that moment, she had faith. Mattie's touch and words felt like they had the power to grant her singular prayer.

"Yep." Mattie nodded. "Real soon." She smiled and her lids came down over her eyes. She whispered, nearly asleep, "It nice to know life gonna keep going." Her head rolled from side to side. "Your babies gonna see things I don' even know how to dream about."

★★★

"How are Samuel and Nora?" Momma asked Jordan about her brother as they prepared supper in the kitchen.

"Good. The same," Miss Jordan replied. "Their three children live near them in Cleveland. His oldest son considered a move to Chicago, but Otis decided to stay put now that we are planning to leave."

"And his grandchildren?" Momma asked. "Your holiday letter said that Otis had a fourth child."

A lovely smile broke across Miss Jordan's face. "Samuel adores his grandchildren. I never see him as excited as when he talks about them."

"That's nice," Momma said. Longing in her voice, she agreed, "Babies are a blessing. Are Samuel and his family coming for . . . ?"

Miss Jordan shook her head. "He can't be here at the end. He doesn't have it in him to see our mama on her way."

Momma nodded and said, "Not everybody can."

"It was the same when our father died," Jordan said in a hushed voice. "Samuel came for a final visit and then left before Pops took his last breath. Samuel says he doesn't want to remember our parents as anything other than strong and alive."

★★★

A week after their arrival, while getting ready for bed, Momma said, "Sadie, as you can see, Mattie isn't in a hurry to leave this earth. I know you told Heinrich we would return in two weeks, but I wish to stay until the end."

Sadie's stomach clenched. Her bleeding had yet to come, but it was still too early to tell Momma. She had lost more than one pregnancy after going this long. And she did not want to draw attention away from Mattie's passing.

Also, it was right that Heinrich learned of their blessing before anyone else. It would be one way to demonstrate that her devotion to him was equal to her attachment to her mother.

She considered telling him in a letter but rejected the idea so she could see the joy on his face when she told him in person.

Sadie was torn between staying with her mother and getting home before her body broadcast the news to the world.

Momma continued, "Jordan has expressed her desire to have me stay as well. I will be fine returning on my own should you decide to leave as planned."

Sadie sighed. "How long do you believe it will be?"

Momma gave her a tender smile. "Only the Lord knows. Death has its own timeline. It does not fit into our schedules, much as we might ask it to," Momma said. "Like birth, it comes when it comes."

"You are very devoted to Jordan," Sadie remarked.

"Jordan was the first baby I ever loved," Momma said, her voice tender and poignant.

Sadie waited, hoping her mother would go on and have a rare moment of speaking about her childhood. Sadie nodded; Momma looked off into the distance, lost in thought.

"How old were you?" Sadie finally asked.

"Hmmm?" Momma thought. "I was young, ten or so, definitely not more than twelve because Mattie left soon after my birthday." Momma looked right at her. "I remember that." Momma shook her head and continued the story. "It was so sudden, the love," Momma explained, wonder in her voice. "Mattie put this precious being in my arms. She trusted me with this tiny baby that was not even a day old." She smiled, reliving the memory. "I remember the feeling like it was yesterday. I touched Jordan's little fingers and my heart . . . changed. It opened up and suddenly Jordan was in it—inside my soul."

Momma laughed with a shrug. "It's remarkable. All this time later and I can still feel it in my body."

"I experienced that when I held Tina for the first time," Sadie said, remembering the birth of her niece.

Momma smiled and nodded. "After that first day I loved to be with Jordan. I'd slip away from the house to sit with her in my lap out in the fields while Mattie picked cotton. It was hot and dirty, but nicer than being lonely in my room."

Sadie's chest swelled for her mother.

"Aunt Emily wasn't a good companion?" Sadie asked.

Momma thought again. "To be honest I just don't remember her well from that time. She was ethereal. Not kind, not cruel. She was present with what I needed—my comb, my dress, my tea—but I never shared my mind with her, and it never occurred to me to ask about her." Momma looked up. "I'm ashamed when I think of it."

"You were young," Sadie reassured.

"I was twenty-one when I left," Momma said. "Not so young. Older than Naomi." Lost in her memories, Momma stared into the distance, then said, "I didn't know she was my sister until I saw our family tree while searching for my baptismal paper."

Sadie nodded, though Momma wasn't looking at her. No words of solace came to mind; the loneliness and cruelty of her mother's childhood struck a painful chord. Fortunately Momma had found a way to leave.

Sadie asked, "You really proposed to Poppa?"

Momma smiled. "I did." She shook her head again. "Oh my, that was the most difficult and the best decision of my life."

"What gave you the courage to do it?"

Momma sat back. She stared at Sadie. Her voice hard, she said, "You know what happened."

Sadie shook her head. "No . . . I don't. You've never spoken of it." She corrected herself. "You have mentioned 'the incident under the willow,' but not the specifics."

Momma looked puzzled. "Truly? I've never told you?"

Sadie shook her head. Longing to hear her mother's deeply held secret swelled her chest.

"You know I was engaged to another man—Edward Cunningham?" Momma asked.

Sadie nodded, then smiled. "Poppa called him 'the best catch on the James River.'"

Momma didn't smile back. She took in a deep, slow breath and sighed.

Looking pained and sounding numb, she recounted the story: "Edward's family invited me to his garden to celebrate my twenty-first birthday. We'd been engaged for a year, and I had grown to admire his mother very much. She was elegant and confident. Everyone felt they had the best estate. I look back and wonder at the notion. In my memory it does not seem so different from the others, but there was fierce competition for Edward. And *I* had won . . ."

Momma shook her head at the memory. She continued, "I remember walking through the grounds, feeling full of awe and gratitude that this would be my home soon. My mother was forced to move far when she married, while I would live near Mary, my dear friend, and my family. I was certain God had blessed me. I stepped off the path to cross under the branches of a willow tree . . ."

Sadie's heart sped up. *The incident under the tree.*

Momma spoke in a calm voice, "I imagined being with my children under its boughs just as I had loved resting and reading with Mattie under the umbrella of our willow tree when I was young."

Momma stopped talking. She looked down and then up again, right at Sadie, and announced, "Under the tree I saw Edward mounted on a field hand."

Sadie sucked in her breath and her hand covered her heart. "Oh, I'm sorry, Momma!"

Momma nodded. "I fled. Edward chased me, apologizing for ruining my birthday, assuming I would accept his actions, but I didn't. I couldn't dismiss what I had seen.

"A few days later I drove a wagon to your Granny and Poppy's house—back then I thought of it as the Johnsons'—to propose." Momma paused at the memory. Her demeanor shifted entirely, and she laughed.

Curious, Sadie wondered aloud, "What is so amusing?"

"Oh my goodness. It took me so long to ask. First I had to determine if your father had . . . with a field hand." Momma flushed red. Sadie hadn't ever seen her so flustered.

"I didn't have any words. *Relations*. I finally asked if he'd had relations with a field hand."

"Oh, Momma." Sadie laughed. "I can imagine Poppa being patient and . . . confused."

"He was." Momma laughed. Then her voice grew tender. "I almost fled from embarrassment, but he stopped me. Showing me the kindness in his heart, after I proposed to him, he got down on one knee and asked *me* if I would give him the honor of becoming his wife."

Sadie and Momma exchanged a moist-eyed smile.

"How delightful!" Sadie gushed. "I can't believe you have never told me this story before."

"It came along with such a terrible tragedy . . . it was hard to speak of." Momma gazed off again, the levity broken. "How could I tell you about the cruelty of men forcing themselves on a woman? I wanted to protect you." Momma exhaled. "I am staying until Mattie passes over. Please do whatever is best for you. I will be fine should I need to journey back without you. Malcolm will ensure my well-being."

Sadie weighed her decision. She did not feel good about her mother making such a trip on her own. Even with Malcolm's attentions, it was a strenuous journey for a woman in her fifties to make alone. Another week or even two should not make a difference. If she was calculating correctly, *and* she held this pregnancy, this baby would have a birthday in October, five months away.

"I'll write to Heinrich to gauge the strength of his feelings, and to Diana to confirm that her cousin is available to continue working," Sadie said.

"Thank you, Sadie," Momma said. The relief on her face confirmed Sadie's belief that Momma preferred company despite her proclamation that she could travel on her own.

★★★

Dearest Heinrich,

I miss you terribly and hope you are faring well without me and Momma. She sends her greetings.

We are enjoying our stay in this lovely city. Downtown Chicago has a lovely river and rests upon the shore of Lake Michigan, which is so enormous it seems to be an ocean. You cannot possibly see to the other side. The architecture of the buildings is exquisite—as is the touch of the perfect breeze. The locals assure us that this weather is not common throughout the year, but only the fortune of our timing.

We visited the Field Columbian Museum this week. It occupies one of the new buildings constructed for last year's Columbian Exposition. You would have enjoyed the exhibits on anthropology, botany, geology, and most especially zoology. There were animals from around the world preserved as if they were still alive.

Tomorrow we are calling on my aunt Emily. She is Momma's half sister on her father's side. You most likely remember her son, Willie—that Pullman conductor who called on us in 1892. We had the pleasure of his company during our eastward journey.

Momma's nurse, Mattie, continues to fade, though her passing is going more slowly than I anticipated. We've been invited to stay through the end, and Momma has accepted that request. I prefer to remain with her, but will leave that decision to you as you have already been inconvenienced.

You have sacrificed your routine as well as your earnings for us to be on this journey. I will return on the next available train if you desire.

    Your loving wife,

    Sadie

Sadie considered her language carefully. Heinrich was not comfortable with overt displays of affection. He found direct expression of the word *love* to be manipulative and overly sentimental, but she felt particularly tender and grateful to him and wanted him to know it. Perhaps he would welcome her affection under these circumstances.

CHAPTER SEVEN

JORDAN

Chicago
May 1894

"Can you accompany Lisbeth and Sadie on their call this afternoon?" Jordan asked Naomi as they were washing up the breakfast dishes.

"They know another family in Chicago?" Naomi asked.

"Emily Smith is Lisbeth's half sister," Jordan explained. "Massa Wainwright was their father."

"*Massa*. That word is repulsive." Naomi shuddered visibly, her shoulders flinching back and her face scrunched together in disgust as she dried a plate.

"I didn't make up his name." Jordan shrugged. "That's what Mama calls him."

"Emily is Negro?"

"She's high yellow, but yes," Jordan explained.

Naomi pressed, "Lisbeth claims her—as a sister?"

"I don't know the nature of their relationship. Mama says Emily was Lisbeth's house slave after Mama escaped. Emily stayed in Virginia through the war, and afterward moved to Richmond with Lisbeth's parents—more likely as a servant than a daughter, from what I understand."

"You've met this Emily?" Naomi asked.

"When I was your age, in Richmond. She and her husband and son left Virginia for Oberlin at the time I stayed in Richmond."

"You traded places," Naomi said.

Jordan smiled and nodded.

"So Grammy lived with Emily on the plantation, and then in Oberlin?" Naomi asked.

Jordan nodded again.

Naomi paused in her work, the damp drying rag hanging in her hand. "I know Grammy was a slave. And you were born one too, but I can't imagine it."

"There's a lot you can't imagine, Naomi. And I hope you never have to. There was so much ugliness toward our people." Jordan swallowed hard. She didn't want to revisit the harsh realities of their family's past; preferring to ignore the pain, she changed the subject. "You take them for the visit. I'll stay with Mama."

"No." Naomi was surprisingly adamant. "I'll take care of Grammy while you go. You haven't been outside for days."

Jordan sighed. She didn't wish to make herself presentable and visit with acquaintances she would likely never see again. She shook her head slowly from side to side.

"Will you say yes if I go as well?" Naomi offered. "Mrs. Chance can stay with Grammy."

Naomi looked eager and confident she had found a solution. Not wanting to disappoint her daughter, Jordan gave a single nod. She forced herself to wash up and get dressed.

★★★

Emily answered the plain wooden door. The years had not diminished her beauty. She was tall and regal, with gray hair pulled into a bun that contrasted with her light-brown skin. Her dress was a simple tan-and-white gingham she had likely sewn for herself.

She looked confused. Her hazel eyes darted between their faces, finally landing on the older White woman. Her eyebrows raised in surprise as recognition dawned.

"Lisbeth?!" Emily asked.

Lisbeth nodded.

"Oh my," Emily beamed at her half sister. "What a lovely surprise. Come in! Is this Sadie? And . . . Jordan?"

Emily hugged them each in turn, even Naomi, whom she had never met before. Jordan did not remember Emily as being so warm, but it had been many years since they had seen one another.

They moved into a living room with worn but comfortable furniture from before the war.

Emily left and soon returned with a tray of biscuits and tea. Jordan listened as Lisbeth explained their purpose in coming to Chicago.

Emily looked at Jordan, her lips pulled down in sorrow. "My condolences. Your mother is a precious soul and the earth will be diminished without her—though heaven will be rewarded with another angel."

Jordan's throat swelled up. It was hard to push out a response, so she just nodded with a bittersweet smile.

"Goodness," Emily said to Lisbeth, "I cannot remember our last correspondence. Perhaps two or even three years ago, when you informed me about your Matthew's passing."

Lisbeth shook her head. "It has been nearly four years since he died."

"Is that so!" Emily said. "Time is an amazing magician, making life vanish all too quickly."

The room grew still as the women took in the truth of

the words.

"How are Sam and his family?" Emily asked.

"Very well!" Lisbeth replied. "He and his wife, Diana, have a produce market in the warehouse district of Oakland. They prefer that to farming and are doing quite well financially. Their three children are our greatest joy."

"Are you in touch with Jack?" Emily asked about their evil brother. Hearing his name quickened Jordan's heart, and bile rose in her throat.

"Jack died from gangrene in 1891. Julianne was kind enough to send a short note to inform me. She alternates between living with her daughter in Charlottesville and her son who remained in Richmond—and followed in his father's footsteps. I fear Johnny is likely as cruel a law enforcement agent as his father was." Lisbeth shuddered as she said his name, making it obvious she shared Jordan's feelings about Jack Wainwright.

Lisbeth changed the topic. "We had the delightful surprise to have Willie working on the train we journeyed on."

"Your son is a porter?" Jordan asked.

Emily shook her head and explained, "He's a conductor."

"Oh, I see," Jordan said, judgment in her voice.

Sadie, in response to her tone, asked, "Is that unusual?"

Emily bit her lip and slowly nodded her head. "It's a White man's job."

"Oh." Sadie looked confused.

Sounding defensive, Emily justified, "Willie went to get a job at the Pullman Company, expecting to follow in his father's footsteps as a coal man. He was told he was in the wrong office and directed to a different department. There he was given a job as a conductor, which pays three times as much as his father makes. They had mistaken him for being White." She shrugged.

"He's passing?" Naomi asked.

Emily nodded. "At work."

Sadie and Lisbeth exchanged a look of confusion. Lisbeth shrugged. Like most White people, they seemed to be ignorant of the practice.

Jordan took in a deep breath and explained, "Passing is when a light-skinned Colored pretends to be White."

Lisbeth drew her eyebrows inward.

Jordan continued, "It is more common than you probably realize."

Sadie asked, "To avoid the harm that can come from being a Negro?"

"Yes," Jordan replied. "And to get the benefits only accorded to White men: safety, respect, higher salaries."

Sadie said, "Momma, it's like the book Diana gave us, *Iola Leroy*."

Shocked, Jordan asked, "You read it?"

"I haven't," Lisbeth replied and then added, "Yet. Sadie is partway through. I wish to read it when she is finished."

Jordan explained, "Then you will learn that passing comes with a cost. Many who pass stop associating with their family."

Lisbeth looked at Emily; concern on her face, she asked, "Willie has not severed his relationship with you, has he?"

Emily shook her head. "Not entirely. He's away for work most of the time. When he's in town, he visits and is generous to share a portion of his wages with us, though he is careful to wear his hat low as he comes and goes so his face isn't seen."

A confusing wave of emotion rose in Jordan. She judged Emily for risking estrangement from her son for financial gain but envied the security that came from a good income.

"Now I better understand the undercurrent in our

conversation with Malcolm on the train," Sadie said. "Remember he cut you off, Momma, when you started to explain that Willie is Colored. He seemed scared and I didn't understand why." Sadie speculated, "It sounds lonely, as if he does not belong anywhere."

"Passing as White comes at a steep, steep price," Jordan agreed. "Some men use it as a means to support their Colored families, while others disappear."

"Does he have a family? Other than you?" Lisbeth asked. "I didn't press him for an answer on the train and he was not forthcoming."

Emily shook her head. "I fear he never will marry. Or if he does, we may not be allowed to meet his bride."

Lisbeth gasped. "No! He is not going to abandon you."

Emily pulled her lips into a tight smile. "We cannot predict the future. For now he seems well enough, and I am grateful to see him when his work brings him back to Chicago. He claims that Oakland does not have racial biases, so he is free to move openly there."

"Does he live there?" Sadie asked.

"Not entirely," Emily replied. "He stays in Pullman, the company town near here. Most of the White workers, even the immigrants, are required to live there."

"But you are free to live where you like?" Lisbeth asked. That sounds like we have an advantage over the White workers, when we don't." Emily considered. "Though with their slash in wages without a reduction in their rent, we may have better housing options"

Lisbeth's eyebrows drew in and she replied, "I don't understand."

"The wages of the factory workers were cut by a quarter, while their rent in the company town remains the same," Jordan explained.

Naomi added, "Mr. Pullman claims it was necessary due to the depression, but only the workingmen are affected, and the investors got a full dividend."

Jordan asked, "Do you believe the rumors of a strike?"

Emily shrugged. "The laborers are furious, but I can't imagine any good can come from walking away from work."

"The porters are striking?" Sadie asked. She looked at Jordan. "Will Malcolm?"

"No. Not the porters," Emily said. "Or the coal men. Only the White factory workers."

Jordan snorted. All eyes turned to her.

She shook her head and explained, heat in her voice, "The White men earn three times what the Colored men make working half the hours. When they organize to ask for more, they keep their lives and their jobs. It's not fair, but that isn't anything new."

She felt the stares of the others. Shame seeped into her body. There was more in her mind, but she stopped herself.

"It's not just," Lisbeth agreed. "But it's changing for the better, right? It takes time, but we will be there soon. I'm certain of that."

Jordan did not share Lisbeth's confidence in the future, but nodded, pretending to agree with her naïve statement. The conversation continued, but Jordan didn't follow it. She ruminated over Emily's son. The thought of Willie passing for White troubled her, though she did not understand why she cared. It was not her concern that he was abandoning his family for financial advancement.

She did not have the energy to tend well to her own family. She didn't need to concern herself with Emily's son.

CHAPTER EIGHT

SADIE

Chicago
June 1894

Sadie crept through the doorway to Mattie's room, not knowing what to expect. Momma, Jordan, and Naomi sat around the bed, so close their knees touched the mattress. Momma and Jordan were still holding hands over Mattie's chest. Had they sat like this all night? Sadie's emotions twisted in empathy.

Mattie had progressively slipped further away. She had slept most of the last three days. Last night her breathing had changed dramatically. Sadie wanted to stay awake with the others, but exhaustion had overcome her, so she'd gone to sleep for a few hours. She'd expected Mattie to be in heaven when she returned from her rest, but that was not the case.

A loud, rattling exhale startled Sadie. Her heart raced hard and fast in her chest. A throbbing silence followed. Was that Mattie's last breath? She waited for the trio to do something besides watch the beloved old woman, but they didn't move.

Pressure built in Sadie's lungs. She inhaled suddenly, involuntarily; she'd been holding her breath. She filled her lungs a few more times. Another loud rattle came from the bed. It wasn't over yet. Sadie slipped out of the room to make tea and toast. They would need sustenance to keep them going after the long night.

She returned with a tray of food. Setting it on the bureau, she poured a cup of tea for each woman. Naomi and Momma took her offering, but Jordan shook her head. Sadie's eyes teared up at the pain on Miss Jordan's face. She wished she could hug her sorrow away, but there was nothing to be done to erase this tender ending. Mattie Freedman was dying and it was causing them pain.

Sadie sat a respectful distance back, poised to be helpful should they need anything. Each time a loud breath ended, Sadie counted until the next one came. It kept her calm and gave her nerves a focus. The numbers mostly grew further and further apart, though not always. She counted to seventeen and then to twenty-three; forty-seven, and then thirty-one. Twenty-two and then twenty-one. On and on she counted, losing all sense of time. And then she got to one hundred. Sadie stopped counting. She waited. And waited. Nothing. That had been the final breath.

The room throbbed in silence. Miss Jordan rose from her mother's bedside, her eyes sunken into her face transformed by grief.

"I'm going to go lie down," she said, her voice flat. She walked out, leaving a void in the room.

Momma and Naomi exchanged looks. Sadie didn't know what happened now. She'd never attended a death before.

Momma suggested, "We can sit here for a bit. There's no rush."

Naomi nodded. Then her eyes welled up and tears spilled out over her cheeks. Momma's light hand took Naomi's.

"Your grandmother was a great woman. One of the best

who ever lived. No book will speak of her, but she will live on in us." Momma's eyes were wet too.

Quiet filled the room. After some time had passed, Momma hummed "Swing Low, Sweet Chariot"—the song she said always brought Mattie to mind.

Naomi smiled and took up the words. Together they sang Mattie's favorite hymn:

> *Swing low, sweet chariot,*
> *Coming for to carry me home,*
> *Swing low, sweet chariot,*
> *Coming for to carry me home.*
>
> *I looked over Jordan, and what did I see,*
> *Coming for to carry me home.*
> *A band of angels coming after me,*
> *Coming for to carry me home.*
>
> *Swing low, sweet chariot,*
> *Coming for to carry me home,*
> *Swing low, sweet chariot,*
> *Coming for to carry me home.*
>
> *If you get there before I do,*
> *Coming for to carry me home;*
> *Tell all my friends I'm coming too,*
> *Coming for to carry me home.*
>
> *Swing low, sweet chariot,*
> *Coming for to carry me home,*
> *Swing low, sweet chariot,*
> *Coming for to carry me home.*
>
> *I'm sometimes up, I'm sometimes down,*
> *Coming for to carry me home;*
> *But still my soul feels heavenly bound,*

Coming for to carry me home.

Swing low, sweet chariot,
Coming for to carry me home,
Swing low, sweet chariot,
Coming for to carry me home.

Naomi said, "Thank you for being here. I'm sorry Mama is so—"

Momma interrupted. "Losing Mattie is a great blow, to both of us."

Naomi nodded. "She hasn't accepted my father's death . . . and now this."

"Great sorrow changes you," Momma said. "It's been four years, but I still miss Matthew every day."

The familiar ache rose in Sadie. The longing for her father that always sat just below the surface rose into her throat. Tears leaked from her eyes, and she did not bother to wipe them away.

"And your mother?" Naomi asked. "Do you still miss her?"

Momma scoffed and drew up one lip. She replied, "My mother was a selfish and bitter woman. She was neither a comfort nor an example for me. I wish for her a peace in heaven she never found on this earth, but I cannot say I miss her."

Sadie put her hand on her belly, aware of the profound devotion she felt toward the little angel that was somehow still growing inside her. Selfishly, she was a little relieved at Mrs. Freedman's passing. She and Momma could return home soon after the burial.

★★★

Alone in Malcolm's room, Momma said, "You are anxious to

be in Oakland. I can see . . ." Momma stopped to consider her words. "Sadie, I have a suspicion that you are eager to return home for a special reason." Her glance traveled to Sadie's belly.

Sadie's eyes welled up. Momma was speaking of the urgent desire, and fear, that weighed on her heart. Sadie rubbed her abdomen and nodded. There was a tiny protrusion now. Of course Momma would notice.

"Yes," Sadie whispered, her voice hoarse. It was hard to share this secret, to have it be real. If she failed, her mother would join her in disappointment and sorrow once again.

Momma reached out a hand. Sadie took it.

"When was your last bleeding?" Momma asked.

"January," Sadie replied.

"Quickening?" Momma asked.

Sadie nodded, though she wondered if she only imagined a tickle in her belly that signaled the movement of a baby.

Momma's lips pulled up; her eyes sparkled. Sadie allowed hope to fill her soul. She felt a delicious chill radiate out from her chest. She smiled back at her momma. Only once before had she made it this far. They could dare to dream that this time might end with a live baby in their family.

Momma declared, "Mattie's burial is set. Let's go to the station to get our tickets home for the following day. I hate to leave so quickly, but Jordan and Naomi will understand when they hear our great news."

Sadie nodded and smiled. "Thank you, Momma."

"Thank you for coming on this journey with me, Sadie. It has been a comfort to have you." Momma's face looked pained. "I wouldn't have accepted your offer, had I known."

"I . . . ," Sadie started to say. She thought for a moment, unsure what she would have chosen had she known with certainty she was carrying a child before they left California.

"And perhaps I would not have made the offer, had I known with certainty," Sadie said. "But neither of us did, so we made our choices in the moment. I do not regret being here with you." Then she added, "Though I long to return home."

★★★

The station was bustling. Sadie thought they might see evidence of the Pullman worker strike that had been going on since May. Yesterday's newspaper reported that the American Railway Union was joining in sympathy with the Pullman workers, but Sadie saw no indication that the strike of the men who built the sleeping cars was affecting the flow of people in all directions. Like Oakland, the crowd was mostly men—American and immigrants from Europe. Unlike Oakland there were many Negro workers and travelers and no Chinese laborers. She'd yet to see a Chinaman in Chicago.

Momma and Sadie purchased two tickets for the Pullman sleeper car on the train leaving the day after Mattie's funeral. As they walked away from the station, relief settled upon her. She imagined pulling into Oakland, the beautiful golden hills on one side and the shimmering bay on the other. She rubbed her belly. Momma smiled at her.

"I'm so happy for you, Sadie," Momma said.

"Me too, Momma."

"Shall we send a telegram to Heinrich to tell him of our arrival date?"

Sadie nodded. In less than a week, her husband would be picking her up at the station. Sadie said, "I look forward to telling him our good news in person."

Momma replied, "Surely any lingering resentment about this trip will be banished at your words."

"No one can maintain a foul mood in the face of a new family member," Sadie agreed. "Can you imagine how excited the girls and Diana and Sam will be?" Sadie beamed, unable to contain her delight.

Momma squeezed her arm; excitement of her own shone in her eyes.

***

Mattie's funeral was held at the AME, the African Methodist Episcopal Church. Waiting for the service to begin, Sadie was acutely aware that there were only a handful of White people in the sanctuary. She'd never been outnumbered by people of another race. As a child in Oberlin, she had worshiped and gone to school in a racially mixed community, but she hardly remembered that. Their Methodist congregation in Oakland was composed of only White people, most of whom were native born. And while her high school had students from all over the world, including China, there was only one Negro, and most of the students were Caucasian.

Sadie was grateful to be sitting with Emily and William. They'd been kind enough to take them in after Mattie's passing. Momma had insisted they give Malcolm's room to Samuel and his family. Initially Jordan had protested, but then accepted the offer with gratitude.

The preacher was lively and personal, telling details about Mattie's life. Sadie enjoyed being carried away by the music and the prayers, and feeling the outpouring of love in the room.

After the worship, a gray-haired Colored man rushed up to Momma.

"Lisbeth!" he exclaimed, a huge grin on his face and his arms open wide.

Momma smiled back at him. "Samuel, it is so good to see you." She leaned in for a surprisingly long embrace.

Sadie studied her mother. She cared deeply for this

person Sadie didn't really know.

"You remember Nora?" Samuel asked Momma.

Momma said, "Of course." The two women hugged briefly.

Samuel explained to the younger generation circled around them: "You remember the stories of the little White girl on the plantation? The one that taught me to read and saved me from her brother?"

His children and grandchildren nodded. Sadie was stunned, and nauseated, by his casual mention of needing to be saved from her uncle Jack.

"This is *that* girl—Lisbeth Wainwright!" Then he corrected, "She's Mrs. Johnson to you."

Momma shook her head. "That was a lifetime ago. Two lifetimes ago. Maybe more than that."

"You are well?" Nora asked.

Momma nodded. They exchanged news about their lives, Momma telling personal details about coping with Poppa's death, ailments, and more. It was at once strange and sweet. Sadie saw a familiarity Momma did not have with friends in Oakland, even after so many years of living there.

She imagined what Heinrich would make of this scene, she and Momma surrounded by Colored people. For Sadie it was self-consciously unusual but also fascinating. She was grateful for this opportunity to learn more about her mother and this lovely family she was so devoted to. In the weeks they had been here, Sadie had grown so very fond of Naomi and Jordan.

Heinrich would likely disapprove because it was not right to make peers out of people who were "socially inferior," a term that made sense to Heinrich but not to Sadie. These were educated people: lawyers, teachers, nurses. She was going to miss them and hoped they would maintain a relationship once they were in Oakland.

★★★

Sadie and Momma finished washing the last dirty plate in the small but functional kitchen. The social hall was nearly empty; it was time to leave. Sadie stepped toward Jordan and Naomi for their goodbyes, but Momma turned the other way, back into the empty sanctuary.

Sadie found her in a corner with tears streaming down her face. Momma shook her head.

"I am silly," she said through a tight voice, "but I will most likely never see Samuel again."

"I didn't realize you were so fond of him," Sadie said.

Momma bit her lip and barely whispered, "Me neither."

Sadie rubbed Momma's back and breathed slowly, like she would with a child who'd fallen and skinned their knees.

"I saw him every day of my childhood, out my window." Her voice broke. She swallowed.

Sadie remembered the window from her only visit to Fair Oaks when she was a little girl. It overlooked the quarters where Samuel lived. Ironically the one time she was there, she had looked out and seen Miss Jordan and Mattie.

Momma continued her remembrance. "Samuel resented me because I had Mattie standing by me each day. And I was jealous of him because he had her greatest devotion. It was such a perversion of family." Momma shook her head.

Sadie listened with rapt attention. Momma so rarely shared anything emotional about her life, especially her childhood.

Momma looked right at Sadie, her eyes red and moist. "I love you. I do not say it often, but never doubt it."

Sadie's heart swelled. "I love you too, Momma. I'm sorry this is causing you such sorrow."

"This pain is the cost for real love . . . and it is well worth the price," Momma said with certainty.

Momma took a deep breath. She wiped her blue eyes and pale skin. She held up a hand, signaling Sadie to give her a moment. Sadie kissed her momma's cheek and stepped away. She waited patiently for Momma's signal that she was ready to say her goodbyes.

Momma and Samuel shared a long, sweet hug. No words passed between them. Sadie watched, full of empathy for her momma, who did not want to make a scene.

Naomi gave Sadie a kind and full hug. Malcolm put out a hand when she opened her arms, polite, but not warm. Sadie felt she knew him well after staying in his room for many weeks, but his visits home had been brief, and she understood that he did not return the sentiment. Miss Jordan patted her cheek after they embraced. It was tender and sweet, reminding Sadie of being her student.

"Goodbye, Miss Jordan. My faaavorite teacher," Sadie said. They both laughed. She imagined how different it would feel to be saying a forever goodbye. She suddenly understood her mother's sadness better and was glad that Miss Jordan would be moving to Oakland so they would see one another again.

Momma stood in front of Jordan, tears glistening in both women's eyes.

"Thank you," Momma said. "I'm so very grateful that I could be here to honor Mattie."

"You . . ." Jordan's voice broke. "I'm glad you were here with us."

They embraced.

"Please call on us soon after you get into Oakland," Momma said. "We want to help you settle in."

Jordan replied, "Thank you. We'll be there as soon as we

get packed up; there's nothing keeping us here now."

Sadie and Momma walked away from Mattie's funeral. Feeling the poignancy of this moment, the young woman looped her arm through her mother's, a small comfort for a great loss, but there was nothing she could do to take away her mother's pain. As Momma said, it was the cost of loving.

★★★

The next day they arrived at the station at the appointed time, but there was no train at the assigned platform. Momma pointed. A train idled down the track. Perhaps that was the one that would take them home. Sadie found an agent.

"Is our train to Oakland delayed?" she asked the young man.

He nodded. "You could say so." He gave a cryptic response without looking at her.

Heat rose in Sadie's cheeks. She longed to be on that train without delay. This man was indifferent to her needs.

"Where should we wait for it?" she asked, striving to keep her emotions out of her voice.

"I'd go home if I were you," he replied.

"That is what I'm here for—to get home." She spoke more harshly than she liked, but his rude dismissal of her concern was galling.

He sighed and looked at her. "You haven't heard?"

"Heard what?"

"This morning the members of the American Railway Union stopped handling any trains that have Pullman sleeper cars attached to them." He looked her up and down. "You were gonna ride in a Pullman?"

Sadie nodded.

"Try to get a second-class ticket," he said. "If I know anything about Eugene Debs, that train is not going to have a Pullman on it—when and *if* it heads to Oakland."

"I don't understand," Sadie said, tears pressing against her eyes.

"Eugene Debs, the head of the Railway Union?" the man said.

Sadie nodded; she'd heard of him. Since the Pullman Strike had started, his name was in the paper nearly every day.

"He's decided none of his workers are touching any cars on any trains that have a Pullman attached to it. The workers are rising up for better pay." He shrugged. "You understand better pay, don' you?"

Sadie nodded and wiped at her eyes.

"I'm sorry, ma'am," the man said, finally sounding sympathetic. "I don't have any more information. This was just sprung on us a few hours ago. Check at the ticket counter. They can assist you."

Her tears had brought out his kindness but didn't get her a path home.

Momma took her hand, and they got in the long line at the counter. It seemed that everyone who expected to be on the westward train wanted to make a new arrangement. After an hour, they were at the counter.

"Tickets." The little man reached out his hand. He looked them over.

"We would like to get to Oakland as soon as possible," Momma declared.

"I suggest that you purchase a second-class ticket from Naperville to Oakland for tomorrow. That train is running today, but you can't get there in time to catch it," he said.

"How far is Naperville?"

"Twenty-eight miles," he replied. "You'll have to hire a carriage."

"You are certain we can get to Oakland from there tomorrow?" Sadie asked.

"No, ma'am," he replied. "We do not know how this situation will play out."

Sadie swallowed hard and pointed down the track. "Is there any chance that train is going out later this morning or afternoon?"

"I can't say for certain, ma'am," he said. "But I do not believe it will be going anywhere today."

"Instead of going to Naperville, can we exchange these tickets for tomorrow's train from Chicago to Oakland?" Momma asked. "We are willing to travel second class."

"All classes are full tomorrow and the next. We have availability in three days," he informed them.

Momma looked at Sadie for approval. Sadie nodded.

"We will take it," Momma said.

As they walked away with their new tickets, Momma spoke. "Hours in a carriage will not be good for the baby nor can we risk being stranded in the middle of Illinois. We'll pray for a swift end to the disruption so we may return home for your confinement." Momma squeezed her hand, not saying more about the fear pressing inside each of them.

Sadie nodded. They joined the line at the telegraph office to inform Heinrich of the change in plans before returning to Emily and William's home.

★★★

In the morning, Momma, Emily, and Sadie stood side by side reading the news from the *Chicago Tribune* spread out on the wooden-plank table.

MOBS HOLD TRAINS.

—

Pullman Boycott in an Alarming Form at Hammond.

—

TROOPS CALLED OUT.

—

Monon and Erie Trains Blocked by Spiked Rails.

—

WRECK ON PENNSYLVANIA

—

Cars Ditched and Several Passengers Reported Hurt.

—

United States Mails Have Been Interfered With and Serious Trouble Feared.

TRAINS ABANDONED IN CALIFORNIA.

Refusal of Men to Handle Pullman Cars Makes the Tie-Up Complete

SAN FRANCISCO, Cal., June 27.—Tonight it is impossible for a person to leave the State of California by rail. Not a train except those engaged in suburban travel is moving in the whole State. The Southern Pacific Company adhered to its determination not to run trains without Pullman cars and the trainmen were equally as determined not to handle the cars bearing the hated name of Pullman. Consequently the hundreds of people who expected

to travel North, South, and East were
forced to return to San Francisco. The
trainmen went to their homes and the
big Oakland mole was deserted except
for the ferry-boat employees and the
suburbaners.

"I'm glad we did not get a ticket from Naperville,"
Momma said.

Sadie nodded, though no one was looking at her.

"Willie is caught in Oakland?" Sadie asked Emily.

"As far as we know," Emily replied, her voice filled with
fear.

Momma patted Emily's back. "I'm sure he is safe."

Emily tried to smile, but it wasn't convincing.

"I don't understand why the railroads don't run the trains
without the Pullman cars," Sadie wondered aloud.

"Those railroad men are sticking together," William
explained from across the room. "If the Pullman laborers
win their strike, then next it will be brakemen, and then the
conductors, and then the engineers. They do not want labor
to organize."

"Their demands are unreasonable?" Sadie asked.

Anger flashed on William's face. Sadie regretted her
words, fearing she sounded as if she were challenging her
generous host—a laborer.

Emily replied, "Pullman expects them to be grateful for
low wages, high rents in a company town, and sixteen-hour
days. He has no regard for safety, then when workers are
injured on the job, their family gets displaced from their
homes because they no longer work for the company." Emily
shook her head. "I don't believe the strike will work, but I
understand the anger of the workers. Dignity and security

are not too much to ask."

Sadie nodded and smiled, wishing to seem sympathetic to their cause. She did want laborers to have good working conditions, but also she resented them for disrupting her life. She just wanted to get home.

"We have two more days until our trip," Momma said. "Let's pray for all of us that this ends before then."

The next day the strike was still in effect, but the story in the paper gave Sadie hope that they would be going home soon. Judge Caldwell of the United States Circuit Court told Debs and the American Railway Union to keep "hands off" the Santa Fe Railroad on the grounds that they were interfering with mail trains. The general marshals of the twenty-one railroad lines that came into Chicago had hired two hundred to three hundred workers to replace the striking men. Federal marshals would give them protection to get the mail moving again. Sadie and Momma kept their trunks packed, and resolved to go to the station in the morning to be on the train home.

Sadie rose early, ready to head out, but William shook his head.

"There's no point in you going," he said. "I just got back from the station. They sent me home. Everything is still locked up tight."

The back of Sadie's eyeballs burned. "What about the replacement men?"

"I hear they had a train ready to head out, but the strikers blocked the tracks, uncoupled the Pullman car, and waved the train on."

"We are traveling second class, so that will not affect us," Momma said.

William shook his head. "Like I said before, the railroad men are sticking together. The owners aren't letting any trains out unless they have the Pullman cars. The workers will not let any train run *with* a Pullman sleeper car."

"But the government is forcing the owners to keep trains going to keep the mail moving," Sadie stated, passion in her voice.

William shook his head. He looked at Sadie as if she were a child.

Sadie asked, "Isn't that what the article said yesterday? The judge's orders."

"The government supports the owners, not the laborers," he explained. "The judges are not going to go against George Pullman."

"But the mail?" Sadie insisted, perhaps sounding naïve.

Emily shrugged. "Soon enough federal marshals will fire upon the strikers. The workers won't be able to stand against the government for long, but for now you are not leaving."

Fire upon? Sadie could not believe the federal government would harm its own citizens.

Momma pulled in her lips and asked, "Would you like us to find another place to stay? We so appreciate your hospitality, and you did not anticipate it would be so long."

Emily smiled and squeezed Momma's hand. "Do not even think of it. You are welcome to stay here as long as you need a home in Chicago."

"Thank you." Momma and Aunt Emily exchanged a smile.

"She's right," Uncle William said. "You are welcome here. And . . . you don't got a lot of choice. Do you know how many folks are stuck in Chicago right now? The hotels are making a fortune." He continued, "I'll be out of your hair soon. Tonight I'm heading to New Orleans. That train is still running. They want extra men on hand in case it gets ugly, so they are doubling us up."

Sadie pored through the newspapers, paying attention as she never had before, her emotions tossed around like a boat in a storm. One day the strike was growing, the workers quitting in solidarity with those who had been fired for not servicing Pullman cars. The next day the federal marshals forced the hand of strikers in Hammond, Indiana. Rather than face bullets, Eugene Debs showed compassion and common sense by directing the men to return to work.

The following day, federal judges invoked the Sherman Antitrust Act and the Interstate Commerce Act and forbade Eugene Debs from communicating with the strikers, almost as if they were hoping for violence to erupt.

On and on it went, day after day: news of mobs, federal troops firing on strikers, court orders, and stranded passengers. Sadie no longer sent telegrams to Heinrich telling him of their plans. She'd already spent too large a sum sending him false information.

Three weeks into the strike, Momma interrupted her as she read about the situation in Oakland. "Let's start making clothes for that little one," Momma said.

"No," Sadie responded without thought. "It's too soon."

"I have to keep busy," Momma said. "Or I will go stir crazy. You too, I believe."

"All right," Sadie agreed reluctantly.

Momma smiled. "Let's get fabric this afternoon. We can start with gowns."

CHAPTER NINE

JORDAN

Chicago
August 1894

Naomi interrupted Jordan's sorting. They'd been organizing and cleaning for days, getting ready for their move. They planned to leave just as the heat of summer was peaking in mid-August, assuming the strike was over by then.

Fortunately Samuel and his family had returned home before the railroads to Cincinnati were tied up. However, Malcolm had been trapped in Chicago, without work or pay, since the funeral. The financial pressure built each day of the strike, but there was nothing to be done. Malcolm did not have enough seniority to be given other routes, and he couldn't find any work in town.

Jordan reminded herself to enjoy this time with him; they hadn't had this many nights under the same roof in years. But she feared that the strike, which made no demands that would benefit her Colored son, would only ruin them.

Naomi called across the room, "Mama, are you certain you wish to pack this?"

She held up the pamphlet from the Columbian Exposition, the cover facing Jordan.

The Reason Why

The Colored American is not
In the World's Columbian Exposition

The Afro-American's Contribution to Columbian Literature

Copies sent to any address on receipt of three cents for postage,
Address Miss Ida B. Wells
128 S. Clark Street, Chicago, Ill., U.S.A.

"I am certain," Jordan replied.

"It only stirs painful memories," Naomi offered. Jordan hated the pity in her daughter's voice.

"Open it," she commanded.

Naomi did. She turned the pages, and then her eyes grew big. She'd found the signature from the great man himself: Frederick B. Douglass. Jordan would never part with that pamphlet and hoped Naomi never would either.

Jordan had worked with him last year as a volunteer for the Columbian Exposition. They'd intended to highlight the accomplishments their race had made in the twenty-five years since emancipation—and to show the practices that were being introduced to tread on the progress of their people. Miss Ida B. Wells, the author of the pamphlet, was especially devoted to publicizing the rising practices of mutilation and lynching that were used to quash Colored business ventures, enfranchisement, and movement.

However, the organizers of the exposition refused to have the reputation of "this great nation" be sullied by the truth, so Colored Americans were not granted any space in the arcade of the United States. Only the small nation of

Hayti, where Mr. Douglass had been the ambassador, allowed them a home for their display.

The small booth had been constantly inundated by Mr. Douglass's admirers. Ladies and gentlemen from all over the world, representing all hues, religions, and backgrounds, lined up to shake the illustrious man's hand. He was the very best of this nation, and yet it refused to give him a place in its representation to the world.

"I understand, Mama. Of course you must keep this pamphlet," Naomi said. "What about this?"

Naomi held up the top half of a broken walking stick. A carved eagle glared at her. Jordan swallowed hard and reached out for it. Naomi passed it to her. Rubbing the worn stick, she thought of its history. It was more than one hundred years old, made in 1788 in honor of the ratification of the United States Constitution.

Cousin Sarah had left it behind in Ohio when she returned to the Fair Oaks plantation. Sarah had not liked living in a town, with so many strangers and choices. She missed her people and her simple routines. It had pained Mama that Sarah couldn't make the adjustment to a new way, and that Mama couldn't prevent her from taking her daughter Ella back to Virginia. Mama had protested, arguing they would not be welcomed back—and maybe even harmed—but she was wrong. Alfie Richards, the current owner of Fair Oaks, celebrated and advertised Sarah's return as proof there was no better life for the freedmen elsewhere.

"This stick killed your great-aunt Rebecca," Jordan said.

Naomi nodded, aware of the story.

And broke my arm, Jordan thought.

After emancipation, Mr. Richards had declared that Cousin Sarah's children, Ella and Sophia, were being sold. Their grandmother Rebecca objected, stating they were free. Mr. Richards met her argument with a hard crack to the head. The girls were sent away, and three days later Aunt Rebecca died from a swollen head.

After the war, Mama had made Samuel and Jordan return to Virginia to rescue Cousin Sarah and try to find her children. Jordan had not wanted to take that journey—back to their ancestral home. Ironically, she stayed in Virginia for years. If she hadn't gone with Mama, she would not have stayed to teach in the Freedman School, would never have met Booker, wouldn't have her beloved children. It was strange how one choice could change the course of your entire life.

Sophia had never been heard from again, but the reunion between young Ella and Cousin Sarah was one of Jordan's most joy-filled memories.

Mr. Richards had repeated his abuse when Cousin Sarah left the plantation with them. Jordan rubbed her forearm, feeling the tender spot where her bones had mended. In an instant, without any forethought, she'd blocked Mr. Richards's blow from striking her mother. Mama twisted the stick from his hand before he could strike any of them again, knocking him to the ground. Mama broke it in two on the side of a wagon and they drove away with it. Jordan had never seen her so fierce.

Mama kept it all these years—*A memento of suffering or courage?* Jordan wondered. Perhaps both. Jordan's throat tightened. She felt torn, uncertain whether she wanted it in her new life.

"Set it aside. I'll decide later," Jordan directed.

She stood up, needing a change of scenery. They'd been sorting for hours. She seemed to want to take everything into their next life. She did not want to decide what was important and what was not, but they did not have room for all of their belongings.

She walked outside for fresh air and sunshine. Sitting on a bench her father had made, Jordan surveyed the backyard. The garden was bursting with life: purple cabbage, lush bush beans, tall tomatoes, and parsnip greens. A few plants had already gone to seed. They'd collected many seeds to start next year's garden. Thin leaves of crocuses, their blooms long gone, popped out at Jordan. Sudden sorrow and fear caused her heart to leap.

She'd nearly forgotten her mama's request that some of those bulbs make the westward journey. She crossed to the cupboard to gather what she needed to transport them. Jordan knelt on the warm ground, a trowel in her hand, and dug down, freeing the bulbs from the earth. She shook off the dirt and placed them in a burlap bag with wood shavings. She repeated the process until she had ten of them. Hopefully one or two would survive to take root and eventually blossom into a sign of spring.

She returned to the living room and handed Naomi the bag of bulbs.

"Pack these," she instructed.

Naomi nodded, though her expression made it clear that she believed Jordan was taking too much. Naomi was still young and did not understand the importance of knowing your heritage, your story, where you come from.

"Do not discard that." Jordan pointed.

Naomi sighed, reached into the waste bin, and pulled out the yellowed newspaper: the *Richmond Dispatch* from February 19, 1880. Skepticism pulled at Naomi's brows as her eyes skimmed left and right across the page; she stopped scanning to read an article. Her face transformed from doubt to disgust to dismay.

Naomi looked up and asked, "Uncle Page?"

Jordan nodded.

"Oh, Mama." Naomi's voice was high. "Lynched?"

That hateful word cut through Jordan. Her mind filled with the horrid image of Page's swollen face, the rope burns on his neck and wrists, his fingers and ears missing—souvenirs for his murderers.

"How? Why?" Naomi took a deep breath. "Why didn't you tell me?"

Jordan swallowed hard and exhaled. She would not let herself be overtaken by emotion.

Sounding harsher than she meant to, she said, "You were young when it happened and we chose to shield you from the ugliness as best as we could. I expected your father would tell you, but then he never did."

"This is why we left Richmond?" Naomi asked. "So suddenly?"

Jordan nodded. Naomi returned to the article.

She looked up and asked, "Did he . . . ?"

"No!" Jordan snapped, interrupting her daughter midsentence. "Do not think for a moment that your uncle Page was murdered for anything besides expecting respect for our people. He did not make advances at that young woman. He was killed because he refused to remove his name from the rolls of registered voters. Uncle Page was a community leader and an outspoken advocate for the Negro franchise."

"Does Malcolm know?" Naomi asked.

Jordan thought for a moment and swallowed back the pain of that time. "We have never spoken of it, but I believe he had an understanding."

Naomi stared at her, looking like she wanted something, perhaps the comfort of a hug.

Jordan said, "It was long ago, Naomi. There is nothing we can do for it now but move on with our lives, but I want to keep the article." She continued, "And the stick. Ask Malcolm to saw off the top. We have enough room for the liberty eagle."

Naomi shook her head and shrugged, not fully understanding why her mother wanted to keep mementos of their family's pain. She turned back to the overwhelming task of sorting their life.

★★★

"Malcolm?" Naomi asked over supper, her voice at once hesitant and challenging.

"Yes?"

"Why are you so subservient and formal when you are around Lisbeth and Sadie?" she questioned. "It doesn't suit you, and it bothers me."

"I don't trust them, and neither should you, despite what you say, Ma." He looked over at Jordan.

Jordan's mind protested at the thought that she caused Malcolm pain by allowing them to be here. "They've been disrespectful to you"? she asked, hoping her voice was neutral.

"The few times I've seen them they treat me just fine, but in my experience the nice ones can be the most dangerous."

"You're being dramatic," Naomi suggested.

He shrugged. "The ones that display their hate are easy. I know where I stand. I understand what they want," he stated.

"How can you live like that, not trusting the people you work with every day?" Naomi asked.

"It's the job," he explained. "Most of the kind ones don't turn against you, but you can't tell which ones are genuine. Not too long after I started on the trains, a White lady made a point of telling me she did not hold to racial prejudices. She was a little too friendly during the journey, if you know what I mean. I pretended not to understand her overtures, but one night she made her desires all too clear. I rebuffed her gently, but she looked at me with such venom that I believe she would have shot me if she had a gun in her possession."

Jordan's chest tightened.

Her son continued his story. "In the midst of the night I heard a scream in the dining car. I rushed to the sound. The White lady stood there, terror on her face, tears in her eyes, reporting I had forced myself upon her. She was such a good actress that I would have believed her myself had she not been speaking of me. Only good fortune spared me my job, and perhaps my life. I'd been with the conductor during the time of the reported abuse. If I had not been with him, he would have believed her."

Jordan's stomach sank as she listened. She wasn't naïve—and was well versed in the humiliations and mistreatment of the porters. Her husband had come home with horrible stories. Still, she'd harbored hope that the treatment would have improved for Malcolm, but once again she was faced with the painful reality that she was helpless in protecting her children from the abuses toward their race.

Malcolm had never spoken of his treatment at work. He'd only glorified Oakland and spoke of his certainty that their lives would be better there—a new start in a growing city that did not hold to the old forms of prejudice. She'd agreed to move there for the weather, but this story confirmed she should not expect them to have all the freedoms they deserved.

★★★

The strike finally ended by the force of the federal marshals. It had seemed nearly endless, but it had been only a matter of weeks from the time the workers walked away from the factory and when they returned to making Pullman cars. The courts had negotiated an agreement with the railroad magnates that allowed the laborers to retain their jobs, though none of the demands for better wages or working conditions had been met. Not even the White men could get a fair wage these days.

Days after the strike ended, the trains ran westward again, but no tickets were available. Malcolm left for work, but Jordan and Naomi lived in a strange limbo, in an abandoned life, with most of their belongings packed. After a few more days their turn had come. In the morning they'd leave Chicago, most likely forever.

Jordan forced the panic down. She did not allow herself to look back at the house. Walking away from it felt like abandoning her beloveds. Her head realized Booker, Pops, and Mama were never coming back, but her heart hammered in protest: *They will not find you when they come home.* She had sudden empathy for Cousin Sarah, who'd wanted to stay on the plantation in case her daughter Sophia returned.

Jordan refused to look at Naomi, who wanted to commiserate. She didn't want to cry. There was nothing to do but walk away.

Sadie and Lisbeth were waiting in the sticky heat. They'd come from Emily and William's home to board together. The two White women had delayed their tickets by two days in order to be on the train with them and Malcolm.

Sadie's belly protruded, revealing to the world the secret they pretended not to see. She looked to be about ten weeks from delivery. It wasn't Jordan's place to bring up a topic that Sadie seemed to want to keep private. Jordan smiled to herself, remembering one of her mama's favorite sayings: "Life goes on even after we are gone."

Jordan led the way down the street until they came to

the nearby station. Booker had been required to live within blocks of the station in case he was needed for an emergency. The train idled at the platform, belching out black smoke. Jordan inhaled the strangely comforting fumes. She ached with the memory of hugging her husband, that smell filling her nostrils as she pressed against his stiff blue suit.

Lost in memory, she heard a voice intruding on her thoughts. "Miss Sadie and Mrs. Johnson?"

"Willie!" Lisbeth said. "What an unexpected surprise."

"This is my route. I'm not surprised that you would be on my train for your return. Please find me if I can do anything to keep you comfortable. Which car are you in?"

Willie was light skinned and strong featured, with sparkling hazel eyes. He was easily able to pass for White but was obviously Colored for those who had eyes to see. Inexplicably Jordan found herself annoyed that they would be sharing the journey with him. Sadie showed him the ticket.

"Malcolm will take great care of you," Willie said. "I'll make certain of that."

Lisbeth sucked in her breath. She replied, "We happen to already be friends with Malcolm. In fact, this is his mother, Jordan, and sister, Naomi."

Willie looked right at Jordan. His colored eyes were lighter than Emily's, but she saw the resemblance.

"Mrs. Wallace, it is very nice to meet you." He smiled in that way men who knew they were handsome did.

He turned to Naomi. "Miss Wallace?"

Naomi nodded at the not-so-subtle inquiry about her marital status. Willie's charm bristled Jordan, but Naomi looked captivated.

"How do you do?" he said with a glint in his eye. "I'm sure Malcolm will make certain you are comfortable."

Naomi shook her head and replied, "Unfortunately there was no room in the Pullman sleeping car for us, so we will not be with my brother."

Willie's eyebrows drew in for a moment, but then he pasted a smile back on.

His hand reached out for their ticket. He looked it over and nodded.

"I'll be sure to ask Cedric to pay you special attention," he assured them. Looking between Jordan and Lisbeth, he tipped his cap and said, "I'll let you get settled in. Please don't hesitate to ask for me if you need anything."

He smiled at Naomi, and an obvious spark passed between them. His light eyes glistened with joy, or lust. Naomi, not normally responsive to the flattery of men, practically flushed. Disturbed at her daughter's outright flirtation, Jordan tapped Naomi's shoulder and pointed down the walkway.

They read the numbers on the train cars until they came to the one they would be journeying on.

"Here we are," Jordan said.

Lisbeth looked up at the car and then down the platform.

"I'm sorry to part ways," the White woman said. "Perhaps we will see one another in the dining car? Or we can visit in the lounge car?"

Naomi shrugged. "I'm not certain of the rules, mixing second class with the sleeper passengers. Certainly we will see you in Oakland . . . in four days." Naomi instructed Sadie, "Tell Malcolm I said you must lie down as much as possible. It is better for your . . . condition."

Sadie nodded fervently, worry in her eyes. Apparently they had spoken about the pregnancy.

Naomi soothed, "I'm only being cautious. Don't let my words cause alarm."

Sadie exhaled. "I will be anxious until this baby is in my

arms. But thank you for the medical advice. Your guidance is welcome." Sadie smiled.

Lisbeth looked uncomfortable as she leaned in to hug Jordan. After their embrace she held Jordan's elbow, stopping her from pulling away altogether.

"If Sadie were not pregnant, I would trade with you," Lisbeth insisted.

Jordan smiled. "Of course, thank you," she replied, as if she believed those words. But she knew better. Offers of generosity were a comfort to those who did not have to follow through with any sacrifice.

She pulled away, stepped onto the low stool, and entered the rail car.

★★★

Sounds startled Jordan awake. She forced herself to take a deep breath to slow down the rush of blood coursing through her body. Over the rhythmic click of the wheels, she heard Naomi whispering. Jordan cracked open her eyes to see Willie leaning over her daughter, his whiskers pressed right against Naomi's smooth cheek. Fury exploded in her chest. She sat up, ready to chastise them, but before Jordan had time to intrude upon their intimacy, Naomi grabbed her arm and shook her hard.

Alarm in her eyes, she whispered, "Sadie needs us!"

Naomi rushed off without conveying any more information. Willie remained, gesturing for her to go ahead of him. Jordan blinked away the sleep cloud in her eyes, rose, and followed her daughter down the narrow aisle.

Naomi waited at the door before the next car. Willie cautioned them to be careful as they passed through. He opened the portal. A gush of air whipped Jordan's face, and soot from the exhaust prickled at her skin. They crossed to the next car, and the next ones, until they came to first class.

The Pullman sleeping car was dark but for a single light on the left side. Malcolm and Lisbeth were kneeling in the dim aisle at the head of Sadie's bed. Lisbeth looked over as they approached, fear riding her features.

"Thank you for coming . . ." Her voice broke. She pointed through the wide opening in the gold curtain that partitioned the aisle from the beds. A pool of blood stained the sheets between Sadie's legs.

Jordan gasped. Her hand flew to her chest. "I'm so sorry."

Naomi rushed to the young woman, replacing Malcolm at her head. She studied Sadie's face, then touched her neck and belly through the blanket. She whispered questions Jordan couldn't make out, leaning in to hear Sadie's answers. Naomi stood up and pulled the curtains closed, separating her and Sadie in the sleeping area from the rest of them in the aisle.

The fabric of the plush velvet curtain moved. Sadie moaned, and then the sound built up into the loud and telling sign of labor. Sorrow swelled in Jordan's throat. It was too soon. How long had this been going on? She was tempted to ask Lisbeth for information but restrained herself. Instead she took her friend's hand and gave a gentle squeeze. Lisbeth acknowledged her kindness with a sad smile and tight grip. Her fingers were cold and trembling. After an unbearably long wait that included another loud moan, Naomi came through the fabric.

Looking at Malcolm, she asked, "Can we move her somewhere private?"

Is the baby alive? Jordan wanted reassurance, but continued her restraint. There was no way for anyone to know the state of the baby inside Sadie's body. It was a kindness to let her daughter do her job. Lisbeth had to be even more anxious to know how Sadie and the baby were faring.

Malcolm nodded, turned to Willie, and spoke in his ear. Willie nodded and walked away.

Malcolm explained, "We can bring her to the smoking car. It has a long couch. It smells of tobacco, but I can keep it private. How . . . ," he started to ask, but Naomi turned away before he could finish his question.

Naomi reached up and pulled down the sheet from the top sleeper.

"Take this." She handed one end to Lisbeth and the other to Jordan. The train jostled; Jordan's body jerked to the side, but she kept her balance.

"We believe Sadie can walk." Naomi instructed, "I will help her up; you two wrap the sheet around her and tie it at her chest. Malcolm, you take one arm; I will take the other."

Jordan nodded. She looked at Lisbeth. Tears ran down the other woman's cheeks, but she didn't wipe them away. She looked poised to follow Naomi's orders. Jordan took a steady breath, knowing that calm was the most helpful stance in this painful situation.

They pulled the cotton fabric open and Naomi spread the gold curtains, revealing Sadie's pale face, nearly as white as the sheet they held out. Naomi took Sadie's hand and cupped her elbow. Slowly the young woman sat up. Naomi cautioned her to stay in that position.

Jordan felt eyes on her. She looked around the car. The passengers were staring.

She shut out the strangers. Naomi must have asked a question, because Sadie nodded almost imperceptibly. Sadie leaned forward slowly and then stood up; Naomi steadied Sadie on the left, and Malcolm took her arm on the other side.

Jordan stepped behind her daughter and reached through

the tunnels of her children's arms to bring the ends of the sheet together. Sadie dipped, but they held her upright as Jordan tied the cotton fabric tight.

Slowly, carefully, they moved in the direction Willie had disappeared. Jordan shuffled behind the awkward caravan that stopped when a labor pain came over Sadie. The laboring woman moaned and swayed from side to side. Lisbeth turned her head away, but Jordan saw her fear. Sadie panted when the pain ended. Naomi whispered in her ear. Sadie nodded and Naomi said, "Let's keep going."

Two more times labor pains stopped them. Two more times they resumed through the cramped hallway until they came to Willie propping open a door. He waved them into the smoking room.

Naomi and Malcolm squeezed Sadie through the narrow portal, leaving Jordan and Lisbeth in the passageway. Ever so slowly, they lowered Sadie onto the couch and helped her to lie down. Willie and Naomi exchanged words too quiet to hear. Jordan stepped back as he rushed out.

"And blankets!" Naomi called to him from between Sadie's legs. "As many blankets as you can find."

Malcolm closed the door in their faces without acknowledging them. Jordan looked at Lisbeth. Fear covered her face. Jordan took her hand.

"We're gonna pray," Jordan declared, sounding calmer than she felt. "For that baby and for your Sadie."

Lisbeth nodded.

Lord help me find the right words, she prayed to herself.

Jordan took in a deep breath and said, "Dear Lord, watch over our Sadie and keep her safe through the birth of her blessed baby. They are both in your strong and gentle hands. We humbly ask you to do all that you can to protect them from harm. Amen."

"God, please save them both," Lisbeth added in a tight voice.

"Amen," Jordan repeated. "Do you know the date of her last bleeding?" Jordan asked.

"January," Lisbeth replied. "The end of January."

Jordan calculated and her stomach clenched; this was a very tiny baby. She nodded slowly, wanting to be kind but not appear unconcerned. She spoke gently. "It's early, but there is a chance that the baby will survive."

Lisbeth nodded, tears in her eyes.

Malcolm came out, closing the door so quickly that Jordan did not see anything, but she heard Sadie moaning.

"I have to get back to my car," he explained, his face flushed and weary. "Send Willie if they need me."

He retreated down the hallway. Jordan watched her son, looking so like her husband in his uniform. Too many times to count she watched the back of that jacket get smaller and smaller as Booker walked away, leaving her to worry for days or weeks until his return; prayers were her only weapon to keep him safe.

Willie returned, burdened by a pitcher of steaming hot water and a pile of blankets. Jordan opened the door to let him in. Her eyes took in the room: Naomi's hands were covered in blood; red smears and a long rivulet trailed down Sadie's thigh. Jordan couldn't tell if it was the "right red" her mama used to talk about. Burgundy blood was a good sign that things were moving along; bright red meant a woman might not make it.

"Lisbeth, help me," Naomi called.

Jordan squeezed her hand. Willie exited as Lisbeth entered, and the door was closed once again.

"Can you tell—" Willie asked.

"No. I don't believe anyone can know how this will turn

out. Not for many weeks, or months or maybe even years, with a baby that small," she said.

"Your Naomi knows what to do," Willie said. "She's impressive."

"Yes, she is. But . . . she's only one year out of school. She doesn't have much experience, though her confidence might indicate otherwise."

He nodded, his eyebrows pulled together in contemplation.

"My mama, her grandmother, was a midwife. Naomi has seen the joy and pain of birth for a very long time. She started helping at them when she was twelve. Perhaps Naomi went into nursing because of my mother."

"Woah, woahhh, woahhh." Sadie's voice crashed through the wooden door.

Willie's eyes grew wide in alarm.

"It's always intense. No matter the circumstances," Jordan explained to the young man who had most likely never heard a laboring woman. "My mother used to say: 'Women roar their first babies into the world. It's God's way of announcing that you've become a mama.'"

Willie smiled, though he still looked concerned.

"Do you need to work?" Jordan asked.

He shook his head. "I only have to be awake when we pull into a station. But I could not possibly get to sleep now."

Jordan smiled and nodded, though her heart burned at the benefits of his light skin. Unlike porters, conductors didn't have much to do at night. It was one of the many advantages given to the White men who worked for the Pullman Company.

In the cramped hallway, Jordan and Willie stood guard over Sadie and the baby, listening for sounds, waiting for news, and offering their prayers.

CHAPTER TEN

SADIE

Train toward Oakland
August 1894

Sadie fought the panic. Her baby was coming. It was too soon, but once again she couldn't stop it. Like the other times, she'd woken to her body's betrayal.

She squeezed Momma's hands and tried to understand Naomi's directions. But the pressure in her was so full, so intense, that she could not understand individual words. Then the force slowly receded until it was over.

There was time for only a few breaths before it started up again. A wave of intensity, building and building. She heard the sound of an animal. Was that her voice?

Panic rose. Momma looked at her.

Momma's mouth was moving. She was saying something. Momma had an encouraging smile. Her eyes were wet. The wave receded.

"Well done, Sadie. Now rest." Momma's words made it through. Her cool, soft hand rubbed Sadie's forehead. Sadie nodded.

Heat radiated through her. Sweat bubbled up on her chest. A wave came again. And again and again. So many, over and over again, until she lost knowing.

Then the urge she'd heard about took over her body. It seemed wrong to do this here, in . . . she tried to open her eyes. Where was she? Her eyes blinked open. She was surrounded by painted wood.

"It's okay, Sadie," Naomi said. "Your baby can come right here. I'm going to do everything I know how to keep you both safe."

Sadie couldn't find any words. She nodded.

The wave built. It was a goat butting with all its strength: She joined with it. There was no holding back. She could not do anything else. The wave subsided. She leaned back, panting. Was Momma gasping too?

She heard voices. Were they talking to her? The wave returned. Bigger, bigger, bigger. This time, when it ended, she did not want to stop. She kept pushing until . . . release. It was over.

Her baby was out. She listened. She looked down. Was it . . .

No sound. The wet baby was on her bare chest. Naomi rubbed the tiny body hard. Hitting it on the back. Her brown fingers were inside blue lips. She rubbed and rubbed.

Sadie heard her momma crying. She wanted to reach for her hand. But her arms were clutching her baby. She jostled the beautiful little body up and down.

"You're here! You're here!" Sadie exclaimed.

The baby jerked, and then shivered. Sadie heard a raspy inhale and a gurgly exhale.

"That's right, baby," Naomi said. "You take your own breaths. You can do it."

The baby jerked with each breath. Lips slowly turned to purple, then to pink.

Naomi exhaled. She smiled at Sadie.

"So far, so good," she encouraged. "She looks like a strong one."

"Really?" Sadie asked. "She's alive? She's still alive?"

"Yes, she is. And look at her breathing on her own. She's hardly bigger than a puppy, but her lungs seem to be working just fine."

"A daughter?" Sadie wondered aloud. She looked at her momma. "A daughter! And she's alive?"

"Yes," Momma said, tears streaming down her face. "You have a daughter. And she's alive."

"What do I do now?" Sadie asked.

"Nothing," Naomi said. "I'm going to pull at you and squeeze you. I'll tell you if you need to do anything besides rest with your darling one on your heart and do what comes naturally."

Naomi disappeared between her legs. Indifferent to what would normally be shameful, Sadie turned her focus on this living miracle. Sadie rubbed her baby's back—her daughter! She'd been covered with blankets so Sadie could not see her very well. Rather than crane her neck, she relaxed and touched a tiny arm, as thin as a fountain pen. Sadie cupped her small head. It was the size of an orange, barely filling her palm. She was so solid and real even though she was tiny. Sadie's hand moved with each jerky breath.

Inside her belly a huge wave came again. Sadie yelled out in pain and surprise. Was there another baby?!

"It's your afterbirth," Naomi explained. "Nothing to be alarmed about."

Sadie nodded and felt the urge to expel it. The wave receded and then returned. She pushed and it was over. Sadie returned her entire focus to the precious being lying on her belly. She rubbed her creamy back. Was that fur on her shoulders? Sadie wished she could really see her.

"Sadie, quick, bite this!" Naomi interrupted.

Sadie bit down on . . . she didn't know what it was. It was soft and salty with a metallic taste.

"It's stopping," Naomi exhaled, relief in her voice.

Sadie looked at her mother. There was terror in her eyes. Apparently something had not gone well but was fine now. Naomi pressed on her belly.

A voice came to her ears. "I'm going to wash you."

Sadie nodded, though she didn't know if anyone was looking at her. She craned her neck to check on the baby. Her skin was mottled, dark red and purple, a shade she'd never seen before on a baby. Sadie's stomach lurched.

"Is she . . . did she?" Sadie managed to stammer out.

Naomi and Momma hovered over her. Naomi lifted the blanket and peered at the baby. She gently touched each limb.

"Let's get her something to eat," Naomi said.

A tear leaked out of Sadie's eye. "I don't have any food."

Naomi smiled. "We are going to get it from your breasts. Lisbeth, please get me at least three teaspoons and a teacup if possible."

Momma nodded and disappeared.

Kindly, gently, Naomi said, "God put food for your baby girl right inside you."

"It's too soon." Sorrow crashed over Sadie.

"I don't think so. Look," Naomi instructed.

Sadie looked where Naomi pointed. The end of her nipple glistened.

"May I?" Naomi asked.

Sadie nodded, though she didn't know what she was agreeing to.

Naomi pushed and squeezed the end of her breast. Astonishingly a shiny glob of liquid rose from her nipple.

"Ohh!" Sadie exclaimed.

Naomi smiled. "God knew just the right time to put that food into you."

Momma returned. Jordan was right behind her with a pitcher of water and a glass.

"Oh, Sadie," Jordan exclaimed, tears shone in her dark-brown eyes. "Congratulations. She's our miracle."

"Thank you." Sadie beamed.

"May I?" Naomi asked, pointing at Sadie's chest.

She nodded. Again, in other circumstances this would have been unthinkable, but Sadie did not care that Naomi was extracting liquid from her breasts in front of other people.

Sadie watched in wonder as the teaspoon filled with thick, clear fluid. Naomi pulled the baby's lower lip away from her gums and poured some into the cave of her mouth. Naomi leaned in with her ear close. She nodded and repeated the process of pouring and listening. Drop by drop she repeated the process until the liquid was gone.

When Naomi was finished, she looked surprised that all their eyes were on her.

"What were you listening for?" Momma asked.

Naomi smiled. "A very quiet sound of swallowing. Some babies make a nice loud click. This one is very quiet, but as you can see—it went down. This liquid gold will keep her strong. Now we keep her warm and let her rest. Grammy always said the best spot for the first few days is where they came from." Naomi looked at Sadie. "She can sleep on you. All right?"

Sadie nodded and put a hand on the baby's back. That would be just fine. She couldn't imagine letting her daughter be anywhere else.

Momma started to hum their favorite lullaby—"Go to Sleepy, Little Baby."

Jordan and Naomi joined in. Sadie felt the sound in her

soul, blessing her and her baby. She smiled at these kind and strong women, so grateful for them. Fear and joy filled her in equal measure. Her baby was here! By the grace of God and the skill of Naomi, she was alive.

★★★

Sadie woke to the sounds of voices outside the compartment. Alarm rushed through her body, waking her fully. She looked at the baby asleep on her chest. The mottled red face of her daughter looked too small and vulnerable to exist. She touched her skin. It was warm. Sadie leaned her head close and heard the barely audible sounds of air swishing in and out of tiny lungs. The baby was still alive. Sadie exhaled in relief.

She heard her mother's voice. "Thank you so very much. You saved my daughter's life."

"That was the most difficult birth I've attended to," Naomi replied. "I'm grateful that Grammy told me stories about the use of the placenta to stop the bleeding; otherwise I would have been at a loss as to what to do. Childbirth does not always go as we hope. And far too much cannot be relieved by modern medicine."

Her mother's voice grew quiet. "What chances of survival do you give her?"

Sadie felt tears at the edges of her eyes, and her chest hammered at the thought of losing her daughter. She listened intently.

"I wish I could be reassuring, but I have no experience or education with a baby born so early. We must keep her warm and fed as best as we can—and pray. Though it is in God's hands—we will act as his hands on this earth. Time will tell."

Naomi, Jordan, and Momma came through the doorway

and squeezed into the small space. Jordan carried a food tray.

"Let's see about getting a bit more colostrum into this little one," Naomi announced. No hint of concern remained in her voice, but Sadie was riddled with fear.

"First the new momma needs to eat something," Jordan said.

Sadie was confused, and then realized Jordan was speaking of her. She was a mother now.

"I can change the baby's napkin to wake her up while you eat." Momma offered.

"Thank you." Sadie was overcome with their kindness. "You have all done so much for me, for us."

"That's our job," Jordan said. "Yours is to keep your girl warm and fed."

Momma took the bundle of baby, and Jordan placed a plate with egg and toast on her lap.

"Have you chosen a name?" Jordan asked.

Sadie nodded while she chewed the bite of food in her mouth. The egg was delicious, from her hunger or the cooking she didn't know.

"With Heinrich's approval, I would like to call her May, after his mother," she finally said.

"What a sweet name," Jordan replied. "I will think of her as May unless you tell me otherwise."

Naomi spoke. "She is too early to suckle directly. Every two hours we are going to get one or two spoonfuls from you and slowly pour it into May. Understand?"

May. Sadie liked to hear the sound of her name. It made it real, as if she were a person who would continue to exist in the world.

"Will she ever be able to?" Sadie asked.

Naomi exchanged a look with Jordan. It was slight, but Sadie saw it.

Jordan said, "I'm sorry, but we just don't know what to expect."

Sadie nodded, biting her lip to hold in her fear and sorrow.

"Each day we will check to see if she has the strength to suck on our finger. When she does that, we'll know she can suckle right from you. In the meantime, we are going to keep pouring food into her for as long as it takes," Naomi explained. "Ready?"

Sadie nodded.

"Lisbeth, can you watch so you can help her with this too?" Naomi asked.

Momma agreed.

They'd done this twice since the birth. The first time, soon after May emerged, the little one eagerly swallowed the thick liquid. But the second time, the baby couldn't be woken up. Sadie wasn't confident any drops of liquid made it into her belly despite Naomi's reassuring words about it slipping down even though they could not hear her swallowing, and they could see milk spill out of her lips.

Sadie sat up. Naomi surrounded her with pillows and blankets. She placed May diagonally across her chest, using gravity to support her tiny body, leaving Sadie's right arm free and one breast exposed.

"Would you like to extract the colostrum?"

Sadie nodded.

"I'll hold the spoon," Naomi offered.

It took a few tries, but soon Sadie was successful. It was not so different from milking the cows and goats on the farm when she was young. She was encouraged as the spoon filled and she poured the liquid into the teacup.

"More?" Sadie asked.

"Yes," Naomi instructed.

After Sadie had filled the spoon again, Naomi said, "I will rub her cheek. When she wiggles, pour a tiny amount onto her lips."

The spoon poised by May's mouth, Sadie waited. Naomi's finger gently stroked against May's skin. She didn't respond.

"Come on, baby," Naomi said. She reached under the blanket and tickled the baby's ribs. Then she returned to the cheek.

May jerked her head toward Naomi's hand.

"Now."

Sadie poured a drop into the fold of May's lips. A pink tongue poked out and licked the shiny liquid. Relief filled Sadie.

"Perfect," Naomi crooned to the baby. "You are a smart girl. Pour another drop."

Sadie did, and May licked it off again. They repeated the process, with Naomi tickling May if she drifted off to sleep. The process took nearly an hour, but eventually they got those two teaspoons, plus more from the other breast, into the fragile infant.

"It's looking good!" Naomi said. And this time Sadie believed her. Maybe this little girl had the strength to survive.

"Lisbeth, can you help her in an hour?"

Momma nodded.

"I'm going to get some sleep," Naomi said.

"You can sleep in Sadie's bed, or mine. Malcolm is leaving them made up so we can get our rest whenever we can."

Naomi gave Momma a skeptical look.

"Willie says he'll stand up to anyone who complains. It's his car and he decides the rules. He's already defended his decision to keep Sadie in here until we get to Oakland."

Naomi nodded. "It will be nice to lie down flat. Thank him for me if you see him before I do."

"Thank you, Naomi." Sadie's voice came out croaky. "For all of this. For everything."

Naomi smiled. "I'm glad I was here. May sure is precious. You both get some well-earned rest—for a bit."

★★★

Three days later Jordan carried in breakfast for Sadie. The three women had provided care for her day and night since May's birth. One of them had attended to them at all times. Sadie had left the smoking car only to use the bathroom.

Sadie sat up. She passed May into Jordan's arms and took the plate. Through the soot on the window, water sparkled. *Home. I'm home.* With a sudden longing she ached to be in her own house, her own bed.

"Is that the Pacific Ocean?" Jordan asked, wonder in her voice.

"No," Sadie said. "It is the bay. You have to go all the way to San Francisco to see the Pacific."

"Is it hard to get there?" Jordan asked.

"You take a ferry across the water. Then walk all day or take a cart to the ocean," Sadie explained. "Or you can take a boat from Oakland through the Golden Gate to the ocean. It's a long journey but so worth it. You can't see the land on the other side. Only the powerful waves rolling in from far away, crashing over and over again on this shore."

"That sounds nice," Jordan said. She got lost in thought and then added, "My mother asked me to toss her shell into the Pacific Ocean. After we are settled, I'll make the journey."

Jordan's face filled with pain. She looked older, and vulnerable. Sadie hurt for her.

"I'm sorry, Jordan. I've been so preoccupied I haven't asked how you are adjusting," Sadie said, feeling as if she'd been a selfish child. She remembered the underlying sorrow that lived in her after her father's death, so close she discovered it at all times.

Jordan's eyes welled up. "It's hard to imagine I will ever adjust to living without her." She shrugged, and changed the subject. "All done?"

Sadie searched for the right words, but finding none, she nodded. Jordan passed May back, took the plate, and left them alone. Sadie sighed and said a quick prayer for Jordan.

Last night she'd fed May without the spoon. She wanted to try again. She drew up her gown to get nourishment for her daughter. A bit of white was mixed in with the clear liquid. Milk was coming in. Sadie soared with joy. Amazingly, her body knew what to do to keep her little one alive.

She unwrapped May and tickled her to consciousness. The girl's eyes opened. Sadie rubbed her cheek and put a drop of liquid directly onto her lips. May's tongue darted out to take in the food. Drop by drop, Sadie gave her daughter what she needed. By the time they were finished, the train was passing Emeryville.

She whispered to her daughter, "May, we're home. You get to meet your poppa. He's going to be so surprised—and happy."

Sadie wanted to believe that Heinrich would be instantly delighted, but he was never one for surprises, even when they were delightful. She might have to give him a few days to make the adjustment, especially since he had had no time to prepare.

As soon as the station came into view, Sadie scanned the crowd for Heinrich's familiar face. Naomi interrupted the search before Sadie saw her husband.

"To keep her warm on the journey through town, I think we should have her right next to your skin." Naomi looked at her for confirmation. Sadie nodded.

"Thank you," Sadie said. "She would have . . ." Sadie's heart was in her throat. May would have died without Naomi. She was certain of it. She was overwhelmed with gratitude but didn't want to start crying.

Naomi smiled, accepting the unspoken appreciation.

Closing the shade for privacy, Sadie bared her chest while Naomi wrapped cloth around them both. It was sweet to have May so snug and secure next to her, almost like she was safe inside again.

She buttoned a dress as high as she could and put a coat on top. The summer fog was thick, and the sun had yet to burn it off. May slept through the process. Her eyes were closed tight, and her sweet face nestled against Sadie's skin, barely poking out between the folds of fabric.

Sadie allowed herself to picture only happiness on Heinrich's face when she showed him what was hidden under the bulge. He was coming to the station expecting two people and would be collecting three. She expected he would be taken aback by the news and then utterly delighted that their dream of becoming a family had been realized. Knowing him, he'd appreciate the efficiency.

Naomi left them alone, giving her time to rest before facing the bustle of life off the train. Sadie looked at the little room where May had been born. *Thank you,* she thought to herself; it was strange to thank inanimate walls and a couch, but she was grateful for them too. She had birthed and then fallen in love with her daughter in this space. She was grateful for its sheltering walls and comforting couch. Sadie imagined that the strong scent of tobacco would forever bring May's birth to mind. She thought about the journey and wondered, had they been in Iowa or Nebraska when May was born? Perhaps Momma or Malcolm knew.

Her mind flashed to the women who had journeyed by

wagon, giving birth along the way on the hard ground or a wooden cart bed. Water was so precious they probably didn't even wash up. She thought of the hastily marked graves of women and infants who didn't make it out of the plains.

She shook her head to push away the morbid thoughts. Neither she nor May were coming back wrapped in a shroud. She stood up and left the chamber she would never forget.

★★★

When the train was empty, Malcolm helped her down from the car. It was strange to be walking with a changed body and for the first time in days.

"I expect Heinrich is waiting with the carriage," Momma said. "Sit here. I'll get him."

Exhausted already, Sadie was relieved to rest. She rubbed the fabric that covered May's back and kissed the black hair on top of her soft head. Momma returned alone, shaking her head to indicate that she hadn't found Heinrich.

Sadie teared up.

Jordan said, "We'll wait with you. It can be difficult to get in and out—especially with a carriage."

Naomi asked, "Does he know you were on this train?"

Sadie looked at Momma, uncertain.

Momma replied, "We sent him a telegram, but it was one of many. Our plans changed too many times to count. And the telegraph lines have been so overwhelmed. We have no way of knowing if it got through."

"If he doesn't come, we will see you home," Jordan said.

"We are so indebted to you for your care," Momma said.

Jordan shook her head. "I'm grateful for the joy you brought to Mama's passing," she replied. "It is the least we can do."

"If Grammy were here, she'd say"—Naomi mimicked

Mattie's accent—"that littl' one is righ' where she belongs. She gonna need to eat 'round the clock at first, jus' like when she was in you. Keep her full of mama's milk and mama's love."

Sadie smiled at the wisdom.

"Got that, Momma? You're going to have to help me now."

Momma nodded and patted Sadie's arm. It was such a comfort to know she wouldn't be caring for May alone.

Malcolm came up to them, having finished his duties.

"Want me to find you a carriage?" he asked.

"Thank you," Momma replied.

"Our home is—" Sadie started to explain.

"I know where you live," Malcolm interrupted. "I delivered the letter there."

"Of course!" Sadie replied. "Excuse me."

Malcolm smiled and walked off in search of a ride. So much had happened between that letter and now. It hardly seemed like Malcolm was the same person as the stranger who had knocked on her door last spring.

★★★

Two hours after she left the sanctuary of the smoking car, Sadie pulled up to her home, shaking with fatigue. Her body was depleted and weak. She leaned on Malcolm's strong arm, feeling silly but grateful for his support.

"Hello?" she called out from the entryway.

Without waiting for Heinrich's reply, she started toward the living room.

"Welcome back, wife," he called out from his study.

Sadie sank into the couch. Malcolm left her side to see to the luggage.

Eventually Heinrich emerged from the study. "I did not

realize—" He stopped, his face pulled into a question as he studied the scene.

Sadie searched his face as Naomi helped her to remove her coat, revealing May's petite face.

"What . . . ?" Heinrich stammered. "Who? You have a . . . ?"

"Baby. We have a baby." Sadie spoke softly.

Disbelief covered Heinrich's face. "I do not understand."

"I wanted to tell you the news in person. She came early."

Heinrich came close and perched on the couch, staring at the infant, then at Sadie. Was he upset? Her throat swelled up. This was too big of a change to take in at once. She should have told him by telegram. He looked back at the baby.

"I am stunned," he stammered out. "Is she? She?"

Sadie nodded. "Yes. We have a daughter."

"She is . . . healthy?" he asked.

Uncertain, fearful that their daughter *was* too small, Sadie looked at Naomi to answer.

"For the moment she seems just fine, Mr. Wagner," Naomi said.

Heinrich startled at her voice.

Naomi continued, "She's eating and staying warm enough. In fact it's time to get more into her. Shall we take you to your bed?"

Sadie nodded.

Hopeful that he was simply too overwhelmed to express joy, but afraid she'd misstepped by keeping this information from him, she said, "I'd like to call her May, after your mother."

"That would be . . ." Heinrich cleared his throat. "She will like that. It will temper her sorrow that she will not know this grandchild. Do not mistake my quiet. I am happy, so very happy, to have a child at last. It is just a large change to understand all at once." He smiled.

Relieved, she smiled back. Tenderness crossed between their eyes. Then, more gently than he had ever been with her, he helped her up the stairs to their bedroom. She could have made it up the stairs using the railing, but she accepted his offer of kindness.

Relief flooded through her when she walked across the threshold of their bedroom. The chair, the washstand, her bedside table welcomed her home.

Heinrich left them in privacy. It took great care for both of them to safely separate May from Sadie. Naomi changed the infant's diaper to wake her up. Sadie settled into the chair and prepared to feed. Naomi brought a pillow for her arm, laid May across her lap, and made adjustments as needed. The process went more quickly now, and in less than an hour Naomi prepared to leave.

Sadie's soul protested at the idea of losing her guide. Of course Naomi would be going to her new home. But Sadie was frightened to be without her care.

"I will miss you. Thank you," Sadie exclaimed.

"Your momma knows what to do, though you may want to hire a nurse as well."

"Are you available?" Sadie asked, desire filling her.

Naomi smiled. "I appreciate the offer. However, I believe you will be better served by a woman with more experience with infants—especially one born so early."

Sadie nodded as if she agreed, but disappointment filled her. Naomi didn't want to be with them. Jordan came upstairs to say goodbye too.

"Thank you . . . words are not enough," Sadie said. "But that is all I have. I am so incredibly grateful."

Sadie wished she could repay Jordan and Naomi.

"You are very welcome. Enjoy your May. She's a blessing

to the world."

"Please give my appreciation to Malcolm," Sadie said. "He has done so much for me—for us—virtual strangers."

"You and your family are not strangers to ours—even if Malcolm does not know you as well as I do, he still shares the connection," Jordan replied.

"Thank you," Sadie replied. "When May is older, I'd like to take you to the Pacific Ocean. And Naomi and Malcolm as well, if they like."

"That would be a welcome adventure," Jordan said. She leaned in to hug Sadie goodbye and rubbed May's cheek.

"I'm going to miss her," Jordan said.

"Please, visit often," Sadie said.

Jordan nodded but didn't respond.

And then Sadie was left alone with her daughter. She looked down at her long and narrow face without a hint of fat. Her closed lids looked bare without lashes. Sadie smoothed her floppy ears back, not yet stiff with cartilage. May yawned and then scrunched up her face. Sadie's heart grew.

"I've been waiting for you," Sadie said. "I love you already, more than I ever knew was possible."

CHAPTER ELEVEN

JORDAN

Oakland
August 1894

Jordan felt melancholy descend upon her as they left Lisbeth and Sadie—and precious May. Caring for them these past few days had given her a focus. Without that, she once again felt the overwhelming ache of loss. Life was an empty tomb without her mama.

She told herself that they could visit, but she knew it would not be the same. Heinrich did not welcome their presence. He'd pointedly told them he appreciated their service and that he would be hiring a German nurse to assist from now on.

Jordan's instinct to protect May had been activated, but there was little she could do now to ensure the infant's well-being. Jordan was grateful Sadie had the financial resources to get good medical care for the baby.

Their home had confirmed Jordan's suspicion about Sadie's social status. The huge, new Victorian had modern amenities that Jordan had never seen in a private home. Water flowed from taps with a simple turn, and the bathroom had a flushing indoor toilet.

Jordan blushed as she remembered the pride she'd expressed that their home had its own private outhouse. She realized that neither Sadie nor Lisbeth had given any indication that relieving themselves outside was an inconvenience. She shook off the memory. That was the past. She was heading to her new home, through the lovely afternoon toward the apartment Malcolm had arranged for them. Unlike Chicago there was nothing sticky in this Oakland summer air.

Naomi suddenly stopped. "Mama, it's the Unitarian Church," she declared. "Would you like to come on Sunday?"

Jordan looked at Malcolm. He shrugged. "I've never attended. I go to the Fifteenth Street AME," he stated. "When I'm in town . . . and not sleeping," he clarified, looking sheepish.

Jordan read the wayside pulpit and saw a familiar name: Rev. Eliza Tupper Wilkes. She had been a speaker at the women's convention and the hall of religion at the Columbian Exposition.

"We can go to both, Mama," Naomi said. "The morning at AME and the seven-thirty here. It will be a good way to meet like-minded people."

Jordan nodded consent but had no actual enthusiasm at the prospect of going to either church. Just the thought of meeting new people tired her. She'd agreed Oakland would be a better home for Naomi and Malcolm but could not foresee that she would find joy in any new relationships.

They continued along Castro Street, following the numbers downward. The brand-new neighborhood gave way to small, older dwellings, but they all had space around them and were well tended.

Malcolm turned east when they arrived at Fifth Street and stopped in front of a nicely painted wooden building. Her mood was cheered by the look of her new home. Their trunks were waiting on the front porch—delivered by the same carriage that had brought them to Sadie and Lisbeth's house.

Malcolm led them through a low wrought-iron gate into a neatly tended front yard. A riot of unfamiliar flowers filled it.

"As you can see, Mrs. King from upstairs enjoys her gardening," Malcolm explained. "I told her you would want to add to it. She's looking forward to meeting you. Her people are from Georgia."

Jordan smiled at hearing a word that was at once comforting and confusing. For fourteen years—after she ran, but before the Civil War—Mama had gone by the name Georgia to evade being captured under the Fugitive Slave Act. Jordan hadn't even known it was a false name until Mama reverted back to Mattie when the war started. It had taken Jordan time to adjust to the change that came easily to Pops and Samuel since they'd known Mama as Mattie before.

Malcolm opened the door to the small ground-floor unit. It cost nearly double what they had been paying in Chicago, but he assured her it was a fair price for Oakland. The living room had an archway to delineate a separate dining area. Behind it was a kitchen.

"You got water with a tap now too, Mama," Malcolm declared, as he turned them to make the water flow.

"You sure we can afford this?" she asked.

"Oakland is so new, just about every house has taps and flush toilets," he said.

Jordan's heart flipped. "We have a flush toilet?"

Malcolm stared at her, looking incredulous. "I told you there were flush toilets."

"You did?" she asked. She hadn't remembered such a conversation.

He nodded vigorously.

"No more going out in the snow in the middle of the night?" Jordan wondered aloud.

"Ma, I've told you . . . there will be no going out in the snow anytime in Oakland. It truly does not snow here. Ever."

Jordan laughed.

"Well, then no going out in the cold in the middle of the night," she said.

"Brother," Naomi declared, "you found us a nice home. Thank you."

"You are welcome, sister," Malcolm said. "I think Oakland is going to be good for all of us."

Jordan was a jumble of conflicting emotions. Delight at a flush toilet mixed with sorrow that Mama wasn't ever going to enjoy it. She looked at the bare walls and empty beds. Booker and Mama would never live here. Without them, would it ever be home for her?

She was tired and just wanted to take a nap in her own bedroom, but she was never going to see her house again. Pressure built behind her eyes. Jordan sighed.

Naomi and Malcolm exchanged a look.

"Let's get unpacked," Naomi said.

Malcolm nodded and fetched the trunks that held what was left of their lives.

★★★

For a few weeks Jordan had felt too unsettled to attend church, but Naomi insisted it was time that they went. Malcolm was on his way back to Chicago, so Naomi and Jordan would attend church in Oakland without an escort. Jordan steeled herself for meeting strangers. It didn't used to feel like a chore, but she just didn't feel up to it.

Naomi called, "We must leave or we will be late, making

a poor introduction to a new congregation."

Jordan carefully considered between her two hats and chose the chapeau with netting instead of the boater. She pinned it on her head and rushed out the door.

Malcolm had instructed them to wear layers, even in the summer. He warned that the chilly morning fog would be gone before noon, leaving her sweating if she wore a wool shirt to worship. As strange as it was to put on a wool coat over her thin cotton blouse in late summer, she was grateful for the warmth of it in the thick morning fog. Mist hung in the air, lending a surreal quality to their ten-block walk up Grove Street.

They stopped in front of the compact church. Like most buildings she'd seen in Oakland, it was new wooden construction painted bright white with dark trim.

A familiar voice exclaimed, "Mrs. Wallace. Miss Wallace. What a lovely surprise."

Jordan turned. Willie Smith grinned at her. He graciously nodded his head in greeting and offered a bent elbow.

"May I accompany you into worship?" His light eyes sparkled with pleasure.

Relieved to see a familiar face, Jordan gladly accepted his gesture despite her reservations about this man and his interest in her daughter. Apparently he was truly able to walk both sides of the race line. She looped her arm through his and followed his lead into the sanctuary.

He bent toward her as he spoke. "I'm going to seat you with Miss Flood if possible. She will help you with the connections you need to settle into Oakland society."

A central aisle intersected long wooden pews on each side. The white painted walls had glass windows, a few stained in brightly colored geometric shapes. The chancel was level to the floor with a simple lectern.

Willie walked most of the way down the aisle and stopped at a pew three rows from the front. A young woman with dark skin and intense eyes sat on the bench. Her hair was pulled into a smart bun topped with a fashionable hat.

He leaned over and said, "Miss Flood, I would like to introduce you to my family friend, who recently relocated from Chicago to Oakland. Like you, she is an advocate for women's suffrage." He looked at Jordan. "You attended the Columbian Exposition, correct?"

Before she could reply, Naomi broke in from behind them. "She organized it."

Naomi sounded proud, but Jordan was less certain that she had accomplished anything of meaning.

She corrected, "I was *one* of the many organizers for the Colored people's section."

Miss Flood put her hand out. "It's a pleasure to meet you. Please, sit with me so we can get better acquainted." The woman slid over to make room in the pine pew.

Willie tipped his hat and said, "I will leave you, then."

Jordan waited in the aisle, gesturing for Naomi to go ahead, but her daughter didn't notice. Naomi was smiling at the handsome young man. Jordan's heart rose up in protest. She glared at Naomi, wanting to chastise her for public flirtation; instead she tapped her arm. Naomi nodded at Willie and slid into the pew without looking at Jordan.

"Has your path crossed with Ida B. Wells?" Miss Flood asked, excitement filling her fresh face.

Naomi inserted, "She and Mama worked together on the exposition."

"I admire her greatly," Miss Flood declared. "I'm delighted that a woman with your political devotion has moved to Oakland."

"I'm afraid my enthusiasm for organizing has waned

after that experience," Jordan corrected. Before she could say any more, the pastor rose in front of the congregation.

In the quiet of the prayers, a sudden longing for her mama jerked at Jordan's chest. Her breath caught, and it was all she could do to keep from crying out. Tears pushed at her eyes. She tried holding them in, but the force was so strong that she surrendered and let them flow, missing her mama with a deep ache.

Naomi took her hand and whispered into her ear, "I miss Grammy too. And Pops."

Jordan nodded. She let the tears flow. Miss Flood was kind enough to pretend she didn't notice. As tears do, they eventually ran out. By the time the congregants sang the final hymn, her soul was more at peace.

After the service Naomi asked Miss Flood, "Will we be welcomed at the Unitarian Church?"

Miss Flood nodded slowly. She said, "I go on occasion. Very few Colored people attend, but there are not many of us in Oakland. They are not hostile in the slightest, and their philosophy is refreshing, but their singing does not stir my soul." She laughed.

Naomi explained, "Reverend Tupper Wilkes is preaching the seven-thirty evening sermon today. Mama saw her speak in Chicago, but I have never experienced a lady pastor."

"Nor have I. If you are going, then I shall too." Miss Flood smiled.

"We will welcome your company," Jordan replied. And she meant it. Miss Flood had a cheerful yet unobtrusive personality.

"I'll see you this evening." Miss Flood left them.

"May I walk you home?" Willie was suddenly at her side. Naomi looked at her, pleading in her eyes. Not wanting to alienate their only connection to the Colored community,

Jordan consented. His actions on the train had been very admirable. He might be a good friend to them, but she hoped nothing more would develop between him and Naomi. She would have to make that clear to her daughter.

Willie extended both of his elbows this time. The mother and daughter each looped an arm through his. Naomi gestured with her head.

"We are staying at 407 Grove Street," she stated.

"That is a lovely neighborhood. Close to the school and shopping district, as well as the train. It's near where I stay when I'm in town."

They walked through the now warm air. True to Malcolm's warning, the fog had burned off, and Jordan was grateful to be carrying her coat and only wearing a light cotton shirt.

Willie appeared to be ignoring Naomi, looking toward Jordan as he spoke, but she knew better than to believe his interest was in her.

"I am glad you and Miss Flood are becoming friends. Her family have been great advocates for our people. They were founders of the church, and her mother was the first Negro teacher in the state of California. Thanks to her father, the schools in Oakland are not segregated."

"Truly?" Jordan asked.

Willie shrugged. "I have not been to them, but that is my understanding. Perhaps you can find employment there."

Naomi's head peered around Willie. "Mama, that would be a good use of your time, now that . . ."

Jordan felt the emptiness of life without Mama with a sudden pang.

"Perhaps." She nodded with a forced smile, but she didn't believe she would return to teaching. She no longer believed that any public institution would accord her respect. Page had been killed for believing the constitution of the United States was real. They had expected Chicago to be different from Virginia, but she lost her position as a teacher for joining in Miss Wells's anti-lynching education campaign. She had no reason to believe that Oakland was any different from Richmond, Virginia, or Chicago, Illinois, despite Malcolm's and Miss Flood's and Willie's assertions. They were young and as naïve as she had been so long ago. She did not intend to take on another Sisyphean task.

Willie stopped in front of the wrought-iron fence that bordered their apartment.

He said, "It was lovely to see you again. I hope you find Oakland to be as welcoming a home as I do."

"Thank you." Jordan nodded at the handsome young man. His charm was disarming.

He turned his focus to Naomi. "Goodbye, Miss Wallace," he said. "May I call on you next time I am in town?"

Naomi's lips spread into a sweet smile, and her eyes lit up. She nodded. "I would like that."

"In ten days, then." He grinned at her. "I will see you in ten days!"

Gleeful longing on her face, Naomi watched Willie walk until he was out of sight. Jordan sighed audibly.

"He is a very nice man, Mama," Naomi responded.

"Yes, he is. A nice man passing for White," Jordan chastised. "Do you know how dangerous it is to play with that? He cannot move between the two worlds without consequences. You would be wise to stay away from his mess."

"He says it is different here," Naomi explained.

"He says?" Jordan exclaimed. "You have already spoken of such things?"

Naomi nodded. "On the train. He understands that in Illinois he must be discreet, but he knows others who are settling down in Oakland and making a family in the Colored community without any dire consequences. The prejudices of the East and South do not have to dictate our lives in the West."

"You are both playing with fire. And being naïve." Fury built inside Jordan. She suddenly felt foolish as she realized they had likely arranged to meet at church this morning. She closed her eyes, took a deep breath, and walked away before she said words to regret.

★★★

The three women walked into the vestibule of the Unitarian Church. Five stained-glass windows had portraits of White men; she read the names under each image. William Ellery Channing was the only one she was familiar with. Reverend Tupper Wilkes shook their hands and welcomed them to the evening worship.

The sanctuary was enormous, like she had imagined a cathedral must feel. Dark wooden beams curved to a line in a high ceiling. Elegant and breathtaking, it drew her spirit upward. Straight ahead, light wooden panels curved around the back of the large chancel. A large round stained-glass window filled the space over it. It was the Sower casting his seeds, his hand reaching out. Far in the background a small figure worked the plow; it could be a woman. Jordan smiled, feeling as if her mother were sending her a message: *Be fertile soil for the word of God.*

Miss Flood led them to a row on the right. Individual wooden seats were separated by armrests. It felt more like a concert hall and less like a church. There was no cross or symbol of Christ.

"As you said," Naomi commented, "not many Colored people."

Jordan looked around. They were the only ones.

"Only eight hundred of us were counted in the last census," Miss Flood said. "In a city of about forty thousand."

"Oh," Jordan replied, struck at the low number. "It doesn't seem like so few from our neighborhood."

"We are concentrated near the station since the rail company requires their workers be close, and they are our best employer," Miss Flood said.

As Miss Flood predicted, the singing wasn't lively. Nothing in this service moved her to aching for Mama. Instead the words of the hymns were inspirational, and the sermon on society was a stirring call to action. Jordan's mind appreciated Reverend Tupper Wilkes's assertion that the sins of the world could be remedied by the touch of human love. She wanted to believe her actions could make a difference; she just didn't. She had yet to find where to place her faith— in God, society, or even herself.

As they parted, Naomi asked Miss Flood, "Will you come to tea soon? We would appreciate any guidance you can offer for us in our adopted city."

Miss Flood replied, "It would be my pleasure."

They seemed to have made their first friend in Oakland and, to her surprise, Jordan was looking forward to getting to know Miss Flood better.

★★★

The next week, Miss Flood called on them for afternoon tea. Their home was still being put in order, but Miss Flood set them at ease. She commented on their lovely garden and the convenience of the location. Her admiration of their teacups felt genuine and made Jordan proud. The bone china with red roses had been a gift from Booker and Mama on her fiftieth birthday.

Naomi peppered Miss Flood with questions that would have been rude to an elder, but Miss Flood happily shared personal details.

"You were born in Oakland?" Naomi asked.

"When I was born in 1862, Brooklyn was a separate town, but now it is an Oakland neighborhood, across Lake Merritt. The neighboring townships are clamoring to join this city. Macadamized roads, underground sewage, public water systems, and the railroad are modern conveniences that attract the nearby communities."

"Is it true you were the first Colored to go to school in Oakland?" Naomi asked.

Miss Flood nodded. "I attended John Swett as soon as the school board declared it would be integrated."

"Was there a controversy?" Jordan asked.

"My father convinced the school board there should be only one system of education for all children. He challenged the segregation laws using the Fourteenth and Fifteenth Amendments as evidence. The prejudices of the slave states are not enshrined here. We are hardly a threat in such small numbers. Have you been out of this neighborhood?"

Jordan shook her head.

"You must see more of this town. Would you like to have a picnic in the cemetery after church soon?" Miss Flood asked. "It is lovely and only a one-hour walk."

Jordan inquired, "We are allowed?"

"Of course. You'll see that all mixture of people are welcome there, in life and in death. We will stroll through the final resting place of paupers and millionaires. In the Civil War section, Negroes are buried right next to Whites. In other parts, Chinamen are laid to rest next to Italians. Only the Catholics have their own cemetery next door. This city does not separate the races and classes. We must fight for that to continue."

Jordan noticed that Miss Flood presumed she would be joining in the struggle for freedom. She did not feel the need to disabuse her of that mistake. While she appreciated the young woman's enthusiasm, she did not intend to devote her energy to politics.

A loud knock on the door intruded upon their conversation. Jordan read Naomi's expression to see if she was excited, perhaps expecting a call from Willie. Her daughter shrugged and headed to the door. Naomi opened it to reveal Lisbeth Johnson.

Jordan smiled. She rose and greeted Lisbeth with a hug. May had been in her prayers each night in the weeks they had been apart, but they had not called on the family. It would be nice to get news.

"How is our little girl doing?" Jordan asked.

Lisbeth nodded once and then tilted her head from side to side, conveying an uncertainty.

"These are precarious days, even when they are full term," Jordan asserted. "She's a fighter. I trust she will be fine."

"I pray you are right," Lisbeth said.

Aware of her guest in the room, Jordan made introductions. "Mrs. Johnson, this is Miss Flood. Miss Flood, this is Mrs. Johnson, an old family friend from . . ."

Jordan paused, hesitant to reveal their connection going back to her birth on a plantation in Virginia. Her parents had thought their history was a point of pride, but over the years Jordan had faced subtle—and overt—superiority from certain people when they found out she had been born into slavery. She was happy to keep that information away from their community in Oakland.

"Ohio. We both lived in Oberlin." Lisbeth filled in part of the missing information with grace.

"Did you attend Oberlin College?" Miss Flood asked.

Lisbeth shook her head. "Unlike Jordan, I did not have the opportunity to enroll there."

Miss Flood's eyebrows arched upward. Admiration filled her voice as she asked Jordan, "You are a graduate of Oberlin College?"

Jordan nodded.

"Mama is a teacher," Naomi declared.

"Was a teacher," Jordan corrected.

In the dramatic, high voice Sadie used as a child, Lisbeth said, "My daughter's faaavorite teacher." Jordan and Lisbeth looked at one another and laughed together.

"My father used Oberlin in his argument to the school board for integration in Oakland," Miss Flood declared. "It seems I may have you to thank for my education as the first Colored to attend public school in this town."

Jordan smiled, but inside she felt a painful mix of pride and sorrow. She flashed on how she felt in her early days teaching in Oberlin. She'd believed that the oppression of her race was nearly behind them, certain that the passage of the Fourteenth and Fifteenth Amendments meant that the degradations of the past would be fully remedied. Back then, her outrage stemmed from women being left out of the Fifteenth Amendment.

But the abuse she'd experienced in the intervening years caused her to lose hope that her people would ever be freed from degradation and unfair burdens. Despite what Miss Flood said about prejudices not being enshrined in this state, Malcolm was working as a porter, not a lawyer.

Naomi said, "Lisbeth, please sit. Join us for tea."

Lisbeth hesitated. "I do not wish to intrude on your visit."

"You are no intrusion. Please stay." Naomi motioned to the worn couch.

Lisbeth looked at Jordan for confirmation. She nodded with a small smile.

"I would enjoy a visit. Thank you." Lisbeth sank into it, rubbing the fabric with her pale fingers. Her usually smooth skin was blotchy, and she had circles under her eyes.

"You are tired?" Jordan asked.

Lisbeth nodded. "As you can imagine, little May requires constant care throughout the day and night. It continues to take two people almost an hour to get her fed and changed."

Jordan explained the extraordinary circumstances of the birth on the train to Miss Flood.

"My goodness," Miss Flood replied. "You are fortunate indeed."

Lisbeth nodded and said, "I thank God each night that we waited to travel on the train with you." She continued, looking at Naomi with glossy eyes. "When Sadie bled from the afterbirth, I believed I was going to lose my daughter. Had you not been there, I am certain I would have. You saved them both, May and Sadie."

A shiver went down Jordan's spine. She had heard the same praise for Mama so many times.

Lisbeth said, "Your grandmother would have been proud."

Naomi said, "I felt her spirit with me in that moment, whispering in my ear." Naomi spoke like Mama: "Placenta. Use the placenta."

Miss Flood spoke up. "I'm certain she is looking down on you from heaven."

Jordan agreed, a mixture of pride and sorrow blocking her throat.

Lisbeth spoke to Naomi. "My purpose in visiting is to see if you can help us once again. At your suggestion we found a nurse experienced with newborns, but the German woman we have hired is leaving Sadie in tears." Lisbeth continued, "She insists that May not be held, saying it is too disturbing to her health. But May whimpers so pitifully from her cradle next to the stove that we cannot agree. We can give you her same pay and would add a debt of gratitude as well."

Jordan's heart leaped when Lisbeth named the sum. It was as much as Malcolm earned with tips. She looked to Miss Flood to see her reaction. The young woman nodded encouragement at Naomi.

Jordan considered asking whether Heinrich had changed his mind, but decided against it. She did not need to complicate matters. Sadie and Lisbeth could manage him.

Lisbeth leaned in, anticipation on her face, waiting for Naomi's answer.

"It would be my pleasure," Naomi agreed.

Lisbeth sat back with a sigh. A grin lit up her face.

"Sadie will be so relieved. Thank you very much," she said.

A jumble of feelings filled Jordan. It was a relief that Naomi had secured work. However, she found it strange that they had come so far to once again be taking care of Lisbeth's family.

CHAPTER TWELVE

SADIE

Oakland
September 1894

Sadie hovered over May as she made a pitiful sound. She was more than a month old, but if May had gestated for the typical amount of time, she would still be inside Sadie. Until recently the baby had slept almost continually, and they'd struggled to rouse her to feed every three hours. Now she woke up on her own, whimpering until she was held.

Over the weeks they'd been home, Sadie had felt more like a failure as a mother rather than less. She longed for reassurance that May was well and would continue to live, but there was no predicting how sickly this little baby was. The doctor had warned her not to get attached until May was six months or even older. But it was too late. Sadie was utterly committed to her precious daughter. She'd never experienced such devotion to anything, and she felt so inadequate to the task of keeping her well.

They were in the kitchen, May in her cradle by the stove. She'd eaten only two hours ago but woke up before her next feeding time at five o'clock. Sadie was confused and uncertain. She longed to pick up May and knew it would stop her crying immediately. But the doctor and their nurse were adamant: no holding her except for feedings every three hours since it would tire her out and spoil her.

Sadie's instincts told her to carry May, but she didn't trust them. Her body had failed her child by giving birth too soon. She'd put May at grave risk. She didn't want to further endanger her sickly daughter or face the withering looks and chastising words of the nurse.

Heinrich wanted her to follow the doctor's recommendations; however, he became irritated when May was noisy.

In contrast Momma advocated for feeding May as often as possible and keeping her warm next to their bodies, not by the stove.

Sadie was torn between these conflicting—and strong—viewpoints. Exhausted and overwhelmed, she found herself on the verge of tears multiple times a day.

Heinrich stood in the doorway between the dining room and kitchen. Framed by the redwood trim, he chastised, "Your tears serve no purpose." His dark brows pulled in contempt, and his lips pursed with judgment.

"I'm sorry," Sadie told her husband. "I will do better containing my emotions."

"You must stop her mewling," he demanded. "I cannot get my work finished."

Sadie took in a deep breath. She nodded.

Relieved to have a clear reason to hold May, she said, "We can go to our room. Her sounds will not interfere with your work from upstairs."

She scooped up the infant. As soon as the girl was in Sadie's arms, she stopped crying. Sadie felt a shiver of relief run down her spine, and her mind calmed. The warm bundle of May against her heart was a joy.

"I am leaving now and will return when I can," Heinrich said. "I may be late for supper, but have it ready in case I am not. There has been an accident; I do not know how long it will take to repair the mistake."

"Where?" Sadie asked.

"Hickmott," Heinrich replied. Anger in his voice, he shook his head and said, "A girl wasn't careful and got an arm caught in the belts. There will be no canning for hours while it is cleaned up, causing more losses. There is blood everywhere and I have to decide what is garbage—"

"Is the girl . . ." Sadie didn't want to say the word *dead*. She blinked back her tears.

"No. She only lost an arm," Heinrich said. "If her parents keep her clean, then she will live."

"Can we help them? Bring them a meal or . . ." Sadie asked.

He smiled. Was it patronizing or tender? "They are Irish. They take care of their own."

"Their own?"

"Catholics," he explained. "It is not our concern. If I worried over illness for each employee in all my businesses, I would only be a full-time nurse."

He started to leave, but then turned back.

"I cannot continue to have my sleep disturbed," he declared. "Tell your mother to make up a bed for me in the study until you have taught May to be less demanding."

A rock dropped in Sadie's stomach, and she felt defeated as a wife. Then a measure of relief rushed in—the nights would be much less stressful without Heinrich in the room. She could focus on May without the concern of disturbing her husband pressing on her. She nodded.

"Where is your mother?" he asked, looking around the kitchen. "She hasn't started supper yet."

"She is calling on a friend. I'm confident she will return soon and you will get your meal," Sadie said, blinking her eyes to once more stop her tears from flowing.

It struck her again that she had married a man who was attached to his routines and had no patience for disturbances. A child hadn't changed that or brought them closer. For Heinrich, May was a disruption to his life.

She'd been foolish to believe Heinrich would be like Sam, doting over his newborns. Truthfully, more men were like Heinrich, taking months or even years to grow attached to their children. Sadie had hoped that fatherhood would change him as suddenly as motherhood had transformed her. In time he might come to love May as much as she did. However, she had to accept that right now he did not share her devotion to their daughter.

★★★

Momma wasn't back by the time May needed to eat, so Sadie decided to manage on her own. First she unwrapped the little girl to give her a clean diaper. Sadie studied the scrawny body looking for changes, evidence that her daughter was growing. The fur that had run over May's shoulders was gone, and cartilage had grown in her ears, keeping the tops up, but May's narrow face still had no trace of fat.

The baby's stomach jerked in with each breath, and her skin was a mottled red and pink. The doctor was surprised that her lungs were so strong. He'd attributed it to her being runted, as if he were talking about a piglet. In the next sentence he'd warned that they should listen for sounds of stress in her breathing, as this was the weakness that signaled doom for premature infants. He'd said it so matter-of-factly, as if he weren't stabbing another fear into Sadie's heart.

May's eyes blinked open. They were still a strange color,

a muddy shade not seen in adult faces.

Sadie brought May and a thin blanket to the rocker where first Momma and then Diana had fed their children. She felt their love and strength when she sat in it.

She massaged her breast until a drop of milk glistened on the end. She held May up against her bare chest, cradling the baby's head in her left hand and her back with the other. May did not open her mouth. Sadie needed to tickle her lips with her nipple, but when she let go of May's head, it flopped away from Sadie's body.

Sadie slid her left hand forward, cradling May's head and body at the same time. She held her breast and tickled the tiny chin to get her to open her mouth. The girl's jaw opened wide and she curled up her arms, blocking access to her mouth. May starting sucking on her own fist.

Sadie sighed. She repositioned May, pulling her arms back. May started mewling in protest.

Sadie let out a large sigh just as Momma walked into the bedroom. Despair must have shown on her face.

"Let me help," Momma said gently.

Sadie nodded, relief surging through her. She simply could not get everything positioned correctly. Sadie held May's head with one hand and her breast with the other. Close at her side, Momma gently pulled May's arm under Sadie's. Momma tickled the tiny baby's cheek until May turned her head into Sadie and opened her small mouth wide. Sadie pulled May forward, placing her nipple as far back as possible. Holding her breath, Sadie prayed that this time she had hit the spot that would cause May to start sucking.

May's jaw moved up and down, followed by the sharp twinge Sadie longed for. A shiver of relief ran through her body.

"Thank you, Momma," Sadie said. "We have been at this for twenty minutes. I feared she would fall back to sleep without getting any food."

Momma returned with a pillow for Sadie's arm. Sadie shook her head at her own forgetfulness. She was incapable of remembering all the details of being a competent mother. Momma patted her arm.

"Your father helped me with Sam for many weeks . . . and he was not nearly this tiny," Momma said. "Be patient. With yourself and with May. She has a lot to learn—sooner than most."

Sadie nodded. Poppa helping Momma feed Sam made sense, but she could not imagine Heinrich at ease in this women's territory.

"Are you comfortable?" Momma asked.

Sadie nodded again. "It's very sweet, once we get settled into it." She smiled at Momma. "I had no idea how it would feel. So close. So urgent."

Momma smiled back, her blue eyes sparkling. "There is nothing so dear as your baby at your breast."

Sadie flashed on a memory of Mattie patting Momma's cheek.

"I better understand Mrs. Freedman's devotion to you now," Sadie said.

Momma smiled.

"It must have been a comfort to have her when Sammy was born."

Momma nodded, a far-off look on her face.

Sadie said, "Before May was born, I never understood the story of Sam's birth. You told me that you didn't realize Mattie was the midwife that saved your lives after two days of labor until weeks later—when you came to pay her. It didn't seem possible that you didn't recognize your Mattie when she walked through the door," Sadie said. "Now it is clear to me that a laboring woman can easily be unaware of her environment. If I had not stayed there afterward, I would have no memory of May's birthing room. I was so overtaken that I didn't know my surroundings. Was Mrs. Freedman a great help after Sammy was born?" Sadie asked.

"No," Momma replied, looking so pained that Sadie regretted broaching the topic. "Before the war we acted as if we did not know one another," Momma explained. "It was too dangerous for Mattie for us to reveal our ties. The Fugitive Slave Act made bounty hunters daring enough to disturb her even in Oberlin."

Sadie shook her head.

Momma continued, "The law was on their side. The Freedmans could be captured and returned to Ohio. It was safest that we treat them like any other Negro family— engaging in business but not being too familiar," Momma said. "Emmanuel and Samuel made this rocking chair. Did you know that?"

Sadie looked at the wooden arm. "I knew it was from Oberlin, that you and Diana both used it. But no . . . you didn't tell me who made it. It's beautiful and so sturdy."

Momma's eyes glazed over. "Enjoy this time. It goes so fast. I know you worry about our May, but she is strong. Little, but so strong. As Mattie would've said: She is going to be jus' fine. I feel it in my bones."

Sadie laughed along with Momma.

"Thanks, Momma. Your confidence means the world to me."

"I return with welcome news," Momma declared. "Naomi said yes. She can start tomorrow."

A shiver ran through Sadie's body. It was the answer she had been hoping for. Gratitude swelled up in her, and moisture filled her eyes. She nodded with a tight smile. She'd given thought to this change in nurse.

"Do not tell Heinrich that we asked Mrs. Schmidt to leave," Sadie instructed. "Say nothing unless he asks, and then our story shall be she was no longer available."

Momma gave her that sad look that reminded her she hadn't married a man as gentle as Poppa. Thankfully she didn't respond and force Sadie to defend or explain her husband.

Momma did not understand the pressures Heinrich was under. The Pullman Strike caused enormous financial losses for his employer and for him personally. He hadn't burdened Sadie with all of the details, but she had discovered he'd borrowed funds to invest in a shipment of fresh peaches and plums, expecting to profit greatly when it was sold in the East. The fruit was loaded onto a train in Martinez but was not permitted to travel due to the strikers, and the investment rotted away in the miles between California and New York.

Heinrich had no empathy for the demands of the laborers; he believed they should be grateful to be given work. Without the Pullman jobs, they would be poor farmers. He railed against their selfishness and was outraged that the strikers were allowed to return to their positions instead of being jailed or deported.

Sadie saw both sides of the disagreement, but she didn't antagonize Heinrich by giving her opinion. Workers needed fair wages, workdays that were shorter than sixteen hours, and a right to a private life. However, they should not be allowed to disrupt travel and the conduct of business for the entire nation. There had to be a compromise.

"Are you all settled?" Momma asked.

Sadie nodded.

"Let me bring you food." Momma kissed the top of her

head and left.

Sadie looked down at her little miracle. May's eyes were closed. Three long, dark lashes had sprouted in the night. Every day this girl changed just a tiny bit. If Sadie didn't look carefully, she'd miss these small benchmarks.

***

"Spreckels is sending me to Hawaii," Heinrich said over supper. He'd waited until Momma had taken May upstairs to share this news. "I leave in three days."

"Hawaii?" Sadie exclaimed.

Sadie still thought of it as the Sandwich Islands. They were purported to be a paradise in the middle of the Pacific Ocean.

"It will take weeks simply to get there," she stated.

Heinrich nodded.

"For sugar?" she asked.

"Yes," he said. "And pineapples. With Britain gone, we are working with a new government being formed by practical men of modern commerce."

"You cannot conduct your business by telegram?" she asked.

He gave her a withering look. "You think there is a wire spanning the thousands of miles between San Francisco and Hawaii magically floating over the Pacific Ocean?"

"I'm sorry," she soothed. Her brain was addled from caring for May round the clock. "I will miss you; we will miss you."

"You abandoned me for months to go to Chicago for no useful purpose. I am traveling for work to keep you fed." He challenged, "You do want to eat, don't you?"

"Yes, Heinrich," Sadie replied. He was mad. She'd overstepped in stating her concerns. "I'm sorry to add my sorrow to your burdens. We will manage while you are gone, and look forward to your swift return."

He nodded and then stared off into space. They ate in silence, as they often did. She chewed slowly, hardly tasting her food.

"Do you imagine you will be home for the New Year?" she asked.

"Sadie, I do not decide these things. I expect I will be, but do not be alarmed if I am not. Or if you do not hear from me. Hawaii is a hostile nation, but there is great wealth to be made there. This is the opportunity of a lifetime. You must appreciate Spreckels for including me."

Sadie nodded, but deep down she didn't feel grateful at the prospect of her husband leaving for weeks, or most likely months. Even with the tension between them, she would worry about him and be left to manage all aspects of the household. But she pasted a smile on her face and pretended to agree.

That night he came to her. It had been nearly six months since they had lain as husband and wife. The part of her that enjoyed closeness with him seemed like a memory from another person. He'd approached her once in the weeks since May's birth, but she'd rebuffed him, explaining that the doctor had told her to wait. Despite her lack of interest, she accepted his advance. Surprisingly, it felt nice to have him close, for them to lie as husband and wife. She had missed his body pressed against hers. Afterward he rested his head on her chest while he casually stroked her skin.

"I am sorry I have been so inconsiderate lately," he said. "There is so much pressure at work. You have no idea. Our family finances are precarious as well. I only work so hard so you and May can have a good life."

Sadie softened. It had been like this many times in the

past. He would become unkind due to pressure from work, but then apologize when he realized he had wounded her. He did not intend to be cruel. He was a kind man working hard for their family in a foreign nation. She must learn to be less demanding and more accepting of his German ways.

★★★

The next morning Sadie could hear Momma at the front door telling Mrs. Schmidt that they appreciated her service but no longer needed it. The woman protested until Momma implied that they could no longer afford to pay her. She was given a generous severance of one week's pay and left without saying goodbye to Sadie or May—which was a relief.

Naomi arrived soon after; Momma showed her to the bedroom.

"May I hold her?" The young woman asked for permission, something Mrs. Schmidt had never done.

Sadie nodded.

"Oh my," Naomi gushed. "She is precious! And she has grown so much! Mama will be glad to hear it. She wants to visit when you are ready."

"We would love that, anytime," Momma said. "Right, Sadie?"

"Absolutely," she replied, and meant it.

Sadie was immediately comforted by Naomi's warmth, kindness, and respect. She gave instructions without reprimanding Sadie for her instincts.

If Heinrich was aware of the change in nurse, he did not comment on it. He left two days after Naomi started with a caution not to expect to hear from him frequently, for he would be busy, and mail took weeks to travel between the two countries.

Naomi's presence made an immediate difference. She

taught Sadie to feed May while lying down, which made it even more relaxing and sweet. It was especially useful at night and allowed all of them to get more sleep, which helped Sadie's mood enormously.

Naomi bathed May, prepared food for Sadie, and exclaimed at May's growth. Her attitude reassured Sadie that her daughter would continue to thrive. When Sadie was honest with herself, she realized that it was not a hardship to have Heinrich on his business trip. She missed him and worried about his well-being, but she no longer had to protect him from the continuous demands of an infant.

First days, and then weeks passed. The women fell into a sweet routine that revolved around the needs of the precious baby, but they also had time for pleasures, such as games of cards, personal conversations, and delicious meals.

One afternoon, a coy smile covered Naomi's face. Sadie smiled and nodded at the young woman, encouraging her without words to share her mind.

Naomi leaned forward and said, "Willie has proposed marriage."

"Truly?" Sadie replied. Excitement filled her voice.

Naomi nodded.

"We shall be cousins!" Sadie declared. "Congratulations."

Doubt covered Naomi's face. Sadie realized her enthusiasm wasn't matched.

"You are not certain you will say yes?" Sadie ventured.

Naomi bit her lip. And nodded.

"Willie is a good man," Sadie said.

A tear leaked out of Naomi's eyes. "He is. My concern is that societal prejudices will cause us harm. As you know, he is passing for White."

"Oh," Sadie replied as understanding flooded her. She considered how to respond.

Quiet filled the room. Naomi looked so sad, like she wanted to be reassured.

"My brother, Sam, and Diana have one of the happiest marriages," Sadie replied. "At first it was not easy for them. Her family did not attend the wedding and refused to speak to her for marrying an American rather than a Greek man. But in time they have made peace with Diana's choice."

"Mama is concerned," Naomi said. "But I love him. I truly do."

Sadie asked, "And you feel he loves you? And will be a good husband?"

Naomi nodded.

"Then the prejudices of the past should not dictate your future," Sadie declared.

"You believe so? Truly?" Naomi asked.

"I do," Sadie replied. "How shall we make progress if we are only limited to the present?"

Naomi smiled. She paused and then she nodded again. "Thank you, Sadie."

★★★

Sadie stepped across the threshold by herself. This once-common practice was strange and exhilarating after so many weeks of pure devotion to May. Momma and Naomi had encouraged her to go, insisting it would be safe for the baby and a tonic for Sadie. The slant of the sun and the color of the leaves made for a stunning late-autumn day.

It was the first time Sadie had been away from her girl since her birth nearly three months before. She trusted Momma and Naomi to take care of her, but it was unsettling. Her life was entirely altered since she'd last walked around her neighborhood alone, but the world continued on without change.

She walked toward the bank to get money to buy flour and sugar at the dry goods store. Sadie paused in front of the imposing building and took in a breath to steady her nerves. She was intimidated by the task ahead of her: speaking to a bank teller and withdrawing money from their account for the first time ever. But the cash Heinrich had left was gone. She had no news about his return. It was up to her to get the funds her family needed. She steeled herself with the reminder that she had every right to be here.

She pulled open the ornate door. Cool air from the high ceiling and marble floor hit her skin. Tellers stood at attention, ready to assist customers. She walked up to an open window, gave her name, and stated her purpose.

A young man in a suit nodded, wrote down her name, and walked away. He crossed to a row of books, pulled one out, and thumbed through the pages.

He returned and said, "There are no funds to draw from your account."

Sadie swallowed. "Are you certain?" she asked, though she imagined he was.

He nodded.

"My husband is away on a business trip. I'm certain he has an explanation," she ventured.

He nodded again.

"We are out of money?" She asked, almost pleading, "Can you extend me credit until he returns?"

"Just a moment," the man said. Sadie could not read his face. He was neither kind nor cruel, simply neutral.

Her heart hammered hard in her chest as she waited for his answer. She wiped her palm on her dress. She thought of the food in their home. There were stores for the winter: beans, dried fruit, and canned vegetables. They would not go hungry, but it would not be appetizing.

An older man returned to the opening in front of her. He shook his head as he spoke. "We've extended all the credit we are able to. I'm sure your husband will explain the situation to you."

Through a tight throat she told him, "My husband is in Hawaii for work. He will not return for many weeks."

"I see," he said. "I'm sorry, but this bank is not able to assist you."

"Are you certain?" Sadie sounded as if she were begging. "Is there anyone else I can speak to?"

The man's face hardened. "Yes. I'm certain. There is no one here that will give you any other answer. Good day." He stared at her, not moving or speaking.

Sadie turned away, blinking back tears of frustration and shame.

CHAPTER THIRTEEN

JORDAN

Oakland
December 1894

Naomi declared, "Mama, I have news. Please don't be alarmed."

That word set off Jordan's heart. She looked at Naomi, raising her eyebrows to encourage her to continue.

"Yesterday was my last day working with May and Sadie."

"They gave you no notice?" Jordan challenged.

"Sadie was apologetic, but they are in financial straits and can no longer pay me. She held out hope that when her husband returns, their finances will allow it, but for now she is out of cash. My final payment was in dry goods from their stores: flour, lentils, and barley."

Jordan shook her head. Concern and annoyance wrestled within her. By all rights, she should have sympathy for Lisbeth and Sadie. But she was more worried about their own financial standing.

Jordan suggested, "Perhaps Miss Flood will be able to assist you in securing another position."

Naomi replied, "Yes, and we should also ask her about the option of you returning to teaching."

Jordan scowled at her daughter.

"She said it pays well," Naomi insisted.

"I do not believe they will hire a Colored teacher in their *integrated* schools," Jordan stated.

"Mama, you have years of experience. How can you know if they will hire you unless you try?" Naomi argued.

Jordan shook her head, uncertain whether her resistance came from the fact that she no longer wanted to teach or a fear that she would not be allowed to. She imagined the thinly veiled lie she would be told: *The position is filled; We have no room;* or simply *No.* She did not want to endure the humiliation of being turned away for her race.

Naomi gazed off into the distance, biting her lip, a sure sign she was nervous.

"What else is troubling you?" Jordan asked.

Her daughter looked down at the threadbare carpet. Her shoulders raised and lowered.

"Yes?" Jordan coaxed.

The young woman looked right at her and announced, "Willie has asked me to marry him."

Jordan's stomach clenched. She could hardly be surprised. What else would come from courting—other than worse trouble?

"I hope you told him that is impossible," Jordan replied.

"I did not."

"What did you say?"

"I would speak to you . . ." She looked like she was about to cry. "To get your blessing."

"You want my support of a marriage to a man who is living a lie? A man who must hide who he is or face dire consequences." Jordan seethed as she asked, "Will he speak of you as his maid when his conductor friends learn about you?"

"Do you want the prejudices of others to dictate my life?" Naomi retorted.

"Killed!" Jordan snapped, rage burning in her. "There are men who will kill Willie after they discover he is deceiving them. More than once a week there is news of a lynching in the newspaper."

The pain on Naomi's face cut through Jordan's anger.

Softening, Jordan said, "I remember believing you can avoid the harsh realities of society, that you can escape from those who will destroy your life to remain in power, but that is not true. You are being naïve and so is he. I'm sorry, Naomi. I should have stopped you earlier. I hoped you would come to this conclusion on your own. Perhaps your father and I should not have sheltered you so much from the hatred. Every time Willie leaves, you will fear he will not return," she explained. "I lived in terror whenever your father was away."

Naomi's eyes grew round and her eyebrows furrowed as she took in her mother's words. Jordan sensed her argument was giving her daughter pause.

She continued, "Oakland is a small town. Where can you live that you will not be discovered?"

"He's convinced no one in Oakland will care," Naomi said.

"Even if they are unconcerned here, even though ninety-nine out of one hundred men will leave you in peace, it only takes the one or two with hatred in their souls to destroy your entire life."

Naomi looked defeated. "I will share your concerns with Willie."

Pushing past her discomfort, working to keep her voice even, Jordan spoke. "After your uncle Page was lynched, we lost all we had worked for: our home, your father's business, my school . . . friends."

Jordan's eyes stung. She paused, blinked, and took a deep breath.

"Lisbeth's brother led the mob that murdered Uncle Page," Jordan declared, revealing a long-held secret to her daughter. She paused to let Naomi take in the information.

Naomi shook her head. "That cannot be."

"Jack Wainwright was the justice of the peace in Richmond." Jordan seethed as she explained. "He had a passionate hatred for our family. I was naïve enough to believe that the words of the constitution—the Fifteenth Amendment—were a shield against his loathing." Jordan continued, fury burning in her, "He lynched your uncle while a crowd cheered him on and then explained the murder as a civic duty to protect the honor of a White woman."

"Lisbeth's brother?" Naomi questioned, still unclear.

"I will never forget the look of triumph on his face when he brought Page's body to my home," Jordan whispered. "He wanted to destroy our family, and Lisbeth's too."

"How can she live with it—be with us—when Grammy . . ." Naomi left the sentence incomplete.

Jordan swallowed and took a deep breath before replying. "She doesn't know."

Naomi stared, her mouth gaping.

"You protected her?!" Naomi sounded incredulous.

Jordan paused, then shook her head and spoke slowly. "I was unwilling to give him that satisfaction. He murdered Page to spread hatred. We refused to add to his chain of evil. Your father and I did not tell Mama or Lisbeth or anyone. You are the first." Jordan continued, "I never told Malcolm, though I wonder if he knows and it is the reason he keeps his distance from Lisbeth."

Naomi took in her words. Confusion and anger wrestled

in her eyes. Jordan nodded, her heart twisting in pain for her daughter.

"Willie is a good man; I am not questioning that," Jordan reassured. "I believe he would make a fine husband for you." Jordan's voice cracked. She cleared her throat. "It is the goodness of other men that I question."

"It's not right," Naomi said. Her eyes glossy.

"We do not live in a righteous world, Naomi," Jordan replied. "As much as we wish it to be, it is not. The reality of this world makes it too dangerous to join your life to Willie's. I fear it will cause you more sorrow than joy."

It hurt to speak the truth so plainly to her daughter. But she had to save her from making a foolish mistake.

CHAPTER FOURTEEN

SADIE

Oakland
December 1894

Sadie rocked in the living room with May at her breast. They no longer needed assistance with this task that occurred repeatedly throughout the day. Each time they sat down to feed, Sadie was confident she could give her daughter what she needed. The months since May had been born had been the most beautiful—and the most trying—time of Sadie's life. She'd been filled with love and fear in equal measure, but now, at last, she believed May would survive.

Momma assured her that soon May would sleep through the night. Sadie hoped Heinrich's return would converge with that milestone and that he would be home for Christmas, though she had no evidence that he would be.

He'd yet to respond to the letter in which she had carefully informed him that the bank said they were out of funds. She imagined he'd had no means of transferring his wages from Hawaii to Oakland. Fortunately Momma had the means to cover their immediate bills.

Satiated, the little girl opened her mouth, pulled her head back, and laid her cheek to rest on Sadie's breast. Sadie rubbed her back but didn't move her up for a burp, having learned that letting the milk settle first helped it to stay in.

Sadie studied this beautiful child. Her eyebrows and eyelashes had come in—long and dark. May's cheeks were beginning to round out. All in all, she looked almost like a healthy newborn. May's eyes popped open. They crossed and then slid outward as she tried to focus. Suddenly she looked at Sadie's face. Her eyes darted around the edges and then landed at her mother's eyes. May's cheeks tugged up. Was that a smile or a burp? Sadie smiled down at her daughter. May's lips stayed pulled up, and her eyes shone back at Sadie. It was a smile! Sadie's heart soared. She beamed at her baby, her spirit so full of love. She had never felt anything like it.

The baby's lips stayed pulled up in a smile as her eyelids slowly slipped downward. May sighed, her lips softened, and she shuddered. Her breaths grew longer as she drifted into sleep.

Sadie reveled in the feeling: her daughter had just smiled at her. A new joy and even more confidence moved into her soul. May would not only survive, she could possibly thrive. Sadie shifted May upward, resting her in the center of her chest. She rubbed her back to get a bubble up if needed. Sadie gazed out the window at the changing leaves, bright yellow and orange. She did not have extra money, and her husband was away for an unknown purpose, but they had enough food stored to survive for weeks if not months; a warm, lovely home; and most important, this healthy and growing baby. She was truly blessed.

★★★

The newspaper spread out before her, Sadie read the notice again. A metallic taste filled her mouth, and she swallowed back bile.

Adjudication of Insolvency.

In the Superior Court in and for the County of Alameda, State of California. In the matter of Heinrich Wagner, an insolvent debtor. Heinrich Wagner having filed in this Court his petition, schedule and inventory in insolvency, from which it appears that he is an insolvent debtor, the said Heinrich Wagner is hereby declared to be insolvent. It is hereby ordered that Robert McKillican, Sheriff of Alameda County, be, and he is hereby appointed receiver of the property of said insolvent, and that upon his giving a bond to the People of the State of California, in the sum of $5500, conditioned as required by law, and qualifying, he take charge and possession of all the estate, real and personal, of said Heinrich Wagner, insolvent debtor, whatsoever and wheresoever situate, except such as may be by law exempt from execution, and of all his deeds, vouchers, books of account and papers, and to keep and care for and dispose of the same until the appointment of an assignee of his estate. All persons having the same or any part thereof in his or their possession are hereby directed to pay the same to said receiver, and that said receiver keep the said property, or the proceeds thereof, till the further order of this Court. And all persons are hereby forbidden to pay any debts to said insolvent, or to deliver any property belonging to such insolvent, to him, or to any person, firm, corporation or association, for his use, and the said debtor is hereby forbidden to transfer or deliver any property until the further order of this Court except as herein ordered.

It is further ordered that all the creditors of said debtor be and appear before the Superior Court of the County of Alameda, Department no. 4, in open court, at the courtroom of said Court, in the County of Alameda, on the twenty-first day of January, 1895, at 10 o'clock a.m. of that day, to prove their debts and to choose one or more assignees of the estate of said debtor.

It is further ordered that this order be published in the *OAKLAND TRIBUNE*, a daily newspaper of general circulation, published in the County of Alameda, as often as the said paper is published before the day set for the meeting of creditors. And it is further ordered that in the meantime all proceedings against said insolvent be stayed.

Dated December 12, 1894

F. B. OGDEN
Judge of the Superior Court
Endorsed: Filed December 12, 1894
JAMES E. CRANE
County Clerk

By N. G. STURTEVANT
Deputy Clerk

Shame and fear buzzed through Sadie's veins. Her mind reeled with the consequences. She hopped from denial to anger to fear.

Momma found her at the dining room table too upset to speak. She pointed at the notice, printed right above the advertisements for coal that had brought her to this page of the newspaper. If not for the cold, she might have been unaware of her own circumstances.

"Oh, Sadie!" Momma cried. "How long? What will we do?"

Sadie shook her head. "I . . ." Her voice caught in her throat. She was too overwhelmed to speak. She had no experience with this type of situation. Momma patted her back.

"We can speak to a lawyer," she said confidently.

Sadie forced out a reply; hardly more than a whisper emerged. "With what funds? As it was, I was going to sell my necklace for coal." She teared up.

"Malcolm will advise us without fees," Lisbeth replied.

She hung her head with a sigh. "They have done more than enough for me."

"Legal advice is not too great a burden," Momma replied. "In fact he may be grateful to put his education to a purpose."

Sadie was too tired to argue. She nodded.

They wheeled the baby carriage that Sam had made for his children down Grove Street. May was bundled up to keep her warm. The perfect late-fall day lifted Sadie's spirits. The crisp air and the sun shining in a clear blue sky were lovely and would soon be gone. Winter would bring rain and gray skies.

Momma pointed out Diana's church as they passed by Fourteenth Street. Tall and stately, it towered over the surrounding buildings.

Soon they were in a neighborhood like Sam and Diana's, with duplexes, fourplexes, and cottages built close to one another. The Wallace family lived in the lower unit of a duplex with a thriving front garden that still had bright blooms.

Sadie felt her nerves as Momma knocked on the door. She feared they were intruding.

Naomi opened the door and beamed with delight when she saw it was them.

"Mama," Naomi yelled. "Little May is here! Come see."

Jordan came into the living room. The grin on her face expelled Sadie's fear that they were not welcome.

"Let me see this precious girl."

Sadie passed her daughter into Jordan's arms.

"My, my. She is looking good," Jordan remarked.

"Thank you." Sadie smiled back.

"What brings you here?" Naomi asked. "Not that you are not welcome to just visit."

Sadie felt shame that Naomi knew they hadn't come just for a social call.

Momma said, "Sadie read this in the paper today." She handed over the notice. "We hoped Malcolm might be home and could advise us."

Naomi read the notice. Then she handed it to Jordan. Jordan shook her head as she read, May still cradled in one arm.

"Sadie, I'm sorry you are in such difficult circumstances," Jordan empathized. "Malcolm isn't home right now. He returns for one night tomorrow. Can we keep this to show him?"

Sadie nodded. They visited, sharing small details of their lives. Neither Naomi nor Jordan had found steady work. The impact of the crash of 1893 continued. Sadie had read about all the people in financial difficulty. It seemed she was now one of them.

***

Two days later Naomi came to their home with Malcolm's legal opinion. She declined the offer to sit down. Instead, she stood on the front porch, framed in the doorway. Sadie could tell from her face that the news was not good.

Kindness in her voice, Naomi reported, "Malcolm says you cannot prevent an eviction and possession once there has been public notification. You might be able to retain your wardrobe."

Sadie swallowed hard. She loved this home and had imagined living here for many years, maybe for the rest of her life.

Naomi continued, "He said to tell you that because you are married, you are obliged by Heinrich's debts, even if you were unaware of them."

Sadie nodded. She pushed out, "Thank you. For asking him and coming to tell me."

"You're welcome. I will leave you to your planning." Naomi patted her arm, a welcome gesture of support, and left.

Their life was about to change entirely. She'd have to tell Momma.

CHAPTER FIFTEEN

JORDAN

Oakland
December 1894

Jordan's warning had proved to be ineffective. Naomi had
consented to Willie's proposal. They were visiting the county
clerk to get a marriage license, intending to marry at church
the next time Willie was back in town.

Naomi argued that the world was changing. Willie
imagined that a private life in Oakland could be kept separate
from his employer in Chicago. Jordan remained unconvinced
and decided to ask his mother to speak to him. Surely Emily
Smith understood that this was a dangerous course. Together
they could dissuade Willie and Naomi from entering into an
enormous mistake.

> *Dear Emily,*
>
> *I hope this letter finds you and William well. We
> are settling into our life in Oakland. I ache terribly
> for my mother, but find the weather and the people
> agreeable as Malcolm predicted.*
>
> *I imagine you are surprised to hear from me,
> but perhaps you already understand my purpose. I*

hope you share my grave concern for the future of both of our children.

Please understand that I hold no disrespect for your son. Willie is a fine man. In other circumstances I would welcome him as my Naomi's husband.

However, I am convinced they will be under constant threat. I have pleaded every argument at my disposal, but they will not listen to me. At this moment they have ventured to the clerk's office for a marriage license, intending to have a wedding perhaps as soon as Willie's next return to Oakland.

It may seem the greatest deceit to ask him to deliver this letter designed to thwart his deepest desire, but I have his well-being in mind. I hope you will agree to my plea and dissuade him from his foolhardy plan to marry Naomi. I am certain his very life is at risk.

Fondly,

Jordan

Sounds from the walkway outside alerted her to their return. Jordan quickly inserted her note in the envelope and wrote Emily's name on the front. She considered signing the back, over the seal, but decided against it. That signal for privacy would only raise suspicion in Willie.

Before she managed to leave the living room, the door opened. She slipped the letter into her apron pocket. She had intended to continue discouraging them with a cold attitude, but the look of despair on Naomi's face raised such concern in her that she abandoned her plan to ignore them.

Willie whispered in Naomi's ear. Naomi shook her head. She collapsed on the divan without looking at Jordan, the silence so painful that Jordan finally broke it.

"What happened?"

Naomi's eyes were hard and sad at the same time. "The clerk refused our request for a license. He claims state law forbids him from authorizing the marriage of a White person with a Negro."

Jordan's throat swelled in anger and sorrow. She nodded slowly, her heart torn in multiple directions. It was outrageous and insulting that California still had the anti-miscegenation laws that Illinois had already overturned. This supposedly more liberal environment seemed to have a mixture of progressive and oppressive laws when it came to her race.

However, she was also glad for the evidence that her fears were warranted. The prejudices of the day could not simply be wished away. She repressed the urge to ask if he had corrected the clerk's mistake. If he was more committed to passing for White than being Naomi's husband.

"I'm sorry. That must have been very humiliating."

Have you changed your plans? Jordan thought, but didn't ask.

"I must go," Willie said.

Jordan's heart sped up. It might not be necessary any longer, but she pulled the note to Emily out of her pocket.

"I took this opportunity of writing to your mother. Can you please deliver it for me?" Jordan asked, working to keep her voice moderate lest she show her nerves. She feared the letter would arrive too late if she sent it through the post.

Willie took the note and sat close to Naomi, his arm wrapped around her shoulders. She leaned against him, obviously comfortable to be touching. Jordan studied her daughter's face and body. She didn't see any signs of change.

Had they crossed that line?"

They whispered to one another. Naomi nodded. Love was palpable between them. Jordan remembered believing that feeling was enough to sustain a family, to keep it safe. But there were forces greater than this couple at work to destroy them. Hopefully the clerk's refusal would demonstrate this.

Jordan wanted to comfort Naomi after Willie left, but her daughter's cold attitude could not be warmed by her efforts.

★★★

"He's unwilling to cross back over the color line?" Jordan asked her daughter over supper that night.

"Willie's wages are three times what Malcolm earns with tips. He works half—*half*—the number of hours. Can you imagine what good we can do with that kind of money? For you, for us, for our children?" Naomi challenged.

"You are still attached to a union?" Jordan questioned.

Naomi nodded.

"Your children will be bastards without a marriage license," Jordan explained. "You will have no legal standing. Is that what you want for yourself? For them?"

"Grammy and Pops never legally married," Naomi replied. "It does not matter to us so long as we are married before God by a minister."

Jordan wanted to slap Naomi. How dare she compare her situation to that of her grandparents? Naomi did not understand that it was her reputation and social standing that were in jeopardy.

Jordan replied, "Willie stands to lose nothing. You might lose everything your father and I dreamed for you—and everything you have worked for. What kind of future will you have, not belonging anywhere ever?"

"In Oakland we can live in the Colored community. Everyone who matters will know the truth of his background. He cannot help the advantages his skin color gives us."

Jordan challenged, "And outside of Oakland?"

"We believe he can advocate to have assignments in the West," Naomi replied.

We. Jordan heard the word like a slap. Naomi was speaking of them as if they were already married.

Jordan rebutted, "You seem certain of his devotion and your future, but I do not share your confidence that his deception will not be discovered—with grave consequences—or that he will not tire of the deceit and abandon you and your children altogether."

The look of hatred in Naomi's eyes hit like a physical blow. Jordan sucked in her breath, immediately regretting her harsh words. The sentiment was not in error, but an insensitive delivery would not win her daughter over.

Jordan teared up. "Naomi, I am sorry that the hatreds and prejudices of our times are causing you pain. I don't agree with them. Willie is a kind man. If the world were different, you would have my blessing. The world is not kind, but instead cruel and unforgiving. You cannot change it."

"You want me to give in to the attitude of the day? If Grammy and Pops had done that, you would be working the fields in Virginia," Naomi replied. "You are a coward! I am not. And neither is Willie."

Jordan's stomach dropped. Naomi stood up, scraping her chair and leaving Jordan alone at the table. She wanted to defend herself, to tell Naomi that she was practical, not a coward, but it was too late. She heard the front door open and then close. Naomi was on the streets of Oakland alone, at night, perhaps finding her way to Willie. She did not return for an hour, and when she did, she did not speak to Jordan.

***

The next morning a knock interrupted Jordan's house duties. Naomi was at the entrance by the time she got there. Miss Flood was framed in the doorway, being welcomed in by Naomi.

Not keeping the bite out of her tone, Naomi explained, "Miss Flood and I are organizing to ask Pastor Summers to speak out against the anti-miscegenation marriage laws. Miss Flood is confident we can get it repealed."

Jordan looked at Miss Flood. Doubt must have shown on her countenance, because Miss Flood said, "My father petitioned the school board for integration, and now that is the law in Oakland. I'm confident we can make a similar impact on the anti-miscegenation laws."

Jordan nodded, less in agreement and more to indicate she had heard the young woman.

"Genuine change is afoot. Mr. Oglesby, from our congregation, is running for the position of justice of the peace in Oakland," Miss Flood told her excitedly. "He will do much good from that position."

"You believe the White men of this city will elect a Colored man as justice of the peace?" Jordan scoffed. "He can run, but he will not win."

Naomi replied, "You may join us if you like, but you cannot stop me from pursuing this course of action."

"Thank you for the invitation. I will consider it."

These idealistic young women reminded Jordan of herself at Naomi's age—certain she could make the world reflect her own desires. She'd been naïve as a nineteen-year-old—convinced that Colored liberation had been accomplished and soon women would have the right to vote along with all the other liberties that men had. Naomi was similarly naïve now to imagine she could simply change the hostility toward their race, and gender, that was enshrined in law.

CHAPTER SIXTEEN

SADIE

Oakland
December 1894

After the discouraging news from Malcolm, Sadie and Momma walked to Sam and Diana's. As usual the kids clamored for hugs and lemon drops from them. Sadie strove to be cheerful and warm, but her throat was so tight she could hardly speak.

Diana took May from Momma's arms. Sitting at the kitchen table, the girls cooed over their cousin, vying for who could bring a smile to her sweet face. She was delighted to be the center of the family gathering. May's joy was contagious and lifted a portion of Sadie's fear.

Diana, sensing something was wrong, shushed the children. Momma looked at Sadie, encouraging her to speak. Sadie shook her head slightly.

Momma spoke out. "Sadie and I find ourselves in an unfortunate situation."

Sadie swallowed the lump in her throat.

Sam and Diana leaned in, concern on their faces. Diana hushed Elena with a stern look. The girl stood close to her mother, May's little hand in her own, and watched the scene unfold.

"It seems that our home is being foreclosed upon. We have no means of getting in touch with Heinrich, so we must find a new place to live . . . and soon. Tomorrow. Sadie has no income or savings that we are aware of."

Diana shook her head. "You do not need to find a place to live. You have a home: here, with us, of course."

Sadie looked at Sam. He nodded.

"But we are so many . . . ," she replied. Left unsaid was that they had only two proper bedrooms. How could three more fit under this roof?

"The girls will sleep on the back porch, and you can have the bedroom," Diana declared.

"It is too cold this time of year," Sadie protested.

"I can finish it," Sam offered. "Turn it into a proper bedroom."

"Are you certain?" Momma asked.

"Of course," Diana said.

"For as long as you need," Sam agreed.

"Thank you," Sadie replied, relief surging through her.

Diana scowled. "No thanks are necessary. You are family."

Conflicting emotions swirled in Sadie. She was furious at Heinrich for putting her and May and Momma in this position. She was scared for their uncertain future. And she was deeply grateful to Sam and Diana for taking them in. It was all too much to hold back. A tear slipped out from her eye. She wiped it away, but the others saw.

"It's okay, Aunt Sadie," Tina said. "It's going to be so much fun to have you live here! I will take care of May all the time."

"Thank you, Tina."

"Nana is moving in?" Elena asked.

"Yes!" Tina told her sister. "And Auntie Sadie and Cousin

May too!"

"Hooray!" The girls jumped up and down, cheering in unison.

Elena said, "Christmas will be even more magical with you here, Nana. And Auntie Sadie. *And* baby May."

Sadie smiled at the girls. Their excitement was contagious. Perhaps joy would be found alongside this tragedy.

★★★

The next day, Diana and Sam arrived with a vegetable cart just after sunrise. The couple was used to being up before dawn and had offered to come even earlier. But Sadie had wanted one last quiet morning with May. Tomorrow they would be surrounded by the bustle of an entire household.

The knock came too soon. They'd packed as much as they could the day before, but between feeding May and needing sleep, they hadn't finished. Most of their clothing was in trunks, but they had yet to sort through which belongings to take and what to abandon. There would not be much space at Sam and Diana's. Sadie and Momma had to take only what they truly needed or loved.

Sam answered the door. Two large Irishmen, maybe father and son, stood on the porch.

Without introduction the older one said, "You need to leave now."

"We have not finished packing," Momma replied.

"There is nothing for you to pack up. All belongings must remain in the house."

The other one said, "Anything you wanted you shoulda gotten out by now."

Sadie's stomach was queasy. "My clothes?" she begged.

"I hate it when you people are here," the older one said. "Why do you do this to us? You knew we were coming.

Now you make us look mean when we are jus' doing what we are paid to do."

"Leave!" Diana declared. "Leave right now. Come back in half an hour."

"Can't do that." He shook his head.

"Yes, you can," she replied. "And you will."

She yelled in Greek. The specifics were lost in translation, but the message was clear.

"Fifteen minutes," he shot back. "We'll give you fifteen minutes."

Sadie sighed.

"Thank you," Sam said to the men.

"Elena," Diana commanded, "take May into the kitchen."

"Come on, girls." Sam waved his daughters upstairs. Diana followed.

Sadie grabbed her sheets and went into the study. She threw a pile of books onto the middle of one and tied up the corners, making it into a pack. She opened Heinrich's desk and dumped the contents of the drawers onto the next one, making another bundle. Tears streamed down her face as she packed up their lives. Heinrich would be furious at the loss of that desk. But she didn't have time to save everything.

"We have all of your trunks from upstairs loaded," Sam said. "What furniture do you want us to take?"

"Really?" she asked. "There is no space in your house for any of this." Her voice broke. She sounded pathetic and ungrateful.

"We have room in the warehouse. Not for everything, but for some. The desk? The table? The couch? What's most important?"

"The kitchen table," she said without hesitation. Momma and Poppa's table. It wasn't the finest piece of furniture in the house, but it held the most meaning. "And if there is space, this desk," she continued.

Momma, Sadie, Diana, and Sam brought the furniture out. The men returned as they were loading the last of the drawers of the desk.

"Hey! You can't take that," he exclaimed. "They want the furniture!"

"Close your eyes," Diana said. "You never saw a desk."

Diana scolded, "Elena, what are you doing?" The girl was bent over, looking at the small patch of front garden.

"Look!" the girl replied.

Diana, Momma, and Sadie examined the ground where she pointed. A bright-yellow flower hugged close to the ground.

"Oh!" Momma exclaimed.

A single yellow crocus had emerged. Sadie smirked at the irony of such beauty on such a sad day. The others they had planted would be emerging soon, but she would not be here to enjoy them.

"It's lovely," Diana said. "Now let's go!"

The girls scampered up on the cart, next to Sam. Elena held May in her arms.

Momma, Diana, and Sadie walked. Diana linked her arms through their elbows, rushing them away from the men. Sadie blinked back tears as she hurried from her house.

"The rocker," she cried out. "I forgot the rocker!" How could she have forgotten the chair that held so many precious memories?

Diana patted her hand. "It's in the wagon. Lisbeth remembered to have Sam get it."

Relief rippled over her panic but not her sorrow.

"Thank you," she said to her home, so quietly no one else could hear. "Goodbye."

CHAPTER SEVENTEEN

JORDAN

Oakland
February 1895

"Mama, listen to this!" Naomi exclaimed. Then she read from the *Oakland Tribune*.

Black Law

> Rev. O. Summers, the colored clergyman who was chaplain of the Assembly of Oakland, has started a new crusade. He is organizing the colored people to fight for the repeal of what he calls California "black law," which prohibits the intermarriage of white and colored people and asserts that there are two hundred white and colored people married by secret contract. These marriages can never be proved up and the children legitimatized unless the law is repealed.

"Pastor Summers knows the members of the assembly,"

Naomi enthused. "He is confident he can stir their outrage to work on the behalf of the children who are currently illegitimate. I told you, Mama. Change is possible. We cast the seeds, like the Sower, and they landed on fertile soil."

Despite herself, Jordan got caught up in Naomi's excitement. She smiled at her daughter and said, "Congratulations. It sure is nice to hear good news coming from the paper."

Naomi smiled back. She looked good, practically beaming.

"Have you been using that hair cream Miss Flood gave you?" Jordan asked.

Naomi nodded.

"I can tell. Your hair looks so smooth. Very nice." Jordan smiled. Then she asked, "Any job possibilities in that paper today?"

Naomi shook her head. "It's the same: German girl, Swedish cook, French maid. Nothing for a Colored nurse."

Jordan would have been surprised to hear otherwise. It had been like that for weeks. "I've decided to apply for the temporary position Miss Flood mentioned."

"Really, Mama?" Naomi asked.

Jordan nodded. It was still unsettling to face the shame of being turned away, but they desperately needed the money. The position as a substitute teacher was temporary, so they might be more inclined to give the job to a Colored woman.

***

The walk to the superintendent's office was a quick ten minutes. Unlike Chicago, Oakland was a small town in population and in acreage, and everything was close.

Jordan continued to be delighted by the weather. Today, all the seasons seemed to be combined. It was the middle of winter, but colorful leaves still hung from the maple trees as if it were autumn, flowers were budding as if it were spring, and the sun was as bright as a summer day. Jordan had to admit that the climate was favorable compared to Chicago, Ohio, or even Virginia.

The one-story building was unimposing compared to the office of education in Chicago. The superintendent had a warm though businesslike demeanor. He shook her hand firmly during introductions.

"Mrs. Wallace, have a seat." The slender White man pointed to an oak chair in his office.

She sat down across from him, intertwining her fingers on her lap to stop them from shaking. Her thumb rubbed the green cotton of her dress. Her heart beat fiercely, though she worked to keep a calm and confident expression on her face.

"Tell me about your qualifications as a teacher," Superintendent McClymonds said. A pen in his hand, he was poised to write notes.

"I studied education at Oberlin College, graduating in 1866," she explained.

"Oberlin!" he exclaimed. "That is a well-thought-of college."

She nodded. "I taught in the Oberlin public school before I moved to Virginia. I was at the Colored school in Richmond for twelve years. Then we moved to Chicago, where I taught for three. I stopped last year to care for my husband when he was ill."

She was pleased to hear him say "You are well qualified." Then he confirmed, "You can begin on Monday?"

She nodded. Was the interview over?

"You understand this is a temporary position in lower elementary while Miss Loughlin is ill. When she recovers, she will return to the classroom."

She nodded again with a smile. "I do."

"Very well," he said. He pulled out two sheets of paper. "Your full name?" Mr. McClymonds asked.

It seemed she'd gotten the position without insult or challenge to her qualifications. She quietly breathed out a sigh of relief.

"Mrs. Booker Wallace," she replied loud and clear.

After filling in her address, he looked at the other sheet.

"Your total experience is seventeen years?" he asked.

"Yes," she confirmed.

He looked at the chart, running his finger across the line until he came to that number. He moved his finger down the chart and said out loud, "The yearly salary would be one thousand thirty dollars. We pay on a ten-month contract."

He did some figuring on a paper and announced $103 for the month. Jordan nearly fell out of her chair. That was Malcolm's salary for six months. She stared at the chart. He smiled at her surprise.

The man said, "You have Miss Kate Kennedy of San Francisco to thank for these high wages. She convinced the school board there that women and men teachers should be paid equally. All of our women teachers assured us they would willingly commute across the bay if we did not make the same policy, so we followed suit."

"I will include her in my prayers tonight." Jordan smiled at the man.

He laughed. He did not seem to consider her race a factor in the pay rate, unlike the treatment she'd received in Virginia and Illinois. Perhaps things truly were different here.

He reached out a hand and said, "Welcome. I wish you the best in your time with us. In case you are not aware, there is concern about a bog that seems to be forming around

Tompkins School. We are aware of the need for repairs and are in negotiations with the public works department for a remedy."

Jordan nodded, though she did not understand what he was referring to.

★★★

Mr. McClymonds's warning hardly prepared her for the stench that poured into her nostrils as she walked up Fifth Street on Monday morning. The odor was a sure sign that dysentery might be caught from this marshy bog. Apparently the school had been built too close to the bay.

A White woman of German heritage greeted her and showed Jordan to her temporary classroom, one of many in this large school. Jordan inhaled slowly and looked around the studentless room. The walls had two maps: one of California and the United States and one of the entire world. The maps weren't particularly old, but they were incorrect—evidence that their nation and the world were changing so rapidly.

The world map showed British, French, Spanish, Portuguese, and Dutch colonies highlighted in various colors. Hawaii, the valuable and disputed land that was always in the newspaper, was labeled Sandwich Islands and as British.

She studied the map of California and the United States from 1883. It was comprehensive, showing all thirty-eight states and nine territories, though North and South Dakota were only labeled as Dakota. The map had many useful facts, including the size in square miles for each state and their populations, as well as a list of presidents up until 1880.

The information about California was more detailed: each California county included acreage, real estate values, population, students, and school funding. Jordan found herself lost in the information when the first students arrived.

"Good morning." Jordan smiled at two girls who looked so alike they must be sisters. "I'm Mrs. Wallace. I'll be your teacher until Miss Loughlin recovers from scarlet fever."

"I'm Suzy. This is Sally." The elder sister introduced them. "Our younger brother, Johnny, is in first form. I can tell you everything you need to know about our classroom."

"Thank you, Suzy. I appreciate your guidance," Jordan replied with a smile.

Suzy's precocious attitude might have been unwelcome to another teacher, but Jordan was grateful to have her advice. As students arrived, Suzy introduced them to their new teacher as if she'd been acquainted with Jordan for ages. She counseled Jordan to separate some of the children, and she made sure to have a seat in the very front.

Suzy reminded Jordan of Tessie, a child she'd been close to in Richmond. Tessie, an orphan who had been deemed contraband in the Civil War, had a bright spirit and confidence that belied her traumatic past. Many of Jordan's former students had struggled, but Tessie had made a good life for herself, sharecropping on a fertile piece of land with her husband and nearly grown children. It was not an easy life, and perhaps Tessie overstated her success, but Jordan found deep satisfaction when she thought of her.

A bell sounded from the hallway. Jordan didn't know what that signaled. She looked at Suzy.

"It's time to begin lessons," Suzy explained.

Jordan nodded. All kinds of faces stared at her: Swedish, German, Portuguese, Italian, Colored, and even a Chinese boy. This was indeed an integrated school.

Her whole being swelled in excitement. She hadn't realized how much she had missed being in front of a classroom of students. Looking out she witnessed the truth of Miss Flood's assertion. She saw for herself that one man's vision and persistence had created this integrated school in Oakland. Changes for the better would come from those who cared enough to make them happen. Perhaps Naomi's quest to overturn the anti-miscegenation laws would be as successful as Mr. Flood's campaign to have one school system for all children in Oakland regardless of their race.

★★★

On Sunday, Jordan and Naomi slid into their usual pew next to Miss Flood. She informed them that Pastor Summers wanted to speak to them after the service. Naomi nodded vigorously and could not hide her excitement. Jordan wasn't convinced overturning this law would keep Willie safe, but at least Naomi would have the social standing and protections that came with a civil marriage.

After the opening hymn, the pastor declared that this was a day of celebration and mourning for the greatest among them: Frederick Douglass. Jordan's throat tightened in sorrow at the great man's name. The news of Mr. Douglass's death was a personal sorrow, though she had not known him well. It was a testament to his stature that news of his passing was in the local paper. He'd died at home quite suddenly after attending the national convention for women's suffrage in Washington, DC.

Pastor Summers read in its entirely the effusive article from Thursday's *Oakland Tribune*. It listed many of Douglass's impressive achievements on behalf of their race, and details of his personal life, including the fact that his second marriage was to a White woman, which many people of all hues found scandalous.

Naomi leaned in and whispered, "Your beloved Mr. Douglass advocated for racial mixing. At least Willie is Colored."

Jordan smiled and shook her head, but did not reply.

"Mrs. Wallace." Jordan startled at the sound of her name coming from the worship leader. She looked at him. He said, "I understand you met the great man himself."

She looked at Miss Flood, who smiled with encouragement. Jordan nodded at the minister.

"Please, come forward and testify," Pastor Summers commanded.

Adrenaline shot through her. She hadn't spoken in church in a very long time. All eyes were on her. Refusing would seem disrespectful—to Reverend Summers and Mr. Douglass.

She stood and made her way to the front on wobbly legs. Standing in front of everyone, she took a deep breath and clasped her hands together to keep them from shaking. She looked at Naomi. Her daughter nodded at her, giving her courage to speak her heart.

"He was kind. And strong," Jordan said through a tight throat. The congregation was listening so intently that it didn't matter that her voice was soft. "He knew he was doing God's work. In his presence you believed in the future of this great nation and the true possibility of liberation. Even in defeat he won because of his unwavering dignity that could not be removed by any harsh treatment. It was a great privilege to shake his hand and stand at his side, if only for a few days."

Jordan returned to her seat, hoping she had honored his legacy adequately. Naomi squeezed her hand. Miss Flood's eyes were glossy. Perhaps she had conveyed the depth of her respect for his greatness.

After worship, congregants lined up to shake Jordan's hand—the one that had been touched by Frederick Douglass's. Jordan was particularly moved by the grandparents who held out the hands of babies and children too young to know their history. But it felt like those children, from the next generation, were receiving a blessing from Douglass through her.

When the greeting line was finished, Miss Flood, Naomi, and Jordan approached the pastor. Before he opened his mouth, Jordan realized the news was going to be disappointing.

Empathy and anger in his voice, Pastor Summers shook his head and informed them, "I am very sorry. The cowardly legislature wouldn't even take a vote on the issue of the black laws. I appealed to their sense of righteousness, but their political futures won the day."

Naomi looked devastated. Even though Jordan was uncertain about the wisdom of Naomi marrying Willie, fury and protection stirred in her. This law was demeaning to them.

"Thank you for carrying our message, Pastor," Miss Flood said.

Jordan and Naomi mumbled their gratitude as well. They walked away from church, defeat in their souls.

Miss Flood announced, "I shall not give up. This fight has only just begun."

Jordan found Miss Flood's passion endearing but naïve. She shook her head.

"White men are not concerned with the needs of Colored women," Jordan replied.

Miss Flood countered, "But women understand the importance of a legitimate family. It is time to vote out men who do not serve our interests." She looked between Jordan and Naomi and implored, "You must join me."

"Join you in what?" Naomi asked, her eyebrows pulled together in confusion.

"The fight for universal suffrage!" Miss Flood declared. Utter disbelief on her face, Naomi shook her head.

"Until the day of his death, Mr. Douglass did not surrender his intention that women should be accorded the same rights as men," Miss Flood said. "How can we surrender the future of our people?"

"To what end?" Naomi said. "He is now dead, and women have no suffrage."

Miss Flood argued, "Women have the franchise in Wyoming and Colorado—why not California? We have a Republican majority in our government. It is time!"

Women's suffrage. Long ago that had been Jordan's passion. In 1870 she'd been certain that the Fifteenth Amendment would be deemed to include women soon. She followed with great excitement and hope when Victoria Woodhull petitioned the congressional Judiciary Committee, but they decided that women were not covered by either the Fourteenth or Fifteenth Amendments.

Jordan's hopes were raised once again in 1878 when Senator Sargent brought an amendment for women's suffrage to the floor of Congress, but that was defeated before any states voted on it. Time and time again, Jordan had been disappointed.

Yet Miss Flood was correct that women in a few states and territories could vote in all elections, while women in even more states voted in local elections.

Jordan looked at her daughter. The young woman had been determined only a week ago. Naomi could not let life's setbacks deter her so easily, or she would be trampled by the many obstacles that society and time would most surely deal to her.

Jordan thought of the faces in her classroom. Boys and girls of all backgrounds. Surely if they could go to school together, they could vote together. Hope swelled in her. She thought of Mama's demand that she keep faith, even if only the size of a mustard seed. She thought of the admiration for Mr. Douglass that she had just expressed. It was time she provided an example for Naomi.

"Yes" leaped from her tongue. "I will join you!"

"Hooray!" Miss Flood cheered. "And you, Naomi?"

The young woman shrugged.

Miss Flood cajoled, "You do know we have a Republican majority, and their platform includes the right for women to vote."

Naomi nodded with a sigh.

Jordan thought back to her arguments with her brother so long ago. Samuel asserted that the men in the family could represent their interests. It was an argument she disagreed with then, but even more now.

"Do you believe Malcolm's one vote should speak for all three of us?" she challenged her daughter.

Naomi looked at her, confused.

"They argue we can be represented by our men," Jordan explained. "But I say we can vote for ourselves!"

"My mother has been encouraging me to start a women's club at our church," Miss Flood continued. "She hopes we can organize a home for the elderly and infirm. I will agree to her request so long as we advocate for universal franchise as well. The Negro women of Oakland will lead in our fight for freedom."

Jordan nodded; true excitement pounded in her chest. She did not know if they would prevail, but it felt right to wage this battle for her own liberation.

CHAPTER EIGHTEEN

SADIE

Oakland
March 1895

Sadie read the *Tribune*, looking for signs of her husband's status. Every week there were articles about Hawaii in the paper, but they were harder to find now that the unrest on the islands was no longer front-page news.

The queen's forced abdication in January was the beginning of instability, not the end. Sadie was past hoping Heinrich would be home soon. She simply wanted to hear from him.

She scanned advertisements promising instant wealth, salacious articles of divorce, and news of looming conflicts with China. On page six she found an article reporting that Hawaiian president Dole was campaigning for the small nation to be annexed by the United States, but others wanted it to remain a separate country, governed by businessmen.

Sadie didn't know Spreckels's stance, and therefore she did not know where Heinrich stood on the issue. Her husband might be one of the men imprisoned for rebellion or even sentenced to death. Would he be allowed to contact her?

Her family wanted to be reassuring, but they were as

uncertain as she was about Heinrich's status. Diana and Sam's continued confirmation that she and May would always have a place in their home was an enormous comfort.

She found more news of Hawaii on the fourth page. The British and United States governments were being asked to intervene with their imprisoned citizens. Heinrich was a German citizen. The United States would be unlikely to intervene on his behalf if he needed it.

Each day she cycled through a variety of emotions: despair that she'd been abandoned; fear that Heinrich was imprisoned; hope that he might return; and sorrow that he was ill or worse: dead. Each time that thought flashed into her mind, she forced it away. It had been only six months. Hawaii was far away and in political unrest. She reminded herself to be both patient and prudent. She hardly knew what to pray for, so she settled on health for May and safety for her husband.

Piece by piece, Sadie had sold the valuables she'd managed to take from the house: jewelry, clothes, and furniture. She contributed to the household by buying groceries, cooking, and cleaning. She'd run out of anything to sell besides her wedding ring; she was unwilling to part with the band of commitment. It was time for her to find a position to bring in income.

"Diana, the news from Hawaii does not reassure me that my husband will be returning anytime soon."

Her sister-in-law replied, "I'm sorry. But I fear you are right."

"I need a job," Sadie said.

Sympathy on her face, Diana looked at Sadie, furrowed her brows, and nodded. Sadie hated that look. Was this to be her future? Pity for being an abandoned wife?

Sadie inhaled and pulled her shoulders back. "I am not

too proud to work," she declared, a challenge in her voice.

"Of course not," Diana said. "What do you have in mind?"

"I've looked through the paper, but only find full-time domestic help. I do not believe I can manage that and care for May. She's too young to wean."

"And too fragile," Diana agreed.

Sadie experienced the too-familiar shameful tingle behind her eyes.

Caution in his voice, Sam offered, "A position has opened up at the produce stand. It is normally done by a man, but I believe you can do it as well. It is physical but not too demanding."

Sadie's heart flew in hope. "I'm happy to do anything you think I am capable of."

"Toward the end of the day, we bring our surplus to a cannery. They give us a severely reduced price, but it is better than letting it rot beyond all use."

Sadie nodded.

"Do you believe you will be able to push a loaded cart?" he asked.

"I did grow up working on a farm," Sadie reminded her brother. "It wasn't so long ago that you were impressed with my skills at a plow. It has been a while, but I'm confident I still have that strength. Is it enough for your cart?"

Sam laughed. "I forget that this pampered lady in front of me is that same girl who used to guide a team so well," he replied.

I hardly remember that was me.

"Can you start today?" Sam asked.

"Truly?!" Sadie replied.

Sam nodded.

"Thank you, brother."

"The pay is not high," he cautioned.

"It will be fine," she said. And she meant it. She simply needed work—to occupy her time and to contribute to the household.

"Come at eleven," he directed. "Diana can show you what to do, and you can start being paid the following day."

Relief surged through her. Once again her brother was providing a lifeline.

"Thank you, Sam," she said. "I'm further indebted to you."

Diana scolded, "You owe him no debt for being a loyal brother."

Sadie smiled and nodded. She agreed with the sentiment, but only wished she were the one doing the giving and not the receiving.

***

Sadie found her nerves as she walked toward the produce district. In a few short blocks she left a quiet residential neighborhood and was in the midst of bustling activity and the unpleasant smell of rotting food. She felt protective of May, tied on her chest. She pulled the thin fabric over May's head to protect her from the stench.

Sadie wore her oldest plain dress but was still out of place. Her fine-grain leather shoes would be forever changed by the muddy earth that caked the walkway. A flash of anger at Heinrich surged through her. It was cruel of him to leave them without protection. Then fear and shame flooded in; it was not a charitable thought about her husband if he was gravely ill, or gone from the earth. perhaps he was ill, or worse—gone forever. She took a deep breath. *This is your life now,* she reminded herself.

Johnson Produce was in the middle of the block just

before Second Street. The market had more roof than walls. Sam said there was no need to finish the walls since they wanted air circulating through the vegetables and fruits. She looked for Sam but didn't see him. A man passed her with a nearly empty wooden cart. She imagined that was what she'd be pushing to the cannery, only laden with produce.

She followed the man. He stood in a short line, waiting to talk with Diana, who was standing at a counter with a large book spread open before her.

The man at the front of the line gave Diana a few bills and a pouch of coins. She counted the money and made a note in the accounting book. Sadie couldn't hear her words, but Diana said something that made the man laugh. Diana patted him on the shoulder and smiled broadly.

The next man stepped up to speak with Diana. She must have felt Sadie's gaze, because she looked up. When she recognized her sister-in-law, she waved her forward.

"I'll be with you in a moment," Diana said to Sadie. "Jusepe will be the last—as always!" she teased.

Sadie watched as the next two men gave Diana their earnings, moved their unsold produce to a cart, and left. When they were done, the market was empty except for Diana and Sadie. And May.

"And now we breathe!" Diana said. She inhaled deeply while Sadie watched. "Join me," Diana insisted. "Deep breaths clean our souls. After the chaos, we need to clear our spirit!"

Sadie laughed and took a deep breath. It was refreshing.

"Two more breaths!" Diana exhorted. "Then we put you to work."

Sadie inhaled deeply, feeling the air move past her nose and into her lungs. She felt May move outward with the breath and then inward when she breathed out. She repeated the action and then nodded at Diana. She did feel much better.

Diana explained, "You will wait until all the peddlers return from the day. They transfer their leftover produce to a cart. Then you walk to the Hickmott Cannery at First and Myrtle. Today I will go with you to introduce you to the manager. Tomorrow you will be the expert doing it on your own."

Sadie smiled at her sister-in-law, appreciating her kind confidence. Diana started to pick up the cart handles.

"Let me," Sadie said. "I want to know that I can."

Diana looked at her, compassion and admiration in her eyes. She nodded once, decisively.

"You want May on your back for this work," Diana said. "Trust me. My children taught me." She laughed and helped Sadie make the adjustment. May was so little that they folded the material around her before attaching her in the new position.

Sadie grabbed the handles and lifted. It took effort, but it was not too difficult. Diana was right; she was glad to have May on her back so she could use her belly to steady the cart. It was wobbly at first, and steering took a few adjustments, but she quickly gained confidence that she could do this part of the job.

Crossing Broadway with the cart was the biggest challenge. Avoiding the holes in the road and the cars took her full attention, but otherwise it was an easy walk to the cannery—one of the ones that Heinrich oversaw. In fact he had arranged for Sam and Diana to sell their unsold produce there. She'd never met the manager she would be working with, Jim Dier, but Heinrich had spoken of him on occasion. It was strange to be coming to this place in this position. She reminded herself to be grateful for the opportunity to earn some money rather than bitter at the need to be working.

No one in this place would know her, so she had nothing to be ashamed about.

Diana marched around the building to the open space in the back. Sadie followed along. The cart was awkward and precarious as she traversed over the very bumpy ground. Her blood raced when the cart nearly tipped over, but she quickly balanced it. The strength and skills she used to plow were still inside her limbs.

"We transfer the produce to this table," Diana explained. "Then we wait for the manager to come. He'll give you a few coins, and then you return with the cart. It is very simple. This time of year it is quiet. In the summer months, watch out! All of the rooms are open. They process fruit almost twenty-four hours a day when the peaches are ripe in August."

August. Five months from now. Would Sadie still have this job? Would Heinrich be back? She had no idea what life would be in five months. When Heinrich left six months before, she had had no idea she'd be in this position now. She couldn't predict the future; she'd make the best of today.

Sadie nodded and studied the workroom. There were long rows of counters with people standing every two feet or so. It was loud from the whir of machinery. Long belts hung through the air, connecting engines and gears.

At the closest table, women were slicing asparagus. Sadie saw men standing in front of a machine, but she could not make out what they were doing. She was surprised to see a child, not more than eight years old, sweeping. A young woman with a hard face and only one arm carried a basket of vegetables. Sadie wondered at the story of these people.

A man walked up to them.

"Mr. Dier, Sadie is going to be bringing our surplus from now on." Diana introduced them.

Sadie was glad her last name was omitted. Then she was ashamed of her own shame. She smiled at the man, but he did not take any interest in her. He handed over a few coins to Diana and left.

Sadie easily lifted the handles of the cart, so much lighter without the asparagus and onions.

"Diana, I didn't realize there were children working in the cannery," Sadie said quietly as they walked away.

Diana sighed. Sadie sensed disapproval.

"What?" Sadie challenged.

"I imagine you read about the girl whose arm was mangled in the belts?" Diana asked.

Sadie remembered the day when Heinrich had been upset about the production stoppage. She nodded.

"That was her," Diana replied.

It was Sadie's turn to sigh. Hearing about a girl was entirely different from seeing her.

"Families need money, Sadie," Diana explained. "Not everyone has the resources we have. Can we blame the poor for using whatever means they have to survive?"

Color rose in Sadie's cheeks. "Children working outside in fields is understandable. But in dark and loud buildings? How many hours a day are they in there?"

Diana shrugged.

Sadie asked, "Is no one concerned that they are not in school?"

"The Unitarian women speak of it—intermittently."

Sadie snorted. "Is there nothing they won't speak of—intermittently?"

Diana defended her faith: "We take up many causes because there is so much that needs reform."

Sadie could not argue with that. She replied wistfully, "I wish the reforms could simply be done with. Why must each be fought for over and over and over again?"

"Come to the Unitarian women's auxiliary with me," Diana encouraged. "You will appreciate the strong women fighting for a better tomorrow for everyone. The topic of our suffrage is our current cause."

A tug of hope along with a stab of fear filled Sadie's chest at the thought of involving herself in political matters. An image of Heinrich's face—incredulous and surprised—popped into her mind. But her husband was gone, perhaps never to return. She had to make her own way now.

Sadie asked, "Can I bring May?"

"Certainly," Diana replied. "You can leave if she becomes a disruption, but we are all mothers. We understand."

"Then I will come!" Excitement stirred in Sadie—at the idea of getting out of the house and meeting like-minded women.

Diana's smile showed her approval.

CHAPTER NINETEEN

Jordan

Oakland
March 1895

Fifteen women boarded the train at the depot on Seventh Street in Oakland. Miss Flood and Jordan were the only Colored people, but they were warmly welcomed by the other delegates. As this was the terminus of the line, the women from San Francisco were boarding here as well.

The National American Woman Suffrage Association had paid the fare for any woman who could make the journey to the capital of California: Sacramento. Dozens of women from many cities would go before the state assembly to claim their right to vote.

Jordan hoped she looked as confident as Miss Flood appeared. She didn't feel as if she belonged with these well-to-do women making demands of the government. Many of them were married to wealthy men and had been organizing for this cause for years. She felt like an impostor, though she shared their ardent desire to see women have the vote.

Jordan was proud to be representing the Colored women of Oakland along with Miss Flood. She'd been surprised when Miss Flood offered this ticket to her, but apparently

Jordan's connection to the Columbian Exposition and Ida B. Wells had been all the information the club needed to choose her as the second delegate. After shaking hands and making acquaintance with the other women, Miss Flood and Jordan searched for seats.

"Would you prefer the window?" Jordan offered, though she dearly wanted to see the view. The last time she'd traveled this route, she'd been too busy tending to Sadie and May to gaze out a window.

"Go right ahead." Miss Flood gestured for her to go first. "I can greet people and chat more easily from the aisle."

Jordan nodded and slid onto the third-class bench. There was no need to be in second or first class on such a short journey. Others on this train would be traveling all the way to Chicago—some in a Pullman car.

Jordan's mind flashed to Willie. Her letter had long since been delivered to his mother, but Naomi had not reported any change in their intention to marry. Hopefully Emily was working to convince Willie that this marriage would be unwise. It would be a painful but temporary blow to her daughter, but better than a lifetime of distress.

Gazing out of the right side of the train, Jordan saw the same mix of people she'd taught in her temporary classroom. She'd been their teacher for only two weeks, but in that time she had experienced for herself the racial mixing that Naomi and Willie spoke about. Out the window she saw people of various shades and hair colors in all kinds of clothing. Most of the Chinese wore American clothes, but a few were in black pajamas or bright silk.

The sight of the porters, in their telltale uniforms, brought up longing for her husband in heaven. He'd be cheering her on, going to fight for her right to vote. Mama too.

Hello, Booker. Hello, Mama. I hope I'm making you proud—

getting on with my life and fighting for the good, she said to them in her soul.

The train jerked away from the station. She waved back at the people on the platform. The familiar sights in Oakland flashed by, and they quickly passed through Emeryville township. In Berkeley she looked for the great university, but Miss Flood said it was too far from the tracks.

At each stop two or three women joined them until she estimated there were twenty-five when they pulled into the station in Sacramento three hours later. The warm, dry air hit her skin, signaling she was in another world. The dramatic differences in the climate of California were perplexing.

On the train platform the women lined up in a formation. Miss Flood hooked her arm through Jordan's. A White woman she'd never met linked elbows on the other side.

"I'm Miss Miller of Berkeley," she leaned in and said.

"Mrs. Booker Wallace of Oakland. And this is Miss Flood," Jordan replied.

The young White woman smiled and declared, "Let's make history."

Jordan's heart hammered as they walked toward the capitol building. Alert for any signs of danger, she scanned ahead. She expected verbal attacks and prayed they would avoid a physical one.

In this moment Jordan sincerely felt her race was no barrier to these women. They were united in their work for the common good of all women. Pride swelled in Jordan's soul; she was fulfilling a long-ago dream that she'd given up for dead.

Soon the capitol building loomed before them. It was stately with its round dome and smooth walls. They marched up the marble stairs, their arms connecting them in rows of three.

A lone White workman snarled, "Women don't get no vote. Especially no Nigger women!"

Jordan's breath caught. Miss Miller gasped.

"Ignore him!" Miss Flood instructed. "He is beneath our concern."

Jordan stumbled over the foot in front of her. The line had suddenly stopped moving forward because Mrs. Gordon had paused at the top.

She bellowed instructions, "Ladies, join hands for a prayer."

Jordan's arms were shaking, and she took a deep breath to settle her emotions. Miss Flood patted her hand.

"He cannot harm you. We are strong together," the young woman said.

Jordan was embarrassed to be so disturbed. She nodded and lied, "I'm fine now, thank you."

Hands clasped and arms hooked, the group of women encircled the stately matron.

"God, give us the strength to do your bidding. In the beginning you said, 'It is not good for man to stand alone.' We are here to fulfill your word. Women's suffrage means every citizen possessing the necessary qualifications shall be entitled to cast one vote at every election and have that vote counted. We do not ask to be elevated above the men. We do not reject our duties for home. We ask for a government that professes to be a republic to be a republic and not pretend to be what it is not. Amen."

Amens echoed back.

Mrs. Gordon declared, "Ladies, we are making history. The women of the great state of California will not tolerate being second-class citizens."

Jordan joined in the rousing cheer and then stepped into the imposing statehouse.

The large meeting room was brimming with energy. Jordan read signs being held up high: "Votes for women," "No taxation without representation," and "Through thick and thin we begin." A chill traveled down her spine and her flesh raised up. Many women held bouquets of flowers.

The crowd of women listened quietly to the proceedings until Judge Spencer of Lassen County introduced the bill. Jordan joined the others in a loud cheer. A gavel silenced them. As Judge Spencer spoke, women walked one by one down to his desk and placed flowers on it.

Jordan leaned in to make out every word.

Miss Flood whispered in Jordan's ear, "That is Mr. Spencer's wife at his side."

Jordan nodded, impressed at the model of equality. As he spoke, she made notes and slid them over to her husband. A number of women were allowed to add their voices to the cause, and they each made their case well, a testament to their sex.

Mrs. Blinn closed the introduction of the bill. "The men have made a mess of our nation. None can argue with that fact. It is our turn to bring the passion and care of a mother's touch to our country. We will have a cleansing effect that will make our state great."

Jordan joined the crowd of women in a brief cheer.

A Mr. Lackman stood up to speak, "What folly we will bring upon our government if we allow illogical and weak women to assume political duties. What would be the effect on affairs of this state today were its governor in the throes of childbirth? I tell you that which might be heaven for this new woman would be hell for old men!"

Jordan was surprised that a raucous uproar of protest greeted his assertion, but she joined in, feeling the power of public dissent.

Mr. Bledsoe spoke next. "As we all know, the constitutionality of this plan is under question. And I wonder at the wisdom of taking such a step. But I shall give women the benefit of the doubt and be adding my voice in favor when we take up a vote."

A cheer went up. And so it went on, with more saying they would vote in favor of the bill than those who proclaimed they would vote against it. By the time the assembly was finished with the topic, Jordan was confident the women's cause would prevail when the time came for a vote.

After the session was adjourned, the women gathered for a picture on the steps of the capitol building. Dozens of petitioners, of many ages and sizes and locations, gathered close. She and Miss Flood were the only Colored faces. It might not have mattered to the proceedings that she was here today, but she was proud that representatives from their race would be memorialized in this historical record of the delegation that fought for women's equality. She grabbed Miss Flood's hand and leaned in close.

"Thank you for including me," Jordan whispered into her delicate ear.

Miss Flood squeezed her hand and they held fast as the delegation posed in the sunshine. It was exhilarating to be a part of history.

★★★

A few days later, Jordan arrived at the women's auxiliary meeting at the Unitarian Church. She scanned the sunny room looking for Miss Flood and was surprised to see her seated near Sadie and May. She sat down by the young woman and scooped up the little one into her arms. A sweet delight spread from her chest outward, like sinking into a warm tub.

"May looks so good!" Jordan declared, grinning at the baby.

May's hazel eyes locked onto Jordan's brown ones. Then her gaze moved around Jordan's face. She returned her focus to Jordan's eyes and slowly, ever so slowly, a tiny smile turned into a huge toothless grin. Jordan beamed back, completely smitten.

Jordan smiled at Sadie. "She's so lovely. I'm so happy to see her, and you, doing so well!"

Sadie nodded with a smile and then pulled the corners of her lips down, a confused confirmation. Before Sadie could explain what she was doing here, Mrs. Gordon, the leader of the women's auxiliary, brought them to attention.

They approved the minutes from their past meeting and turned to new business.

"Great news—with the suffrage bill passed in the state assembly, we are halfway to our goal. There is a groundswell of genuine support."

Jordan cheered with the women and smiled at Sadie.

"We must not let up. The state senate will be voting on our cause. We must be there in large numbers. The National American Woman Suffrage Association does not have funds to cover our expenses again, so, ladies, we must pay our own way."

Jordan's hopes sank. Neither she nor Naomi had found steady employment. Though it had paid well, the temporary position as a substitute teacher did not give her the means to pay for a ticket to Sacramento. Even with a regular income, the cost of a ticket for such a journey would be too dear. She'd so very much wanted to be there on the historic day when the California Senate voted to enfranchise the women in this state, setting an example for the nation.

Miss Flood stood up. "I shall take up a collection at

church. Fifteenth Street AME will support us!"

The group cheered.

"That is the precise spirit that will see our cause won!" Reverend Tupper Wilkes proclaimed. "Who else can pledge to be there?"

Miss Flood leaned in to have a private conversation. "If the church will support us, I trust you will join me again?"

"Certainly," Jordan agreed with genuine desire. "Thank you."

The larger conversation continued with women pledging their presence, their financial support, or both, until they had a delegation Oakland could be proud of.

When the meeting ended, Jordan reluctantly handed May back to her mother. The little one had happily stayed on her lap for the entire gathering.

"What a joy to have both of you join us," Jordan exclaimed.

Sadie explained, "Diana, Sam's wife, encouraged me to join in. She attends this church."

"We do as well. Their lady preacher is refreshing," Jordan said. "What did you think of the meeting for our great cause?"

"It's quite exhilarating," Sadie replied. "It recalls the debates from my childhood about women's, and the Negroes', franchise. You will be there next week? For the vote?"

"It seems so," Jordan said.

"I suppose there'll be no more need for meetings like this after that," Sadie said. She looked disappointed.

"I imagine we will meet to support other causes," Jordan replied. "Our franchise will just be the beginning to a great social movement of liberation. Perhaps your mother will join in too."

"That would surprise me," Sadie said. "She has never

been one for politics."

Reflexively, Jordan raised one side of her mouth. *Some people have that luxury,* she thought to herself.

"Please give her my very best," Jordan said as they bade one another farewell.

Jordan rushed home, excited to share the news about the vote. Naomi had been glum in the many months since the visit with the county clerk. Perhaps this information would cheer her spirits.

Mrs. King was bent over in the garden. They exchanged pleasantries, and then Jordan went into her house.

Naomi was standing at the door, a look of hatred on her face. Jordan's throat clenched tight.

"You are determined to undermine my very happiness, aren't you?" her daughter hissed.

Jordan's heart beat hard in her chest. She swallowed. *The letter!*

"How dare you write to Willie's parents," Naomi seethed. "They shared your betrayal with him, and he had no choice but to tell me of it."

Jordan stammered out, "I only have your well-being in mind."

"You cannot determine the course of my life," Naomi replied, her hand over her womb.

With sudden certainty, Jordan's fear was confirmed: Naomi carried Willie's child.

Naomi glared and spit out, "Your duplicity won't be rewarded. Emily and William are coming to Oakland to swear before the clerk that they are Willie's parents so that we may get our license. Despite your interference—perhaps because of it—we will be married soon."

Naomi stormed away, leaving Jordan gasping for breath. Her mind was swirling in confusion, and her heart sank in pain. Naomi had already leaped off a cliff. Jordan no longer trusted her daughter. And Naomi did not trust Jordan.

CHAPTER TWENTY

SADIE

Oakland
March 1895

Sadie rushed home from her errands, hoping to beat her baby's hunger pangs. Now that she was seven months old, May loudly broadcast her need for food. It was at once a burden and a joy to have her daughter be demanding. With each week that passed, Sadie was more confident in May's strength and her own ability to give her what she needed. Her little one had a fierce determination that inspired.

Sadie went through the back door, set the bags of produce on the counter in the kitchen, and put away a few items with May still tied to her body. It was a habit she had yet to end. She felt most comfortable with May close.

"Hello, Sadie." The low voice startled her.

Adrenaline shot through her body. She looked over. Standing in the doorway to the dining room was her husband, the man she had feared dead. His cheeks were chiseled and his suit hung on his body. He'd lost an enormous amount of weight.

"Heinrich?" Sadie questioned. Confusion delayed her rush of relief, but then it came. "Heinrich!" She rushed to him and wrapped her arms around him, May sandwiched between them.

He exhaled with a snort and patted her back as they embraced. Her lip trembled. *He's alive.*

When they pulled apart, she wiped a tear.

"Are you so sad to see me, wife?" he teased.

She shook her head. "I thought you were . . . dead," she squeaked out.

"You cannot be rid of me so easily," he replied with a smile.

"Why didn't you write?" Sadie asked.

"Surely you have read about the situation in Hawaii?"

She nodded and bit her lip.

"Mail was interrupted. Then I became ill, and by the time I could hold a pen, it was time for me to come home."

She forced a smile. She was relieved to see him, but anger welled up in her chest as well. Four months without word. He'd left her wondering if she'd been abandoned or widowed.

"Are you mad at me, wife?" he asked, sounding as if he were angry himself.

She shook her head to clear it. "I'm sorry, Heinrich. I am behaving horribly." She pasted a smile on her face. "Come." She took his hand and led him into the living room. "You can hold your daughter and tell me about your time away."

He shook his head. "Can you make me lunch to eat while I finish my work?" he asked.

Sadie felt those words as a blow to her chest. He had no time for either of them. She wanted to protest, but instead nodded.

"Good girl," Heinrich said. "I've found an apartment for us. I will need to visit it this afternoon to confirm. If it is suitable, we can move there tonight."

Sadie worked to take in the information. Of course they would not stay here now that Heinrich was back, but tonight? So soon.

"How did you find us?" Sadie asked.

"Where else could you be?" he asked. "You have no means to support yourself."

"When you left, did you know we would be removed from our home before your return?" Sadie challenged.

Heinrich looked at her, his eyebrows pulled in. "I'll take my lunch in the other room," he replied, ignoring her question.

Sadie exhaled. She rubbed May's back and blinked away tears. She'd imagined a joyful reunion with Heinrich many times, but she should have been realistic. Her husband was a practical, not sentimental, man. She returned to the kitchen to cut bread, cheese, and apples. She piled the slices on a stoneware plate.

Sadie carried the food into the other room and set it on the table in front of Heinrich. He patted her hand and smiled at her. She leaned over and kissed him.

"I am so very glad to see you alive and well," she said.

"Would you like to come with me?" he asked.

"Where?"

"To see the apartment?"

She nodded.

"It will only be temporary . . . until we are ready to move to Hawaii. For maybe two months—three at the most." He smiled and turned back to his papers.

Her stomach turned over. "We are moving?" she stammered.

"Sadie, I must finish this," he chastised.

She watched him sitting calmly at the table while her body churned. Live in Hawaii? Anger and sadness in equal measure swirled within her. She couldn't imagine moving to another country, leaving Sam, Diana, and the kids. Would Momma agree? She waited, hoping Heinrich would notice her anguish and be willing to discuss the matter, but he continued working.

May stirred. He hadn't even looked at their daughter. She left her husband alone in the dining room. Sadie brought May upstairs to their bedroom. They were in the rocking chair nursing when Heinrich found them to say he was ready to go.

"She's not finished yet," Sadie explained.

Heinrich tsked impatience. "Very well. I'll wait for you two downstairs."

Sadie sighed. She'd longed for Heinrich to return, but now that he had, she remembered the difficulty of living with him. As the head of the household, he expected her, and now May, to follow his wishes without complaint or request.

It was going to be a hard adjustment for Sadie.

★★★

The apartment was a few blocks away on Twelfth Street. Heinrich climbed up four flights of stairs without slowing for her. When Sadie caught up to him, her heart was beating hard. She didn't know if it was from emotion or exertion. There were two doors to the right. Heinrich opened the one on the left.

The large living room had a couch on one side and a mattress on the other. A little stove and sink were against the opposite wall. It must be a one-bedroom apartment. She supposed Momma would be willing to sleep in this space temporarily.

Sadie opened the door on the right. It was a storage closet. She opened the left door expecting to find a bedroom, but it was a water closet.

She looked around for another door, but there was none. Perhaps Heinrich expected Momma to stay with Sam and Diana until they left.

"It is small, but adequate for our needs, don't you agree?" Heinrich asked.

"I see there is no space for my mother."

"Lisbeth can stay with your brother."

"She's very helpful with May," Sadie replied.

"You will not need her anymore," Heinrich said.

Was he offering to help with the baby?

Sadie said, "As you mentioned, it won't be for very long."

"In Hawaii you will have all the help you need. You will never have to care for her again."

"I like to take care of her," Sadie replied.

"You were the one who complained that you needed your mother for assistance. Take care of her yourself, or use one of the maids. I do not care. As you like."

"Maids?" Sadie asked.

"Yes," he replied, and satisfaction shone from his eyes. "You will have all the maids you like. One for each room if you wish."

She drew in her eyebrows.

"Are you angry again?" he questioned. "Maids are not enough for you?"

"No," she said, keeping her voice calm. "I'm confused. I know nothing about our future circumstances because you have not told me."

Heinrich replied, "You do not need to understand anything. We will have every comfort we need in Hawaii. Spreckels is extremely pleased with my work there. I have secured my place in that new land."

"You've struck gold?" she asked.

"What?" he replied.

"You've been disappointed that you were born too late to make a fortune in the Gold Rush," Sadie explained. "Is this your opportunity?"

"Yes! You understand now." Heinrich smiled. "I have struck gold."

Sadie pulled up the sides of her cheeks, hoping to show excitement. Heinrich had found what he'd wanted for so many years. Perhaps he would now be satisfied with his life and their family.

She said to her husband, "Congratulations. That is good news indeed. My family will be happy for you—and for us."

★★★

When they returned to Sam and Diana's, Momma was there.

"Heinrich!" Momma exclaimed when she saw him. "Welcome home."

"Thank you, Lisbeth. I'm glad to be back, if only for temporary."

Momma looked at Sadie.

A wave traveled down Sadie's back; she sighed and swallowed before telling her mother their bittersweet news.

"We are moving to Hawaii." Sadie looked at her mother's blue eyes as she spoke.

"Oh," Momma said. She bit her lip. Her eyes filled with moisture. Sadie saw her take in a deep breath. Then Momma smiled and said, "I imagine that means your business is going well there. Congratulations, Heinrich."

Heinrich grinned at Momma. "Yes, very well. There is great wealth to be made there. I am fortunate to be a . . . ." He paused, muttered to himself in German, then asked, "How do you say, in English, first to arrive?"

"Pioneer?" Sadie said.

"I am fortunate to be a pioneer in Hawaii. There is almost nothing there—but great opportunity for business. Unlike here, where all the land is owned already."

Momma repeated, "Congratulations. When do we leave?"

Heinrich replied before Sadie had a chance. "We do not need you anymore. Sadie will have servants."

Sadie's stomach lurched. She searched for the right words to convey to her mother that she was more than a servant—much more. That Sadie valued her companionship and wisdom and . . .

Sadie looked at her mother. Momma's face was calm and hard. She nodded and said, "I understand."

Heinrich, oblivious to the insult, said, "We have an apartment, so you will be free of the burden starting tonight."

Momma closed her eyes and took a slow breath. She gave one nod and left the room.

***

Sadie found her mother in the room the three of them had shared for several months. She could not imagine how May would have survived without Momma's care. Momma was on the bed. Sadie sat down in the rocker.

"Momma, you know a servant cannot possibly replace you?" Sadie said.

Momma nodded, her eyes moist like Sadie's. "And you know you are not a burden?"

Sadie nodded.

"Do you want to come with us?" Sadie asked, uncertain what answer she wanted to hear.

If Momma desired to leave with them, Sadie might be torn between her mother and Heinrich. She could not tell whether Heinrich was indifferent or preferred to have Momma stay in California. If Momma wished to stay in

Oakland, Sadie would miss her terribly and be very lonely. She wanted her momma to *want* to be with her and May. On the other hand she did not want to force her mother to leave Oakland, choosing her over Sam and his family.

Momma sighed. Sadie's heart twisted.

Sadie asked, "Momma, why did you and Poppa decide to move to California?"

"Opportunity," she replied. "We thought you and Sam would have more choices here. Your uncle Michael praised the weather, the soil, the crops. Fruit seemed easier to grow than corn or wheat." Momma looked at Sadie. "I believe we made the right decision, as sad as it was to leave Granny and Poppy Johnson. Do you know we invited them as well?"

Sadie shook her head. She hadn't thought about it, but it made sense.

"And Uncle Mitch. But they chose to stay in Charles City." Momma shrugged.

May leaned back and patted Sadie's breast, signaling a desire to eat. Sadie smiled at the baby and unbuttoned her dress. May kicked her legs in delight and grinned up at Sadie. They settled into a feeding.

Sadie looked down at her daughter, savoring the closeness between them. Momma rubbed May's head and then kissed it.

"I'm going to miss you. So much," Momma said. "But you need to do what's best for your family. I'll . . ." Momma's voice broke. Sadie looked at Momma, sorrow closing her throat.

"I need to give thought to my answer," Momma whispered.

Sadie looked at her mother, holding her gaze and nodding. It would be an enormous change. It might be an adventure in paradise for all of them, or it could be a nightmare—living in a new land without any friends or family besides each other.

"Can I take the rocker?" Sadie's voice broke.

Momma smiled and nodded. "Of course." She blinked back tears and asked, "Would you like me to start packing you two up?"

Sadie nodded again, her throat too tight to speak. Momma left the room to get a trunk.

Sadie smiled at her daughter, who'd switched sides and was fully satiated. May reached up and patted Sadie's cheek. Then she put her hand to Sadie's mouth. Sadie took it and kissed her palm. May beamed up at her. Sadie leaned over and kissed the sweet space between her ear and her shoulder.

May's eyes blinked closed and then open; closed and then open. She was falling asleep for the last time in this room. Momma returned.

Sadie asked another question. "What gave you the courage to break your engagement to that man in Virginia?"

Momma took in a slow breath. Sadie waited. Momma opened the wardrobe and pulled down a dress. She folded it and placed it in the trunk.

Momma teared up. Without looking at Sadie, she stated in a quiet voice, "Loving Jordan. It was that girl's eyes—I'm ashamed to say that I don't even know her name. I could have found out from Sarah. But would it have mattered? I couldn't help her."

Sadie was confused. "Loving Jordan?" she asked.

"The girl, under the willow, that Edward . . . mounted, her eyes were like Jordan's—I could not get them out of my heart, my soul."

Sadie felt ill as she imagined the scene.

Momma explained, her voice at once flat and in pain, "My mother and my dearest friend, Mary, told me I was foolish to have concern for her. They felt it was God's will, but I could no longer pretend that there was no harm in this *natural order.*"

Momma stared at the wall, pulling in the edge of her lip, thinking. She shook her head and finally spoke. "I didn't take Emily with me. I was so foolish that it didn't even occur to me that I could rescue her. Her freedom wasn't part of my understanding. It was impossible for me to imagine Emily's life other than it was."

Sadie sucked in her breath. She'd never considered that time from Aunt Emily's viewpoint. Her parents spoke of rescuing Aunt Emily, Uncle William, and Cousin Willie after the war. She hadn't thought about Momma abandoning Aunt Emily before the war.

"Aunt Emily doesn't seem to hold it against you," Sadie offered, hoping to assuage her mother's pain.

Momma nodded. "I don't know how, but I think you're right. Perhaps she never considered it for herself. We have never spoken about it."

"You did it for love, Momma—left your home and everything you ever knew," Sadie said. "I think that's better than leaving from fear."

Momma replied, "I suppose."

Sadie said, "I'm glad you did. Thank you for finding the courage."

"I caught it from Mattie," Momma said with a small smile. "Jordan was a baby, just toddlin' a bit, when they left Virginia. Mattie tied Jordan on her back and walked into the woods—alone. I didn't understand how she could abandon me and *put themselves in peril*—to sound like my mother— until I saw that girl under Edward." Momma inhaled deeply and continued, "Mattie was willing to risk it all—their very lives—rather than surrender Jordan's fate to a massa or his sons or an overseer."

Sadie had heard the story of Mattie's escape many times but had never imagined how it actually had felt—the fear, the courage, the faith it took to walk away from her home and her family. Sadie's admiration for Mattie grew.

Sadie gazed at May, asleep in her arms, fully trusting in Sadie to care for her. She hoped she would take the same risk to protect her May in similar circumstances.

Sadie looked at Momma. She had also made a brave choice—ending an engagement despite her own mother's fury.

She felt her mind loosen and then come back together in a new way. Sadie would do it as well: find the courage to leave her home and family to make a life in Hawaii with Heinrich and May. It was terrifying, but she would find the strength in the example of Momma's and Mattie's lives.

CHAPTER TWENTY-ONE

JORDAN

Oakland
April 1895

Jordan returned home from the AME women's club meeting and found Naomi in the kitchen. They'd been cautious around one another in the few weeks since Naomi's harsh words.

"Good afternoon," Jordan said.

Naomi did not turn around from the sink or reply. Jordan sighed. She ignored her daughter's rude behavior and spoke as if there were no tension between them.

Jordan explained, "Miss Flood has procured the funds for us to travel to Sacramento once again. She made a stirring speech about the need to have our people represented in this fight and that no other club would have the means."

"Congratulations, Mama. I'm happy for you," Naomi said, but her tone did not match her words. She was still angry.

Jordan took a deep breath to calm herself. How long could Naomi withhold her forgiveness? Their home had been without any warmth for too long. Jordan did not want to stir up more arguments, but she found her daughter's attitude intolerable.

"Would you like me to grease your hair tonight?" Jordan asked.

"No."

"Naomi, you must forgive me," Jordan said. "I am very sorry. I made an error. But we cannot continue to live like this."

"I agree, Mama," she replied. "It is too difficult to live like this."

Naomi bit her lip, blinked hard, and left the room. Jordan sighed. She rubbed her eyes, hoping she had not made the situation between them worse by trying to address it directly.

★★★

Jordan boarded the train to Sacramento again, this time with the confidence that came from familiarity. Their hopes of success were high. She greeted familiar companions, the energy and excitement in the car palpable.

"We shall walk together into the polling place next June!" Miss Flood declared.

Jordan said with a laugh, "I feel like a girl again!" She would not let her fight with Naomi sully the joy of this day. She rubbed the shell she had put in her pocket this morning. Today was the day she would get her freedom. After this she could fulfill her mother's wish that she throw this shell in the Pacific Ocean.

Miss Flood said, "I'm so delighted that Naomi will be living on my street."

Jordan's stomach clenched. Naomi was moving out? Confusion must have shown on her face.

"Oh dear," Miss Flood said. "I did not know it was still a surprise for you. Please do not tell her I revealed her secret."

Jordan nodded and gave a tight smile despite the pit in

her stomach.

"Mr. and Mrs. Smith moved in yesterday," Miss Flood continued. "They are charming."

Emily and William had moved to Oakland? Jordan felt ill but hid her distress from Miss Flood and simply agreed. "They are."

Jordan took a deep breath to steady her nerves. It wasn't surprising that Willie and Naomi were moving forward with their plans, nor that Naomi had decided to move out. But it pained her deeply that her daughter was not sharing her plans with her. How many secrets did Naomi have? And would she ever find a way to forgive Jordan? Jordan feared that her well-intentioned comments would forever create a breach between her and Naomi.

"Look at the hillside!" Miss Flood interrupted Jordan's thoughts, pointing at the window.

Jordan turned around. A riot of orange covered the rolling hills as far as the eye could see. It was breathtaking. The golden poppies were in full bloom. Her soul soared at the magnificent sight.

"Amazing!" Jordan declared. "Does this happen every year?"

"I have never seen quite so many at once," Miss Flood said. "I will take them as a sign of hope that our cause will flourish and win the day."

The grandeur raised Jordan's spirits. In the face of such beauty, it was hard to hold on to her personal concerns. The scene was so big and beautiful that she felt assured of the goodness of creation. Surely Naomi would come to forgiveness soon.

The journey east was a bustle of goodwill. Women from all of the clubs introduced themselves to one another. Jordan joined in the conversations of hope and excitement. She would set aside her family concerns to enjoy this day.

The crowd of women in Sacramento was even larger than the last gathering. People from as far as San Diego had come to bear witness to this historic moment when the franchise would be granted to women across this state—one of the largest and most modern in the nation. The packed room was hot and stuffy despite the open windows, and Jordan was grateful for her fan.

The chair called the gathering to order. The women quieted down as the business of the chamber unfolded. Jordan didn't know the order of the proceedings. Each time they finished a vote, she perked up in anticipation of the suffrage bill. More than two hours had passed before she heard the chairman call out the bill number.

Her heart leaped. This was it! Miss Flood grabbed her hand. Anticipation rushed through Jordan's veins. She was about to have the right to vote. A chill rushed down her spine and radiated through her body. She and Miss Flood exchanged looks, their eyes beaming excitement.

"Motion to table," a bald man said.

A cry of protest rang out from the crowd.

"All in favor," the chairman said.

"Aye," the majority of senators shouted in unison.

Stop. No. Jordan protested in her mind.

"All opposed?" the chairman asked.

"Nay," a few voices yelled loudly.

"Motion to table carried," the chairman said.

Women in the balcony cried out in protest. Jordan did not understand what had happened. Just a few minutes ago they were confident that the vote was going to go in their favor.

A chant rose from the crowd: *"Votes for women! Votes for women!"* Trying to be heard over the chanting, the chairman yelled, "Assembly bill . . ."

The women did not quiet their chant; Jordan joined in. *"Votes for women! Votes for women!"*

The chairman, red in the face, yelled, "You will be silent or asked to leave this assembly."

"VOTES FOR WOMEN! VOTES FOR WOMEN!"

He banged his gavel and waved to the marshal. The man stood and glared at the women in the balcony. He walked toward the exit of the chamber, ready to make his way upstairs.

Voices dropped from the chanting, including Jordan's, until the hall was nearly silent. Jordan looked around at the faces. Many women were glaring, clearly furious. Others had moist eyes or even tears. One woman stood up and put a hand over her own mouth. She glared at the men on the floor of the senate.

Jordan tapped Miss Flood's arm and pointed to the standing protester. Miss Flood nodded. They rose together and assumed the same stance, Jordan grateful for a means of showing her outrage. One by one, the women around them did the same. For the rest of the proceedings, they stood tall and proud—a balcony of women protesting in silent rage.

★★★

Jordan was exhausted as they made their way to the train station. Thirsty and sweaty, she boarded the car and sank onto the seat by the window. The hot and stuffy room, the defeat of the bill, and the news about Naomi conspired to drain her soul. From the faces around her, she could tell that some women shared her sentiment, but others seemed even more determined to fight.

"If they think we can be deterred so easily," Mrs. Gordon declared, "they are mistaken. We shall return for each vote."

The White women nodded in agreement.

Jordan's spirits sank lower. She was not a woman of independent means or married to a rich man like most of these women. Their congregation would not continue to invest in tickets to Sacramento for this lost cause. With Naomi moving out, Jordan and Malcolm's finances would become even tighter. She needed to be working steadily—even if it meant turning to domestic work. This had been her one opportunity to be there for the historic moment.

Jordan felt Mama's shell in her pocket. *Not today, Mama. We're still not free.* She looked out the window, not wanting to engage with the women around her. Her deepest hopes had been dashed once again.

***

The next morning, Naomi spoke to Jordan with unwelcome information. "Our plans are settled. Emily is coming today to accompany me to the courthouse. Afterward . . ." Naomi's voice broke.

Today? That word hit Jordan hard. She'd had her last night under the same roof with Naomi and didn't even know it.

Naomi looked as if she might cry. Why was she doing this? Jordan nodded, but then a knock intruded. She left Naomi to answer it.

Jordan forced a strained smile and gestured. "Emily, please come in. Have a seat."

Naomi entered the living room. "Good morning." She smiled at Emily, though Jordan felt tension in the air. "There is no need for you to sit," Naomi said. "I'll be back in a moment."

As soon as Naomi left the room, Emily glared at Jordan. Standing tall and proud, she spoke slowly. "You think my son isn't good enough for your daughter. You say you care about his safety, but I know you look down on him because he did not attend college."

"You are mistaken," Jordan replied. But her voice quavered. Perhaps there was truth to Emily's accusation.

Naomi returned to the room before more words could pass between them. Jordan's stomach lurched at the sight of the satchel in Naomi's hands. The magnitude of this transition hit her in full force. Naomi was moving out. Right now.

Ignoring Jordan, Naomi said to Emily, "I'm ready."

Jordan stepped forward. Naomi took a deep breath, her bosom rising and falling visibly. She furrowed her mouth and her eyes narrowed.

"Mother, you are not invited," Naomi said, her voice so high that Jordan knew she was holding back tears. "Only those who *celebrate* my marriage will be there when Willie and I pledge ourselves to one another."

Those words a devastating blow to her soul, Jordan collapsed onto the couch. Hot tears of anger and frustration filled her eyes. She searched for words, but the two women were out the door before she found any. How had her life come to this?

She was alone in her home: her husband and mother dead, her son gone for work, and now Naomi had abandoned her. Jordan had entirely miscalculated Naomi's reaction to her disapproval.

Instead of Naomi seeking acceptance from her mother, Jordan was being shunned.

CHAPTER TWENTY-TWO

SADIE

Oakland
May 1895

Sadie did not want to further agitate Heinrich. He wasn't accustomed to living in such small quarters—especially with a child. While May was a good baby, she could not always be kept quiet. He had no means of escape and was on the edge of disapproval at all times. Many weeks of living in this single room had been difficult for all of them.

She did not have much to do during the day. She'd stopped working as soon as Heinrich had returned. He was mortified to learn that she had delivered produce to Hickmott, though grateful that no one seemed to be aware of their connection. After cooking and cleaning up after breakfast, she most often went to Sam's to be with Momma. Other days, like today, she went to the women's auxiliary meeting at the Unitarian Church.

She kept her tone light as she told her husband, "May and I will leave you to work in private."

"Very well," he said. Then he looked up. "Where are you going?"

"Church," she answered.

"Very well," he repeated. Then he questioned, "What church meets in the day?"

"I'm attending the women's auxiliary," she replied. She would have left the explanation at that, but he stared at her, encouraging her to continue with his expression.

"We are planning for Miss Susan B. Anthony and Reverend Anna Shaw's upcoming visit to organize for suffrage."

Her heart hammered, though she had no evidence that Heinrich opposed universal suffrage; they had never spoken about it.

Indifferent, he nodded and went back to his work. Heinrich was still a puzzle to Sadie. She could not predict what he would care deeply about.

★★★

Sadie scanned the meeting room at the Unitarian Church. She'd come to know quite a few of the women from these meetings and felt a genuine devotion to them and to this work. A lump rose in her throat at the thought of leaving this behind.

Jordan sat alone, a sad expression on her face. Her friend Miss Flood must be otherwise engaged. Sadie walked up to her, and Jordan reached for May, a greedy grin lighting up her face. Sadie smiled and passed her daughter to her former teacher. It was remarkable that this was the same woman Sadie had adored as a child. Time and circumstances were strange tricksters.

"I have to hold her before she gets to toddling all over the place," Jordan declared with a smile. "And you move away." Jordan pulled her lips down. It was going to be a sad transition for all of them.

Sadie nodded. "I was so worried about her for so long.

And now I miss that tiny baby, gone too fast. I wish I could go back in time to tell myself to enjoy her more and fret about her less."

Jordan smiled, a wistful look in her eyes. "I'd like to be reassuring that the concern stops, but I will not deceive you—a mama always worries about her babies. No matter how old they get, no matter where they are."

Sadie's breath caught, and she was filled with strong emotion. "I didn't realize how much my mother loved me until May was born."

"God is amazing, isn't he? He made mothers love so much it hurts," Jordan said. "But we will do anything to protect our children."

"Do fathers ever love that much?" Sadie asked without thought.

Jordan gave her a sad smile. She sighed and said, "In my experience, most, but not all."

Sadie nodded, feeling foolish for bringing up such a personal topic.

"Is Heinrich slow to warm up to May?" Jordan asked.

Tears burned Sadie's eyes.

"For some men it comes eventually," Jordan stated. "For others . . ." She paused. "For a few it never comes. I guess for some mothers too if we are being honest."

Jordan looked sad, like she was holding back emotion. She patted Sadie's hand.

"I'm sorry this is a hard time in your marriage," Jordan empathized. "It is normal in the course of a large change for the bond between a husband and wife to be strained."

Her kindness felt like a knife slicing Sadie open. Sadie's hand flew to her own heart, pressing the sorrow inside. This was not the place or time to express the painful disappointment of her marriage and her fears about moving to a new country.

Reverend Tupper Wilkes and Mrs. Harrison, the organizers of the meeting, stood up and faced the group of women.

Mrs. Harrison said, "Reverend Shaw and Miss Anthony have eagerly accepted our invitation!"

A few cries of *wonderful* and *hooray* met the announcement. Sadie joined in the enthusiastic clapping.

"They believe Oakland is the perfect location for the organizing meeting. The National American Woman Suffrage Association has pledged to fund Reverend Shaw for full-time organizing until November, when the proposition will be on the ballot.

"Reverend Shaw will be traveling up and down the coast of our state, so inform your friends and family to greet her with zeal. We need everyone's support in order to secure its passage."

The meeting continued. Sadie would have joined one of the teams but did not volunteer, since she would be in Honolulu by November. She offered to bring cookies to the organizing event at the Unitarian Church, but she wasn't certain she would even be able to fulfill that commitment in less than a month.

Her life in Oakland, near her family and friends, was coming to an end.

"I hope you will invite Lisbeth to the gathering," Jordan said. "We need as much support as possible."

Sadie nodded, though she wasn't confident her mother would agree. So far she had declined any invitation to these meetings. But the prospect of seeing Miss Susan B. Anthony speak might draw her into politics.

"Tell her it is important to me," Jordan said. "Perhaps that will persuade her."

Sadie laughed. "She does like to please you."

"Apparently she carried me around for much of the day when I was this size." Jordan patted May's back. "My mama told me that we used to 'love on each other,' in that voice of hers. I guess that feeling is still there."

"I hope you do not find this statement insulting," Sadie said. "I know you and Momma lived on a plantation together. I know you were born a slave. But I still cannot believe it in my soul."

Jordan shrugged and then nodded. "You lived in Oberlin and now here. You've lived a sheltered life when it comes to the ugliness of racial hatred."

Sadness fluttered across Jordan's face. Sadie's heart clenched in empathy.

"I envy you your innocence," Jordan said. "Your freedom from the worst of human cruelty."

Sadie nodded, aware that she had experienced her own form of ugliness, but it did not compare to the suffering of enslavement, so it felt indulgent to even consider bringing it up.

Sadie replied, "I'm just grateful those times are behind us."

Jordan nodded, but a flicker of doubt showed on her face.

"You do feel fully welcome here, do you not?" Sadie questioned, trying to keep the challenge out of her voice.

Jordan smiled. "Yes. Everyone has been entirely gracious to me and Miss Flood. I have the sincerest hope that the prejudices I've faced are all behind me."

Sadie was grateful to be reassured that the women's auxiliary, and perhaps all of Oakland, were forward-thinking.

★★★

Over supper that evening Heinrich stated, "Earlier, I did not understand what you meant when you said you were going to this meeting at this church. But later I realized you were speaking of women voting? Correct?"

Sadie nodded.

"No." Heinrich shook his head. "You do not need to vote."

Sadie's heart sank. She responded, "But we believe we can create better social good. End child labor . . ."

Before she could finish her sentence, his hand flew across her face. Sadie's head jerked to the side. Her eyes stung and her cheek burned.

"Women do not vote," Heinrich declared. "Do you understand me?"

She nodded, not wanting to provoke him further.

"The women do this so they can control the men," he yelled. "Not let us have our beer houses. Say no to liquor. Is this what you want?!"

She put a hand to her cheek and shook her head. The shame of being talked to like a child hurt as much as the physical blow.

"There is no reason for you to vote," he repeated. "You may not go to one of those meetings again; do you agree to this?"

She nodded, scooped up May, and walked out. Thankfully he neither called to her nor followed them. She walked it off on the street, breathing deeply. The physical pain of the slap was already gone, but the shame lingered.

When they were first married, he had slapped her often to get her to stop speaking. Her outrage did not dissuade him from the behavior. He argued it was a normal way for a German husband to silence his wife. And he was a German husband.

Soon she'd learned how to make requests so as not to

provoke him, to stop speaking as soon as she saw a particular look in his eyes. It had been many years since Heinrich had touched her like that.

In the months while he was gone, she'd become too frank. She had forgotten when to keep things private from him and how to manage his strong feelings. These too-close quarters were trying for all of their nerves. She would have to readjust if they were to have a peaceful future.

★★★

Sadie woke to her breast throbbing in pain. She touched one; it was rock hard. May must have slept through her usual feeding. Leaning over the edge of the bed, Sadie looked at the little girl lying in her bassinet.

Before Heinrich had come home, May had slept tucked between Sadie and Lisbeth. But he did not care to have the baby in his bed, and Sadie feared Heinrich would harm May by rolling over onto her in the night, so the still-petite baby slept in a bassinet on the floor right by her.

Sadie put her hand on the girl's head. May was cold to the touch. Sadie's heart beat hard in her chest. She picked up the girl and tried to rouse her. May was not responsive. Sadie's breathing grew shallow. She laid the girl on the bed and unwrapped the swaddle with shaking hands. Sadie brought the baby to her chest and tickled her cheek like when she was a newborn. She leaned over and whispered fiercely, "Wake up, little one. You need to eat."

May's eyes blinked open and then closed. Relief surged through Sadie. Pink lips opened wide. May leaned forward and latched on. In a moment Sadie felt the tug and release of milk; her breath released with it. May was fine, just a bit cold and sleepy. Moisture streamed out of Sadie's other breast. A dark spot grew on her gown.

Heinrich's voice intruded. "That is unattractive."

"She slept through her feeding. We are thrown off."

"Can't you do something about it?" Heinrich questioned.

"Please get me a rag," she asked, still mad at him for his treatment earlier in the day.

Heinrich sighed, threw the covers off, and got out of bed. He returned with a cloth.

She wiped her gown and pressed the cloth against her breast. When that did not stop the stream, she inserted her pinky into May's mouth to remove her from the left breast. She repositioned her to get milk from the right side.

Heinrich leaned his head on her arm. He watched May suckle and rubbed her sweet, soft head with his finger.

"She's so soft," he said. He picked up the girl's small hand. "And so tiny."

Sadie nodded, though Heinrich could not see her. Perhaps he felt her movement. She breathed in his scent. She felt her anger soften. It was sweet to have him be a part of this.

"She is still very young—only a few months past her due date," Sadie ventured.

He nodded; perhaps he was open to a conversation.

She explained, "I worry how she might do on a long sea voyage."

He sat up. "Truly?"

"Yes. Can we perhaps consider if moving is best for all of us right now? May is still weak. She might grow ill on such a long journey. Perhaps in the fall when she is more than a year?"

Heinrich glared. She'd gone too far in her request.

She soothed, "Of course we will do whatever you believe is best. You have a great opportunity in Hawaii."

He got up from the bed without responding; he dressed

and left their cramped apartment to go out into the dark night.

Sadie felt sick. She had not handled that well. It was still too soon for him to understand May's needs. She wiped away a tear. Her daughter looked so fragile and vulnerable. She rubbed her soft cheek. Love welled up inside her. She would do anything to protect her May. Heinrich did not seem to feel the same. She hoped that his fatherly love would grow, even if slowly.

★★★

A sound penetrated her sleep. She rolled over and took a deep breath, hoping to go right back to dreaming. The noise came again. It was Heinrich clearing his throat loudly. She did not want to fight, so she pretended to be asleep.

"Sadie," he demanded in a harsh whisper.

She opened her eyes. He wasn't in the bed. She sat up and looked around the room. Her heart flew into her throat, stopping up her breath.

Heinrich stood at the wide-open window, his arms reaching into the cold night with May dangling between his hands. A wave of terror crashed over Sadie. Her arms shook, and she forced down the impulse to scream. Her chest nearly burst.

"I am the head of this household!" Heinrich growled slowly in a deep voice.

Sadie nodded frantically.

"Do you understand me?" He glared.

Sadie swallowed bile and nodded again.

"I decide where we go and when we go there," he declared.

Sadie tried to speak, but nothing came out, her eyes glued to the precious bundle in his hands. A tear slipped from her eye.

Pausing between each word for emphasis, he spit out, "Do . . . you . . . under . . . stand . . . me?"

She clenched her hands willing herself not to lunge for May.

"Y . . . yes," she stammered out. She pleaded, "I'm sorry, Heinrich. I was wrong. You know best, of course."

She looked at him demurely, hiding the hatred that filled her chest. If it would keep May safe, she could have killed him in this moment.

He glowered at her. She averted her eyes.

"Anything you want, Heinrich. I promise. Anything," she whimpered. She glanced up at him through her eyelashes.

"All right, then," he agreed.

A horrid silence filled the room. She swallowed, desperate for him to bring May to safety. He did nothing.

"Please," she begged.

Eventually he nodded and slowly pulled her baby inside. Sadie exhaled and her shoulders dropped. May stirred. Sadie reached for her daughter. Heinrich shook his head. Sadie dropped her arms. He placed the awake baby in the bassinet.

Heinrich loomed over the bed and jerked the covers off of Sadie. He stood over her like a challenge. She knew what he was demanding. Despite her revulsion, she inched up her gown.

"I don't want to look at your disgusting face," he said. He pointed a finger at her and then twirled it in a circle. Sadie rolled onto her stomach. A cry started from the bassinet. Sadie buried her face in the mattress.

He mounted her from behind, pounding over and over as May's screams built ever louder. *He'll be finished soon. He'll be finished soon. He'll be finished soon.* Sadie silently chanted to herself and to May.

Her body jerked forward and back until he finally shook and collapsed heavily on top of her. Sadie resisted the impulse to flinch, though she was desperate to get away. She forced herself to lie still. Heinrich panted against her cheek; his breath hot and filled with alcohol. She feared she might suffocate. She worked to take in tiny amounts of air through compressed lungs.

He'll be gone soon. He'll be gone soon.

Heinrich pushed himself up from the bed, using her head to brace himself, forcing it into the hard mattress. She felt him standing over her. Too terrified to move or make eye contact, she acted as if she were dead.

Just leave. Just leave.

Heinrich snorted. She heard the sound of his pants being pulled up. Footsteps tapped across the floor, and the sound of the door opening and then closing told her he was gone. She exhaled but did not move. She forced herself to count to ten. Sadie sat up and reached for her distraught daughter.

As soon as May was in her arms, sobs overtook Sadie. Tears streamed down her face, and her shoulders jerked up and down. Rocking back and forth, she comforted both of them. Gratitude and fear pulsed through her veins in equal measure.

Thank you, God, for keeping her safe. May, I'm so sorry. I didn't know. I didn't know he'd do that to you. I will never let him treat you like that again.

Sadie knew with certainty that she had to protect May from the monster she had married. She would rise above her shame and fear to leave Heinrich.

CHAPTER TWENTY-THREE

JORDAN

Oakland
May 1895

One day turned into two. Before she knew it, a week had passed. That turned into weeks, and now it had been nearly a month since Jordan had seen Naomi. Each day that went by without contact confirmed that Naomi did not want her in her life.

Despair and sorrow waxed and waned. Malcolm insisted she was foolish to stay away from Naomi. When he was home, he went to visit his sister in her new home. He encouraged Jordan to join him, but the invitation had come from him, not Naomi. Jordan didn't want to face being rejected and humiliated—especially in front of Naomi's new family. *New family.* The thought hurt.

Mrs. King yelled from the kitchen door, "Come see."

Jordan smiled. Her neighbor, noticing that Naomi had moved out, had turned their neighborliness into a true friendship that included meals, gossip, and gardening. Most days they spent time with one another.

Jordan walked into their shared backyard. The vegetable plants were already knee high. In Chicago they would just be starts. Their bounty would sustain her through the summer and fall.

"Look." Mrs. King pointed.

Jordan was delighted to see bright-yellow flowers bursting from the ends of some tall green stalks.

"Tomatoes!" Mrs. King declared. "Last year I didn't water enough and we never got any. Without summer rain we have to do it ourselves."

Like Jordan, Mrs. King was a transplant. This was her second year in Oakland. This garden was getting the benefit of learning from Mrs. King's previous mistakes.

Jordan nodded.

"I hear three or four times a week will do it," Mrs. King said. "Can you take that on?"

"Gladly," Jordan said. And she meant it. She was grateful for any meaningful distraction.

"Hello!" a man's voice called out from the front.

A confused look passed between Jordan and Mrs. King. Neither one was expecting a visitor. They came around to the front, where Jordan was surprised to see Superintendent McClymonds.

"Good afternoon, Mrs. Wallace," he greeted her.

"Good afternoon," she replied, and then made introductions. "This is my neighbor and friend, Mrs. King."

He reached out a white hand. "How do you do. I hope I am not coming at a bothersome time," he said.

"Not at all," Jordan replied. "Please come in." She was burning with curiosity but would not be rude by asking why he had come.

"I appreciate the offer, but I cannot stay for long," he said. "May I come right to my business?"

Jordan's heart beat in hopeful anticipation. She nodded with a smile. "Certainly."

"We have an opening at Tompkins for next term. Everyone agreed you would be a great permanent addition to the school."

A shiver caused goose flesh to rise on Jordan's arms.

"Are you available?" he asked.

Her eyes sparkled as she replied, "I am, and it would be my pleasure."

"Wonderful. Thank you. Come by my office next week and we can sign the contract."

He reached out a hand and she took it. A warm and firm handshake clinched their agreement. She would be a teacher again.

"Congratulations, Mrs. Wallace," Mrs. King declared. Jordan smiled at her friend.

***

An unexpected knock startled Jordan. Alone in the night, as she was most of the time now, she hesitated to answer. Jordan took comfort knowing the Kings were upstairs should she need anything.

Jordan questioned through the door, "Who's there?"

"Willie." His deep voice was muffled by the wood.

Emotion surged in her. Jordan's nerves raced—in anger, perhaps fear. She hadn't heard from Naomi in the many weeks since their marriage. And she sent Willie? Or was Naomi hurt? Jordan pulled the front door open. Willie's colored eyes were glassy, confirming her concern that something *was* wrong with Naomi.

"Come in." She welcomed him by pointing to the couch, not wanting to pounce, though urgency pulsed in her mind.

He sat, his hat held between his hands, his head hanging down.

"Naomi lost the baby," he whispered in a hoarse voice.

He looked up, right at Jordan. Her heart twisted hard and painful. "I thought it only right you should know," he said. "She's your daughter. That's your grandbaby."

Jordan bit her lip. A tear slipped out the side of her eye.

"Naomi misses you so much," Willie continued. "She's a proud woman and won't come to you, but I know she wants her mama."

"Does she know you're here?" Jordan asked.

He shook his head. "If I asked, she might have said no. I don't want to go against her, so I left without telling her why."

"When did it . . . ?"

"Two days ago. It happened fast. Not much pain for her body, but it's hard on her spirits." He looked at Jordan again. "Like I said, she misses you."

Jordan imagined the scene; she pictured her daughter's distress at the cramping followed by a bright-red smear. Feelings swirled in Jordan; gratitude and sorrow made strange companions.

She said, "Thank you, Willie. For coming to tell me."

He nodded. Then he pleaded, "Could you just come by? With hock soup?"

Naomi doesn't want me. The thought pierced through Jordan. Confusion pressed on her.

Willie continued, "Don't tell her I was here. Act like you are ready to"—he stared at her, longing in his eyes—"accept me."

"Oh, Willie." Jordan's stomach lurched. "You are a good man. My objections have nothing to do with you. I hope you know that."

He shrugged.

"Truly!" she declared. "If you had decided to live only as a Colored man, I would not have expressed any concerns.

However, I know—I know in my bones—this deception is not safe for you."

"I can take care of myself . . . and Naomi," he said.

"You believe that. I don't. The world is more cruel than you imagine," Jordan replied. Page's face popped into her mind. Then she sighed. "But what is done is done. You are married now. You and Naomi will make your way as best as you can. So yes . . . I will make her hock soup and bring it over tomorrow as a peace offering."

"Thank you," he said, a sweet smile on his face. He was a handsome man, even though he was so light.

Through her jumbled emotions, she smiled at him. "Thank you for coming to me."

He stood to leave. She rose with him. At the door he put his pale hand out. She looked at it. She opened her arms, inviting him in closer. He stared at her, perhaps confused, maybe refusing her peace offering. She lowered her arms to put her hand out. A small smile pulled up his lips. He nodded and then met her embrace.

★★★

Jordan's heart pounded as she knocked on the shiny door. Naomi's new home was in one of the modern developments along the Colored section of Seventh Street—west of the railroad station, as the Pullman Company required.

Emily answered the door to reveal a tidy living room with an archway that led to a separate dining room.

"I'm so glad you came," Emily said with a surprisingly warm smile. Perhaps she had forgiven Jordan's insult to Willie. "Naomi's spirits are low."

Jordan teared up. "Thank you for taking care of her." Her voice broke. She took a breath and whispered, "I brought hock soup as Willie suggested."

Emily patted Jordan's hand and gestured with her head. Jordan followed her past whitewashed walls in the dining room to the kitchen.

Emily ladled the still-warm soup into a metal bowl, filled a glass with water, and handed them both to Jordan. They went to the door off of the dining room.

Emily knocked and then called through the wood, "You have a visitor." Without waiting for a reply, she opened it and waved Jordan in. The door closed behind her. Emily had left them alone.

The room was dark and stuffy. Naomi was lying in bed, her eyes puffy and barely open. Jordan stood uncertain and hopeful.

Naomi's brow furrowed. Was she angry to see Jordan? Then her eyes opened wide and her lip began to quiver.

"Oh, Mama . . ." Naomi cried.

There was true longing in Naomi's eyes. Relief rushed through Jordan's bones. She set the food on the stand, sat on the edge of the mattress, and opened her arms. Naomi sat up and sank into Jordan.

Jordan rocked Naomi as her daughter sobbed.

"I'm sorry you lost your baby," Jordan whispered into her daughter's hair.

She felt Naomi take in a sputtering breath, and her head nodded against Jordan's chest.

"There'll be others, I'm certain of it, but you'll always miss this angel," Jordan said.

Naomi pulled away, looked right at Jordan, and said, "I missed you, Mama."

"Me too, baby," Jordan replied. If there was more to say, she didn't find the words. She just said, "I missed you."

CHAPTER TWENTY-FOUR

SADIE

Oakland
May 1895

"Momma, I need your help." Sadie teared up as soon as she saw her mother. They sat in Sam's living room together two days after *the incident*. She'd acted as if nothing had changed between her and Heinrich the following morning, but her heart was set on an entirely different course.

Momma leaned in and nodded. "Sadie? What is it?"

"I can't go with him to Hawaii," Sadie stated. She took a breath and said, "He threatened to kill May!"

Momma's face lost its color. "Heinrich?"

Sadie nodded.

Fury hardened her momma's eyes. "Did he harm you?"

Sadie's lip quivered. She gave a slow, shallow nod as shame filled her up and seeped out of every pore. She couldn't look at her mother as she explained, "Nothing I could not bear. But I will kill him before I let him harm May."

Sadie waited for her mother's response. When none came, she looked up.

Momma's eyes were closed tight. Eventually she took a deep breath. When she opened them, they were hard and glistening, somehow angry and sad at the same time.

"You are not surprised?" Sadie asked.

"I suspected," Momma replied, "but you hid it well."

Sadie's cheeks flushed. Tears spilled out as she whispered, "I'm so ashamed."

"You have nothing to be contrite about," Momma protested. "He is a self-centered and unkind man."

"How could I have misunderstood his true nature?" Sadie asked.

"He was charming," Momma reminded her. "Very solicitous when you met him. He proved his devotion and respect with a fast proposal and wedding. He fooled me as well. But I fear as soon as you were married, his attitude changed."

Sadie nodded. She thought of the contemptuous words, the criticism of her housekeeping, and the slaps. But the worst was the silence that might go on for days when she expressed her mind. Each cruelty, large and small, was followed by apologies, kind gestures, and a justification. Sometimes he faulted her for being too demanding or incompetent. Other times he blamed the stresses of his work.

Whatever the reason, she was no longer willing to live with his erratic behavior. For herself or for May.

Momma said, "How could you have known his soul before he revealed it to you?"

Sadie nodded, but still felt she was at fault for being in these circumstances.

"I had learned to work around his temper, but I do not want to anymore. I cannot risk moving far away to another country with him," Sadie explained.

"What will you do?" Momma asked, fear in her voice.

"I will pretend I am leaving for Hawaii, but we won't get on the ship. Instead I'll hide where he can't find us."

"Won't he come for you?" Momma asked.

Her mother disagreed with her decision. Despair crashed upon Sadie.

"You believe I should go with him?" she questioned.

"No!" Momma declared. "I'm sorry to confuse and overwhelm you with questions. You are right to hide."

"Here?" Sadie asked, doubt filling her voice. She shook her head. "This is the first place he will come for me."

"Perhaps Diana's mother will conceal you?" Momma suggested.

Sadie sighed. "He knows where they live. I wish there were a home where he has never been."

The two women looked at one another—perhaps Momma had the same idea. Was it too much to ask?

"Jordan will protect you, Sadie," Momma declared. "And he would never think to find you there."

***

Heinrich commanded, "Use this to have light dresses made. You will need them in Honolulu."

Bills were folded neatly in his outstretched hand. She smiled at him, her heart softened by this thoughtfulness. They hadn't spoken about what had happened that horrible night, but he had been extremely affectionate in the days since, buying sweets for her and toys for May.

"Thank you, Heinrich—that is very kind," she said.

"And for the baby," he added. "She too will need clothes for the warm temperatures."

Sadie nodded, her stomach in her throat as she thought about her deception. She was packing as if she would be going with him, all the while plotting her escape. Was it right to raise May without her father? Had she truly done what she could to ensure the success of their marriage? Her eyes welled up.

"What are you upset about now?" Heinrich challenged.

She blinked. Her mind searched for an excuse for her feelings that would not betray her intentions and imperil their safety.

"I am silly, Heinrich," she soothed. "I will miss my mother and family in Oakland. That is all."

"You know I do not like your tears," he scolded.

Anger surged through Sadie, banishing any sorrow she felt at the loss of her marriage.

"I understand," she said in a flat, stone voice.

"That is better," he said with a smile. "Good girl."

Sadie turned back to her packing. She said goodbye to each item as she put it in a trunk. They would be loaded onto the ship, but when it sailed, she and May would be hiding. She counted on the expense of the tickets, and the pressure from work, to outweigh Heinrich's desire to control her.

She prayed that he would sail without her, but wasn't confident that God would grant her most fervent wish—that Heinrich would leave them forever.

CHAPTER TWENTY-FIVE

JORDAN

Oakland
June 1895

"Mama, listen to this!" Naomi exclaimed. She held the *Oakland Tribune* in her hand.

Jordan looked at her daughter, gratitude still flooding through her. They hadn't spoken about the breach in their relationship but seemed to have come to a sweet understanding since the day Jordan had brought hock soup over. Even Emily had moved on, accepting her as part of their extended family. Jordan was welcomed for Sunday supper at the Smiths'. Naomi came for supper at her home most Wednesdays. Willie too, when he was in town.

Jordan's home was not the center of their family. She was adjusting to her new place in Naomi's life. She'd learned a dear lesson from their conflict and was not going to risk another. While she still believed the marriage was unwise due to societal prejudices, she also saw that Willie was a good husband for her Naomi. From now on she would express only support for Willie and Naomi's choices. Unless asked, she would keep her opinions to herself.

Jordan was not entirely satisfied with living alone most

of the time, but she was making her way. The Unitarian women's auxiliary, the AME women's club, Mrs. King's companionship, and the garden kept her occupied. Malcolm returned for a night every few weeks. Soon she would have the meaning and purpose that came from teaching.

Naomi read out loud:

THE MISSION OF A NEGRESS

Ida B. Wells, Whose Life Has Been Devoted to Getting her Race a Square Show.

TEACHER, JOURNALIST AND LECTURER

She Supported Five Young Brothers and Sisters When She Was Fourteen—

Warned Not to Return to Memphis.

Miss Ida B. Wells, the young colored teacher, journalist and lecturer of Chicago, is on a visit to California and at present is in Santa Cruz. Miss Wells is a clever young woman who, while many of her sex are crying for the ballot and equal rights with men, is devoting her time to the interests of her race. Her crusade is in special against lynch law.

Miss Wells, finding that the northern people ignore the negro question altogether, accepted an invitation to lay her cause before the English public. While in England she created a furor, and newspapers on both sides of the ocean [are] printing columns about her. Her mission received the support of clergy, nobility and commoners.

Naomi kept reading the detailed and stirring tribute that told of Miss Wells's history as a teacher, a newspaperwoman, and an activist on behalf of their race. Jordan was particularly struck by the truth of this sentiment in Miss Wells's own words:

"There is throughout the whole United States this caste prejudice which is unknown in any other part of the civilized world. It differs only in degree North, East, South or West. If they do not lynch the negro in some of the States, they refuse him accommodations equal to those of other travelers; try to freeze them out at the public schools; give him no adequate political representation; and refuse to employ him in any other than the most menial capacities. It is almost as great a cruelty to educate youths in the public and industrial schools of this country and then shut the doors of the factories, mercantile establishments and trade unions in their faces because they are black, as it is to deny them trial by jury and lynch them. In one case you kill the body, and in the other you murder all the higher aspirations which distinguish man from brute creatures.

"America has much to learn

before she can be the justice-loving, Christian progressive nation that she deludes herself into thinking she now is."

Naomi stopped reading and looked up at Jordan. "Your friend is famous!"

"I'm not surprised. She is as devoted as she is inspiring," Jordan said. "We must invite her to call on us when she is in Oakland."

A mischievous smile came to Naomi's face.

"What are you plotting?" Jordan asked her daughter.

"If she says yes, let's invite Miss Flood and surprise her with Miss Wells's presence," Naomi said with delight shining in her eyes.

Jordan agreed wholeheartedly. She grew excited at the possibility of introducing those two fine women. She felt she could not thank Miss Flood enough for her persistent encouragement that had returned Jordan to teaching *and* revived her passion to work for her own franchise.

Surely Miss Flood would be moved by meeting Miss Wells, an inspiration for all of them whether they were fighting for suffrage or Colored rights.

★★★

A few days later, Miss Flood, Naomi, and Jordan were sitting on the couches in Jordan's house. Miss Wells would arrive at any moment, though Miss Flood was entirely unaware that they were waiting for an esteemed guest.

A knock at the door startled Jordan so greatly that she did not have to feign surprise. She opened the door and welcomed dear Miss Wells with a long hug. The woman had matured in the few years since they had organized the Columbian Exposition, but she had the same sparkle in her eye.

Jordan stepped back and turned so she could see Miss Flood's expression when she became aware of Miss Wells's presence. The young woman's reaction did not disappoint— her mouth was nearly on the rug with astonishment.

"Miss Wells, do you remember Naomi? And this is our dear friend Miss Lydia Flood."

"It is an honor to meet you!" Miss Flood said. "And quite the surprise!"

Naomi clapped, her face shining in excitement.

Jordan ushered Miss Wells to a seat and poured her tea. They shared pleasantries and caught up on their lives. Their conversation turned to the news of the day.

"I have been reading your verbal war with Miss Willard with great amusement," Jordan said.

Miss Wells had publicly chastised Miss Willard, the president of the Woman's Christian Temperance Union, for her lack of support for the anti-lynching campaign. Rather than support equality among the races, Miss Willard had abandoned Colored people to gain favor with Southern Whites.

Miss Wells laughed. "She is outraged that I am speaking the truth. But she has been indifferent to the suffering of our people. That is all I said. Now that she is being condemned for her attitude, she claims that it is not true, as if she had been a friend to our people like the dear Miss Susan B. Anthony. She is no Miss Anthony, I assure you."

"Have you met Miss Anthony?" Naomi asked.

"Met her?" Miss Wells exclaimed. "She and I are good friends. And she is a dedicated advocate for our people. Would you like to hear a story that exemplifies her attitude toward our race?"

They all nodded. Jordan reveled in Miss Wells's presence.

"Just last August, we stayed together in Chicago. She not only showed no animosity toward me, she proved she would take a stand on my behalf."

Miss Wells continued into a story she obviously enjoyed telling.

"One morning Miss Anthony was unable to use the stenographer she had hired because she had engagements, so she directed the woman to record my letters. The girl refused, saying, 'It is quite all right for you, Miss Anthony, to treat Negroes as equals, but I refuse to take dictation from a Colored woman.'

"'Indeed!' said Miss Anthony. 'Then you needn't take any more dictation from me. If this is the way you feel about it, you needn't stay any longer.' The woman stared at Miss Anthony, quite confused as to her meaning. Miss Anthony made herself clear, instructing, 'Come, get your bonnet and go!'"

"That is a true friend," Miss Flood agreed.

Jordan delighted in the story and the storyteller.

Miss Wells continued, "There is a reason the great Frederick Douglass held her in such high esteem."

A respectful quiet filled the air.

Jordan sighed. "I miss knowing he is in the world."

"Yes," Miss Flood agreed. "Though I never had the pleasure of meeting him as you did, I feel I owe him a debt of gratitude that I cannot now pay."

"We honor him by continuing the work of liberation," Miss Wells said. "If he had not taken me under his tutelage at the Columbian Exposition, my campaign against lynching would not have its current publicity."

"Did you read about the White man who was flayed and lynched in New Orleans this week?" Naomi asked.

Bile rose in Jordan's throat. She forced away a horrid

image of the poor man. It was so painful to contemplate; the cruelty unfathomable. She could not let herself think of his mother and the other people who loved him.

"That was no White man," Miss Wells retorted. "The Southern papers report it as so only so they can pretend that this disgraceful act is not used to repress our race. But I'm certain if you saw him, you would recognize him as a light-skinned Colored man."

Jordan looked at Naomi. Her daughter had blanched and looked like she might faint. Jordan swallowed hard. *This* was the pain she wanted to protect her daughter from.

But Naomi had made her decision. She was married, her life joined with Willie's. They would make their way just as she and Booker had made theirs.

In truth, there was no path in which Naomi would have a pain-free life, as much as Jordan wanted that for her children. Jordan thought back to Mama's words: "Our Lord is jus' like a mama. He wanting what's best for His children but not always able to make it so."

In these past weeks, Jordan realized how strong Mama had been to hold her tongue when Jordan had stayed in Virginia in 1868. The risk had been high, but she had been set on living there. Mama could not have dissuaded her, even if she had tried.

Was the risk to Willie passing truly any higher than what Booker had faced as a Colored man? Or what Malcolm still faced? Jordan had acted as if there were a safe path, had argued for it as if it were real, but there was no guarantee of security for any of them. She took Naomi's hand and squeezed. Neither of them knew what lay ahead. There would be pain—and joy. Whatever came, Jordan was grateful she and Naomi would face it together.

"We are very excited that Miss Anthony and Miss Shaw

are coming to Oakland," Miss Flood said.

"I am sorry our paths will not cross here," Miss Wells replied. "If you like, I will write a letter of introduction. They will be delighted to know the women's club at the Fifteenth Street AME Church is ready to fight for the cause of women's suffrage."

Jordan nodded and Miss Flood clapped her hands.

"That would be most welcome." Wonder in her voice, Jordan said, "To think that I will meet a woman who met the great Sojourner Truth."

A chill traveled down her spine as she imagined it. Jordan filled with gratitude at God's grace. Only weeks ago she had felt alone in the world, facing two painful setbacks—one personal and one political. It seemed her life was devastated, but she had not succumbed to despair. Now she was in this room with her beloved daughter and other strong women, fighting for a better tomorrow for all of them.

She sent a silent message to her mother: *I found my faith again, Mama, and lovely people to join with.*

★★★

Jordan heard the door in the living room open. She was not expecting anyone.

"Mama?" Naomi's voice called.

"In here," Jordan replied from the kitchen. Surprised but pleased, she dried her hands and reached for the kettle. She stopped short when her daughter came in. Naomi looked terrified. Jordan's heart rose into her throat.

"Is Malcolm home?" Naomi asked.

"Yes," Jordan replied. "He's washing up."

"Willie didn't come back," Naomi said, her eyes round in fear.

"Are you certain?" Jordan asked, hiding her rising

concern.

"He's not home," Naomi replied. "He's not at the station."

"Malcolm!" Jordan called to her son through the bathroom door.

"What, Mama?" he answered.

"Was Willie on your train?"

"Yes," he said, "as usual."

"Naomi says he never made it home."

The door opened. Wiping his wet face with a towel, he looked at Naomi, then at Jordan, a question in his eyes.

"When was the last time you saw him?" Naomi asked.

"Reno," Malcolm replied. "He and I shared a laugh about a rider getting off with too many bags."

"Did you see him on the train after Reno?"

Malcolm thought and then shook his head. "I don't have any recall of him after that stop." He offered, "Let me go to the station . . . see if Cedric knows anything."

Naomi nodded. "Thank you."

"Do you want to stay here or go home?" Jordan asked.

"I don't know," Naomi said, on the verge of tears.

"Are Emily and William there?" Jordan asked.

Naomi nodded.

"Let's sit with them. It will be nice for all of us to have company," Jordan decided. "Malcolm, go there when you've learned what there is to know."

They stepped into the foggy June night. Walking arm in arm, Naomi said, "I can't do this, Mama. I'm so scared. What if he . . ."

Jordan patted her daughter's arm. "Take deep breaths, keep yourself calm, and do *not* borrow trouble."

Despite her words, Jordan's heart beat fast and her palms were sweaty. Naomi's fear was contagious.

"When we get to your home, we'll pray with Emily and

William. It will be a comfort to all of us," Jordan said. "He probably got caught up in work. There is no need to think of the worst possible thing; it will only cause you unnecessary suffering."

It was easy to say, but harder to do. Jordan's body and mind were racing with fear. She took deep breaths to keep herself as calm as possible. When they got to the house, Emily and William looked as alarmed as Naomi. Jordan and Emily exchanged a tight smile. Jordan was doing her best to act calm in the face of their concern.

They sat at the table in the back of their large kitchen, drinking lemonade, playing dominoes, and pretending that there wasn't a furious buzz coursing through them.

Jordan heard the door open and close. Was it Malcolm?

Willie poked his head into the kitchen.

"Hello, family!"

Relief surged through Jordan.

Willie beamed at them, read the emotion in the room, and then his face fell into concern.

"What's wrong?" he asked. "Are you . . . ?"

Naomi flew to him.

Willie held her at arm's length, fear on his face, and asked, "What happened?"

"I thought you were dead!" Naomi said. "We all did."

"What? Why?" he asked, fear transformed into confusion as he looked from person to person in the room. Jordan shrugged.

"You were not on your train . . . ," Naomi said with tears streaming down her face.

"I'm sorry, Naomi. Sorry to trouble you, Mama." Willie explained, "In Sacramento I was called into the office. I missed my train. The next one was delayed . . ." He shrugged. "I never imagined you'd be so affected, so frightened."

William said, "I'm glad you are all right, son. I've been in your situation many times. Right, Emily? They call you in, you got to go." He shrugged.

Naomi looked at Emily and then Jordan.

"You've experienced this?" Naomi asked. "More than once?"

They both nodded.

"I told you not to borrow trouble," Jordan reminded her.

Emily said, "I'd like to tell you that the fear goes away, but it doesn't."

"Over time, you get better at living with it, not letting it disrupt your life entirely." Jordan explained, "You set your fear right next to your hope until you know which one is the truth."

"You felt like this?" Naomi asked, looking at Jordan. "Every time Pops was *late*?"

Jordan nodded.

"Every time he was *away*?"

"Not every time, but many." Jordan shook her head. "I can't tell you why sometimes I was terrified and others only afraid—for your pops and now for Malcolm."

Jordan looked at Willie and William. Two men who made a living venturing far away toward imagined, and real, risk. She'd been foolish to believe she could protect her daughter from pain. Naomi would know moments of fear for her husband whether he was passing for White or living as Colored.

Jordan stayed until Malcolm arrived. The tension on his face melted away when he saw Willie. He joked as he hugged his brother-in-law, but it covered a painful truth.

Jordan rose. "Let's leave you be."

She hugged each of them in turn, holding on a little longer than normal. All of their hearts had been pained tonight. Jordan and Malcolm walked back home through the foggy night, her arm looped through her son's. They didn't speak of the fears that brought them out.

She focused on being grateful that Willie was home safe and sound, rather than on her anger that they were forced to live with the burden of this feeling. Thankfully only a case of the nerves had caused her daughter to seek her out for comfort. She felt the blessing that Naomi had turned to her, a blessing she would never take for granted.

And she prayed that the terrors they imagined would never come to be.

CHAPTER TWENTY-SIX

SADIE

Oakland
July 1895

"I'm taking these to Momma. She will be glad to have these sentimental items I don't want anymore," Sadie lied to Heinrich.

The bag held her most treasured mementos: a family photo that included Poppa, the christening gown that had been in the family for two generations, the locket from Aunt Julianne. Most of her possessions were being packed in trunks that would be loaded onto the boat. She didn't want these precious items to sail across the ocean, never to be seen again.

She walked to Sam and Diana's with May on her back, her mind buzzing. She had less than a week to get everything in order. She hoped she would not feel this strongly until then, but she feared she would. Her nerves had begun to impinge upon her sleep. She would wake in the night with a pounding fear she had forgotten an important detail.

Her stomach lurched as she handed the belongings to Momma. Her mind was muddled by questions.

"Momma, you truly believe I am making the right choice?" Sadie asked.

Momma looked at her, her eyes shiny.

"I fear he will not get on the boat without me," Sadie said. "We cannot hide at Jordan's forever."

Momma's face grew hard. "In truth he has no power over you, as much as you feel he does. He cannot compel you to move to Hawaii, though he wishes it were otherwise."

Sadie replied, "You are correct. Nevertheless, I believe it would be wise to move south for a time if he doesn't leave or he returns. He has business interests to the north, west, and east, but nothing below Monterey. Perhaps Los Angeles. We can be anonymous there."

Momma pulled her lips inward. She looked like she was trying to stifle tears. Then she nodded.

"I hope it doesn't come to that. I just feel it is best to have a long-term plan in case I need it. I would miss living in Oakland—terribly."

Momma shook her head. "*We* would miss living here."

We. That word rang out in Sadie's heart.

"You would come with us?"

Momma replied, "Of course."

Sadie cleared her throat. "Thank you, Momma."

Momma hugged Sadie and said, "Go. The meeting has already started."

Sadie rushed away, her spirit buoyed knowing that Momma would be with her whatever came to pass.

★★★

The room at the Unitarian Church was so crowded that every chair was filled. Miss Anthony's visit had greatly increased interest in their activities. Sadie slipped to the right and stood in the back. She looked around; Jordan was there, in the middle, her back to Sadie. Sadie nodded to herself. She would have to wait for the meeting to end.

Sadie alternated between listening to the speakers and discussion and thinking about her own life. They had tickets to sail in five days. Heinrich was so focused on his own needs that he did not seem to have any understanding of her plans. Momma's words were a comfort, but Sadie still had many unanswered questions. The most pressing was how they would get food and shelter—especially if they needed to move away from Oakland. Even here she hadn't found work that earned a decent wage. She didn't want to survive off the charity of others indefinitely. If they moved to Los Angeles, it would be even more of a challenge.

Sadie felt May stirring in her wrap. She was waking up and would be hungry. The girl cried out. Sadie left the room and found a chair in the entryway. She untied May and brought her to her breast.

What kind of life can I give you? Sadie wondered as she stroked the soft brown hair on her daughter's head. She felt the burden of responsibility for this precious life.

You kept her safe and healthy before, she reminded herself. *You can do it again.* Sadie swallowed. No matter how much she questioned the wisdom of marrying Heinrich, she could never regret that her daughter had been born.

The meeting ended, and Jordan found her and May.

"Can I hold her before you move on with your day?" Jordan asked. "This might be my last chance before you sail." Jordan turned down her mouth in sorrow.

Sadie nodded, holding back her emotion.

Jordan patted her arm and took the baby. "She is a dear," Jordan cooed.

Sadie took in a deep breath and steeled herself. "I have a large favor to ask you," she said.

"Certainly," Jordan said.

"I cannot go with Heinrich," Sadie declared, sounding

stronger than she felt. "He has shown me cruelty that I cannot abide for May."

Jordan's eyebrows drew together. "Oh," she said. "I'm so sorry."

Shame flooded in. Sadie took a breath and said, "He may not let me go easily, so I wish to hide when he sails away."

Jordan nodded.

"He knows everyone I trust . . . except for you," Sadie said. "Will you . . ." Her voice broke. "Can May and I take shelter in your home on Friday, the day we are supposed to sail? I would not ask if I had an alternative, but I cannot think of one."

Sadie studied Jordan's face for a reaction. She looked confused. Uncertain. It was an enormous request.

Jordan gave a single decisive nod. "Yes. Of course. I will do whatever I can to ensure you and May are safe."

A chill ran down Sadie's spine. "Thank you. For me, but most especially for her."

Sadie smiled at Jordan. Tears glistened in both of their eyes.

★★★

"Tomorrow morning I walk you and May onto the boat at nine a.m. It will take an hour or more to journey to the dock. Be ready to leave at seven thirty," Heinrich declared.

"You mean Friday?" Sadie replied.

He stared at her. *Is that a challenge in his eyes?* "Tomorrow." He drew out the word and nodded slowly.

"You told me the fifth," she replied.

He shook his head and tsked. "I told you many times— the first. We are leaving the first. I don't know why you cannot remember."

The hair on her scalp rose. Heinrich knew what she

thought she'd been hiding. He'd been lying to her just as she had been deceiving him.

"We haven't said our goodbyes to my family," Sadie said, her voice shaking.

He stared through slits. Taunting, he replied, "If you are ready by seven, we may have time to go there before we get on the boat."

She swallowed. "Thank you, Heinrich," she forced out. "I'm sorry I confused the dates. I'm grateful we can go first thing in the morning to say our goodbyes."

He continued staring at her, intentionally making her uncomfortable.

Sadie soothed, "I know you do not understand my attachment to my family. I will be sad for a few days, but then I promise I will be a cheerful wife."

His lip raised—in a smirk or a smile she could not tell. She hoped he believed he had triumphed. Though anger burned inside, she'd continue the ruse and act defeated, but in the middle of the night, she and May would sneak to Jordan's.

***

She put the last of her belongings in her trunk, bidding farewell to each item as it went in. Porters were coming this evening to transfer their things to the ship. Soon they would be left in the apartment as she first saw it with only a bed and a couch.

Sadie fed May in the family rocking chair for the last time. *Sorry, Momma. I'm losing your beloved rocker.* She rubbed the wood, thinking of the hands that had touched it. Emmanuel and Samuel had chopped down the oak tree and worked the trunk into a chair. Poppa and Momma had rocked her and Sam in it. Sam and Diana had done the same for Tina, Elena, and Alex. All that history would be lost because of her. Tears pushed at the backs of her eyes. She blinked. She would not give Heinrich the satisfaction of seeing her cry.

Two porters arrived, both very small Chinese men. She hoped Heinrich would supervise their transfer to the ship at the dock in San Francisco, giving her the opportunity to escape in the evening rather than in the middle of the night. But he did not give up his guard over her. Instead he waved two bills at the porters and told them they would get it tomorrow, on the boat, if all of these belongings arrived safe and secure.

★★★

Her heart pounded as she lay in bed, May asleep next to her in a box on the floor. The bassinet had been taken away. Sadie rehearsed her plan. *Slip on my shoes. Get my coat. Grab May. Walk out the door.* She would not take anything else. Anxiety flooded through her; she wasn't worried about falling asleep.

She listened for Heinrich's sounds, waiting for the snore that indicated deep sleep. Long after she lay down, she heard it. Her back to him, she rose up. She turned to look at her husband.

He was sitting up, his eyebrows raised in a challenge. Her throat clenched. Heinrich was not going to let her go so easily.

"I have to use the water closet," she lied.

When the door was closed to the bathroom, she forced herself to take deep breaths. Sadie reminded herself, *You are not sailing yet. You still have time to get away.* She had many hours before the boat sailed. She would look for any opportunity to get away from Heinrich—even if she had to run into a crowd in San Francisco.

★★★

The morning was a blur, made more confusing by the lack of sleep. At Sam's, no one had to feign surprise or sorrow as they said hasty goodbyes. Heinrich watched with a look of triumph as Sadie hugged each family member in turn.

"Do not come to wave farewell at the dock," Heinrich ordered. "Sadie is having enough trouble with this transition. We will not add theatrics to our departure, so she will not be standing on the deck."

Momma looked defeated as she nodded to Heinrich, but when she gave Sadie one last hug, she whispered in her ear, "You get away from him. We will be waiting."

Sadie hugged Momma hard and whispered back, "I will."

Sadie welled up watching her family pass May around for hugs. The little girl had no concern or fears. What was going to become of their lives if she failed—or if she succeeded?

Heinrich stayed close to her side on the journey to the ship. He did not like May to be tied to her, so she carried the wiggly girl in her arms. It was not so easy now that May was older.

It took more than an hour to get from Oakland to the pier in San Francisco. She was not familiar with the ferry system, so she carefully observed the route so that she could get back.

Her throat swelled as they walked up the gangplank. The boat was large and forbidding. She noted another gangplank boarding people with dark hair and dark clothes. Chinese laborers would make their way home after the boat stopped in Hawaii, one of the first on this journey.

Heinrich held her elbow as he guided her to their stateroom. He opened the polished wooden door. It was a small but elegant space with a bed taking up the majority of the floor.

"Spreckels is expecting me," Heinrich declared. "You will wait here for me to return."

"Of course, Heinrich." This was her chance to escape.

"Do not explore the boat without me," he commanded.

She sat on the bed and looked at him demurely. "I have my book. I will read and take care of May."

"Spreckels is on the boat. I will not be far," he warned with a glare.

She nodded and clenched her lips downward, fighting her own emotion. He left, and she let her lips rise. She heard the turn of the key and a click. Adrenaline flooded her body. She swallowed hard. She crossed to the door and listened. She let five minutes pass before she turned the knob and pulled. The door did not budge.

Acting quickly, Sadie tied May to her back. She pulled a pin out of her hair, bent it, and went to work on the mechanism with the thin metal rod. Rather than turn the lock, the pin straightened. She needed a stronger tool. She looked around the room. A hair comb sat on the vanity. She pressed at some of the teeth until they broke away, leaving a gap with a few at the end.

She inserted the makeshift key into the lock and turned it until she felt resistance. She pushed steadily until the mechanism turned with a satisfying click. Slowly she opened the door. The hall was empty.

She stepped out, locked the door behind her, and walked away. Adrenaline coursed through her as she made her way cautiously to the exit; her eyes scanned the scene, on the lookout for Heinrich.

A porter reached out his arm to stop her at the top of the gangplank.

She jumped.

"Excuse me, ma'am." He asked, "Do you have your boarding papers?"

She nodded and lied, "Yes. I do. Thank you for taking care of me."

"We do not want you to be left behind," he said.

She smiled over her fear. "Of course not."

"You would be wise to return by five p.m.," he said. "After that it gets too busy."

"At night?" she asked.

He nodded. "We sail around eight, but the gangplank is pulled up by seven."

Sadie forced a smile and agreed. That was hours from now. Heinrich would have plenty of time to discover that she had left the ship.

CHAPTER TWENTY-SEVEN

JORDAN

Oakland
July 1895

The violent pounding on the door startled Jordan. She wasn't surprised that he'd come. Men like Heinrich did not give up so easily. She took a deep breath, hoping to slow her galloping heart, but it had no effect. She'd have to act calmer than she felt.

"Hello?" she called through the door.

"Do not pretend you do not know why I am here!" his voice screamed from the other side. The door jerked inward, accompanied by a loud bang. He was kicking it.

She yelled over the sound, "Give me a moment to unlock it!"

He stopped kicking. She turned the latch and opened the door. Framed in the sunlight, Lisbeth stood next to him, sorrow and defeat on her face. His hand grasped Lisbeth's arm so tightly that his fingers made deep indentations in the fabric. He thrust Lisbeth inside.

"Where is she?" he screamed, red-faced.

"Who?" Jordan feigned calm as well as innocence.

He leaned so close to her face that she felt his hot breath

as he growled, "Do not play with me!"

She resisted the urge to pull back. She was not going to let this man see her fear.

Without waiting for a reply, he stormed past her to the bedroom. Throwing open the door, he yelled, "Sadie, come here at once!"

Panic in her eyes, Lisbeth grabbed Jordan's arm. Jordan patted her hand. She put her finger to her lips and shook her head. Lisbeth must give nothing away.

Jordan heard sounds from the room as he overturned furniture and looked in the closet. He stormed out and looked around the open space. He crossed into the kitchen and opened the back door.

"Sadie! You must come with me," he yelled out. "The boat sails in four hours. There's no point in hiding."

Lisbeth clawed at Jordan. Jordan took her hand and brought her to the couch. "Sit here," she whispered. "Do not say a word."

Lisbeth nodded.

Mrs. King, Mr. King, and two people she didn't know came through the front door. Two men and two women stood around Lisbeth on the couch, a wall of support and protection.

Heinrich returned, bellowing, "Where is she?!"

"Mr. Wagner," Jordan said, "your wife is not here."

"I can see that," he said. Then he took notice of her neighbors.

"Are you hiding her?" he demanded.

"As the lady said, your wife is not here," Mr. King said. "I'm sorry you are having a hard time keeping track of her. You've interrupted our peace enough for today. Time to move along."

Heinrich stared at Mr. King, hatred burning in his eyes.

He opened and closed his fist. Then he looked down. They'd won.

He turned and stormed out of the house, leaving Lisbeth behind. Jordan held up her hand, signaling silence. She walked to the window. Heinrich was still out front. She went onto the stoop so he could see that she was aware of his presence.

"Good day, Mr. Wagner," she said, and gave him her most stern teacher look.

He turned away and walked toward downtown. She waited until he was out of sight before she went inside.

"He's gone—for now at least," she reported. She looked at her neighbors. "Thank you for coming over."

"You warned us you might need us." Mrs. King laughed.

"Where are Sadie and May?" Lisbeth whispered, her voice tight.

The door burst open. Jordan jumped along with the others. The crazed White man stormed to the couch, fury in his eyes.

"She is dead to me!" Heinrich leaned over Lisbeth and screamed—his finger striking her in the chest. "You tell her that she will not hear from me ever again."

And then he left as suddenly as he had come.

Jordan's heart beat so hard she felt it might explode. She looked around. Others looked as alarmed as she felt. She took a steadying breath.

"Are you hurt?" she asked Lisbeth.

Lisbeth's body was visibly shaking. She also took a breath and blinked back tears. She shook her head, as if to clear it, and whispered, "Where is my daughter?"

Jordan smiled. She looked at Mr. King, who was by the window.

"Is he gone?"

Mr. King nodded.

"With Naomi," Jordan replied. "Safe and sound."

Relief washed over Lisbeth's face.

"Thank you," Lisbeth said, tears in her eyes. "You knew better than we did."

"I know men like him," Jordan declared. "They go to great lengths to keep what they believe is theirs. I knew he'd remember us: The family who called Sadie to Chicago. The nurse that worked in his home."

He would not use that polite a term, but Jordan was not going to say the hateful word in her own home.

"Think it will be the last you see of him?" Mrs. King asked.

Lisbeth shrugged. "Perhaps he will keep his promise to never see Sadie again," she said. "Sam is at the docks, watching to see if he stays on the boat. We'll know in a few hours if he did. We believe he is too proud to admit to his employer that he could not control his wife. We hope he will leave and make up a story that suits his ego. If not . . ."

Lisbeth let the thought hang in the air. Jordan didn't know what they would do if Heinrich forced the issue.

"Thank you for coming," Lisbeth said to the Kings and the others.

Mrs. King said, "Any friend of Mrs. Wallace's is a friend of ours."

She introduced the others as they all left with assurances that they would be right upstairs if they needed anything.

When they were alone, Lisbeth asked, "We should stay here?"

Jordan nodded. "We don't want to lead him to them. Does Sam plan to come here after the boat sails?"

"Yes," Lisbeth said. Then she sighed. "This is going to be a long wait."

Jordan studied Lisbeth. She looked young and frightened.

Jordan suspected Lisbeth wasn't familiar with being in this situation: waiting to be reassured of a loved one's well-being with nothing to be done but pray.

Jordan was too well practiced at it. She was at once resentful and envious of Lisbeth's innocence. Without the constant underlying fear for her family's safety, life would be more joyful.

Lisbeth said, "I can't thank you enough. You've saved them once again."

Jordan smiled at Lisbeth.

"We owe so much to your family," Lisbeth remarked.

They sat in a comfortable silence, each in their own thoughts.

A tear in her eye, Lisbeth spoke up. "I miss knowing that Mattie is in the world."

Jordan's breath caught. "Me too."

"I know it is worse for you," Lisbeth said. "You saw her each day, so you cannot pretend she is still on this earth as I can. I often forget she is gone, and then it hits me with a fierce and sudden painful blow."

Jordan replied, "She visits in my dreams with a hug or a kind word. It is deeply comforting, until I wake and remember she is gone with a sadness so intense I cannot stop the tears."

Lisbeth smiled a bittersweet smile at Jordan. "We are two old women, missing so much—our husbands and our . . ." She looked uncertain as to what to say and stopped speaking.

"Yes, we are," Jordan said. "After Mama died, I thought I would never find delight ever again. And then I held your little May, and I knew that joy continues right next to the pain."

Lisbeth nodded. "Ordinary pleasures are sweeter after the pain of loss. I wondered how I could possibly go on without

Matthew, but I have found a way. I honor his memory better by finding hope rather than giving in to despair."

Jordan said, "We know Mama would want us to notice the beauty in each day and do all the good we can with the gift of our lives."

Lisbeth laughed. "She would indeed."

Jordan squeezed Lisbeth's hand. She and this woman had such a strange connection. It wasn't clear what they were to each other, but it was a comfort to have someone who loved and remembered Mama too.

"Should we put up green beans while we're waiting?" Jordan asked.

"It would be lovely to have a distraction," Lisbeth agreed.

CHAPTER TWENTY-EIGHT

SADIE

Oakland
July 1895

Sadie didn't realize her heart could beat so hard for so long. It had started racing when they'd left their apartment this morning and it had yet to stop. She felt she must move or she would burst.

May and Sadie had been with Naomi for several hours. Sadie had made her way to Jordan's without incident. Then Jordan had brought her here—to Naomi's—which was also Aunt Emily, Uncle William, and Cousin Willie's home. Aunt Emily was at work for the day, cleaning houses by Lake Merritt. Uncle William and Willie were away until next week, as was typical for a coal man and a conductor.

It was still strange, but delightfully so, that Naomi was now her cousin. They had not visited often since the marriage, but Sadie kept abreast of the news of Naomi's life from Jordan.

Sadie said to Naomi, "I am finding it difficult to contain my emotion. I'd like to take May for a walk, perhaps all the way to the cemetery."

"I'll join you," Naomi replied, "if you would care for

company."

"That would be most welcome," Sadie replied, relieved. "Thank you."

An hour later they walked through the gates of the Mountain View Cemetery. In the distance tall stones marked the burial place of the wealthy. Close by, small headstones lay flat on the ground. Sadie studied them as they walked in silence. Most of the words engraved on the stones were in English, but scattered among them were the languages of the world: French, German, Swedish, Turkish, Chinese. In death they were made the same. Husbands, wives, little angels. Some had long lives, others died too young.

"I'm sorry about your lost 'angel,' as your grandmother said to me," Sadie looked at Naomi.

The younger woman nodded, pain on her face.

"I'm so grateful for May," Sadie said, patting her daughter's back. "But she doesn't entirely erase the pain of my lost ones."

"Thank you for saying so," Naomi said. "I don't want to burden Mama or Willie with my sadness, but it is still there."

"I understand," Sadie replied. "I only shared my ongoing pain with my sister-in-law, Diana. Speaking with Momma only made my sorrow worse. I worried for Momma's sadness for me. And Heinrich . . . well, now I understand that his attitude was simply selfishness, not pain for us."

In silence, they climbed up a hill. Sadie thought of Heinrich and the many times he'd lashed out—and the explanations she had made for him for too many years. She'd been certain that once external circumstances had changed, he would become kinder and more respectful. She'd been a fool.

Spidery green leaves of poppy plants popped out of the surrounding grass. The glorious flower that covered the land only a few months ago had fallen away. The bright petals were gone, and the poppies had gone to seed. The top of each stem was dotted with tiny black orbs ready to fall to the ground. Many would never transform into anything else, but many would land on fertile soil at the right time. They would sprout, take root, and blossom into new golden poppies.

"I'd like to collect seeds," Sadie said.

"Wonderful idea," Naomi agreed. "I would love some as well."

Sadie pulled out a handkerchief. She bent over a green stalk and flicked the end. Dozens of dark balls flew into her hands. So many from just one plant. She repeated the process until she had hundreds of minuscule seeds piled up in the center of the white fabric. Naomi had collected an equal amount.

Satisfaction filled Sadie as she tied up the corners. She said, "In the fall I will scatter these."

"Right here in Oakland," Naomi declared.

Sadie smiled and nodded. *In Oakland,* she prayed.

They continued walking upward. At the top they looked out.

Naomi exclaimed, "It is beautiful. I've never climbed this high before."

Oakland spread out below, and the bay sparkled behind Sadie's beloved city. San Francisco rose from the opposite shore. She saw a small dot on the other side. That might be the boat she'd been on just a few hours before. *Dear God, please compel Heinrich to sail away—forever.*

"Where is the university from here?" Naomi asked.

Sadie pointed to her right and said, "I have never visited Berkeley—the town or the university." Then she looked ahead and pointed west—the direction she was desperate to avoid. "Through that opening is the Pacific Ocean."

Naomi gasped. Awe in her voice, she said, "I'm the first." She looked at Sadie, her eyes glistening. "I'm the first woman in my family to ever see the Pacific Ocean."

Sadie smiled and asked, "Did your mother tell you of our plan to cast Mattie's shell into it?"

Naomi nodded.

"I look forward to that outing," Sadie said. She didn't add *If we are able to stay here.*

May woke up. She leaned sideways, signaling her desire to eat. Naomi helped Sadie untie her daughter. They found shelter under the canopy of a large oak tree. As Sadie fed May, the little girl smiled and patted, unaware that her life was changing forever.

They stayed in the cemetery until they had just enough sunlight to make it home before dark. As they walked, fear rose in Sadie's throat. Heinrich might be in Oakland—lying in wait for her. *He cannot force you to move to another country—even if he is your husband,* she reminded herself.

She couldn't imagine he cared enough for her to surrender his position with Spreckels to be with her. He might argue and demand, but now that she had decided to be free of him, he no longer controlled her. She could even sue for divorce if she chose to, a right that many women in California exercised in these circumstances. She feared for her future, was uncertain about how she would possibly provide a home for herself and May. But she chanted silently with each step, *Our life will be better without him than with him.*

★★★

Well after dark, Jordan walked in, followed by Momma and Sam, who was dressed in the traditional black clothes of Chinese laborers. Sadie filled with joy to see them. As they stood in a circle in the living room, she stared at Sam, a question in her eyes.

"I followed you as we planned," Sam told her. "Did you see me?"

"I made myself ignore the possibility that you were there," Sadie replied.

Sam told the group, "One time Heinrich turned around, but he did not register any recognition. These pajamas were a good disguise. I watched you three board the ship.

"My heart was in my chest when I saw you speaking to the porter, and it was hard to let you walk away without me, but I stayed to track Heinrich." He continued, "About two hours after you left, Heinrich stormed off the ship. I followed him to our house, then to Miss Jordan's." Sam teared up. "Momma, I'm sorry I didn't stop him."

"What did he do?" Sadie demanded.

"Nothing I couldn't handle," Momma replied to Sadie. She looked right at her son. "You did what I asked, Sam. I may have a bruise tomorrow, nothing more. It is well worth it to have kept you two away from him." Momma nodded at Sadie, looking certain.

Another wave of shame passed through Sadie. How could she have put her family through this?

Sam returned to the story. "When he left your home"— Sam gestured toward Jordan—"Heinrich practically ran back to San Francisco and up the gangplank. I watched intently until the ship sailed away. I didn't see him get off." He shrugged, then declared, "I think he's gone!"

"Thank you, Lord!" Jordan exclaimed.

Relief surged through Sadie. She looked at Momma, who nodded.

Her blue eyes shiny with emotion, Momma looked at Naomi, Aunt Emily, and then Jordan.

"Thank you, all of you," Momma said. "And bless you."

The women smiled and nodded, their eyes shiny too.

"Mama would be proud of us!" Jordan said. "Like when we stood up to Mr. Richards to rescue Cousin Sarah from the plantation in Virginia."

Momma asked, "Do you remember that day, Sadie? You were so young."

"It's like a dream," Sadie replied. "I remember helping Miss Jordan up the stairs." She thought back. "Did we have a conversation about liberty?"

"We did." Jordan laughed. "My mama was impressed that a six-year-old girl expressed an opinion about the rights in the constitution."

"I remember the feeling of that day," Sadie said. "The triumph and the excitement. I suppose this day feels the same."

Momma looked at Sadie. "Are you worried Heinrich will return to cause trouble for you?"

Sadie said, "I'm telling myself there is no need to borrow trouble. If he comes, I will handle it. In the meantime, I'll hold on to hope that he is gone forever."

She looked at each face, gratitude filling her. These wonderful people had rallied around her and May. She would find a way to make a good home for her daughter. It would be hard, but she was determined that they would be a family like this one, full of generosity, kindness, and respect.

CHAPTER TWENTY-NINE

Jordan

Oakland
July 1895

They were gathering in the sanctuary at the Unitarian Church to organize the strategy for the campaign. Members from the Congregational, AME, Unitarian, and Presbyterian churches were meeting with Susan B. Anthony and the Rev. Anna Shaw. The vote would not occur until November of 1896—in more than a year—but they were marshaling every possible resource to ensure the success of the campaign.

Miss Anthony seemed a queen holding court. Excited to meet the acclaimed activist, Jordan stood with Naomi in a long line of women, and a few men, to greet her.

"It's an honor to meet you," Jordan said when she got to the front of the line. "I'm all the more honored to shake this hand, knowing you touched the great Sojourner Truth."

Miss Anthony sandwiched Jordan's smooth hand between her aged ones. She was commanding and powerful. Jordan's breath caught at the intensity of her gaze.

"She was a powerful soul. I am forever in her debt . . . and her service."

Jordan nodded, unable to find a verbal response. Miss

Anthony continued staring while grasping her hand. The esteemed woman's eyes glazed in thought.

"All I do is in service of the greater good for all," Miss Anthony said, sounding as if she were making an argument. Then she asked, "You are Miss Wells's colleague?"

Jordan nodded.

"I admire her greatly. Never doubt it," she commanded.

Jordan was confused by her statement. But before she could respond, the woman released her hand and reached out to Naomi.

They entered the large sanctuary, and Jordan scanned for Sadie and May, hoping for an opportunity to hold the baby. They were close to the front on the right side, and they were not alone. Lisbeth and Diana were sitting with them. Jordan and Naomi filled in the row, being certain to reserve a seat for Miss Flood, who had promised her attendance. Jordan reached out her hands, and Sadie passed May into her arms.

"Lisbeth, what a surprise!" Jordan said.

"I could not miss this opportunity to see Miss Anthony," Lisbeth replied. "I may not be as devoted as you all, but I am a supporter of the cause."

Diana declared, "This turnout is inspiring. With so many women organizing, we will win the day."

Not wanting to sully the mood with his name, Jordan did not ask about Heinrich. She trusted she would hear if he returned. In the weeks since the boat had sailed, he had kept his promise that he would abandon Sadie.

"Momma and I have decided to open a boardinghouse!" Sadie declared.

"That is a splendid idea," Jordan responded.

Sadie leaned in. "It seems the best way for two reputable women to support themselves in this town."

"Do you have a location?" she asked.

"Eleventh and Clay," she replied. "Momma signed the papers today. I will not be on them." She sighed.

Confusion must have shown on Jordan's face, because Sadie explained, "We do not want Heinrich to have any claim."

"You are clever to think of it," Jordan said.

"I have learned that I must be," Sadie said. "After we are settled, I would like to finally take you on that trip to the Pacific Ocean that you promised Mattie."

Jordan felt the shell in her pocket. She'd brought Mama's spirit along to this historic meeting.

"I look forward to that day," Jordan said, "though I believe we need to wait until we have the vote. How can I tell the ancestors we're free when we do not have the franchise?"

Sadie sighed. She took Jordan's hand and squeezed. "December 1896, then."

Jordan nodded with a smile.

The back of the room got suddenly quiet. Jordan turned. The leaders of the meeting marched down the aisle and onto the chancel. Reverend Tupper Wilkes opened with a stirring invocation that did not mention Jesus, only God, as the Unitarians were inclined.

Then woman after woman stood before them and spoke of their plans. The focus would be on organizing in the large cities. Resources had been pledged from around the nation. The example of women prevailing in California would then lead the way for the rest of our nation. Emphatic arguments declared that the time had come for women's participation in civic life.

When it was over, the crowd in the pews stood in ovation. Jordan clapped, carried by the spirit of hope and faith. She looked up at the Sower window. Seeds had been cast on fertile soil today. These women would take the message from this place and spread it around the great County of Alameda. Miss Anthony stood before them nodding in encouragement and appreciation. Jordan felt a tap on the shoulder.

A young German woman surprised Jordan by stating, "Miss Anthony would like to speak with you and your party privately. Please wait for her in the Starr King room."

The command was made without any doubt of their cooperation. They were to have a special meeting with Miss Anthony. Miss Wells's message must have brought them to her attention. Excitement stirred in Jordan.

★★★

After the applause ended, they made their way to the other side of the building to an empty room. Jordan, Naomi, Miss Flood, Lisbeth, and Sadie waited in hard wooden chairs. No doubt Miss Anthony would be detained by a long line of admirers.

Little May sat on Jordan's lap. The growing girl was all smiles. It was hard to believe how precarious her beginning had been. Her bright hazel eyes and round cheeks were like a magnet that pulled out delight.

Jordan and May were partway through a game of patty-cake when Miss Anthony entered. Jordan felt the urge to rise in her presence, but Miss Anthony sat down immediately.

"I have a duty that is both unpleasant and necessary." Miss Anthony spoke without making any eye contact; instead she looked between their heads to the cloud of invisible witnesses. She declared, "Unlike too many of my colleagues, I do not hold to the notion of the superiority of the Anglo-Saxon race."

Jordan's stomach rose high and hard into her throat.

"For decades my mind, heart, body, and soul have been set on universal suffrage," Miss Anthony continued. She stopped and looked intently first at Miss Flood, then at Naomi, and finally at Jordan. "You know Mr. Douglass was a dear friend, despite his willingness to put the good of the men of his race over the rights of our gender. I believed the Fifteenth Amendment should have included us; he was willing to take a partial victory."

Jordan felt dread spread into her limbs. She knew what was to come next.

"We must strategize for the long term," she explained. "I am a practical woman whose patience has ended. I will see that women have the vote before I leave this earth by whatever means necessary. Universal suffrage for all is still the goal. When I have achieved the franchise for myself, I will have achieved it for you as well.

"To that end, you must remain in the background. It is the only way for us to achieve success. I am sorry that the painful truth of this nation is that we are still not resolved to living in unity with each flourishing of their own accord. But I am confident that with the franchise, women, all women, will chart a better course for our nation. Miss Wells has been told of this painful plan."

Shame and sorrow swelled in Jordan. She wanted to argue, but didn't. She couldn't even look at her daughter.

Miss Anthony looked at them, her face hard. "Good day. And thank you for your understanding."

She ended, making it clear that this was not a discussion, simply a fact. Jordan's brown skin was a liability to the cause. She and others like her must be made invisible for women to win the vote.

Miss Anthony had assumed Jordan would be understanding. Modern technology meant images from the events of today, in California, would be published in newspapers throughout the country. The suffragist did not want Jordan's face to result in Southern White women abandoning the cause.

This was no different than the message conveyed by the planners of the Columbian Exposition. The plight of Negroes could not be publicized for the tarnish it would put on the shining nation on a hill.

Fury rose in Jordan. Her chest tightened and her head pulsed in rage. She took a deep breath to appear calm.

She had once again imagined that *this* time, in *this* place, she would not find abuse on account of her race. And once again she had been wrong. She touched the fabric over the shell in her pocket. *Sorry, Mama. We're still not free.*

★★★

They walked from the stone building, each lost in stunned silence. Jordan still held May in her arms. She looked at the White baby; despite her innocence, it was hard not to revile her, knowing that she too might cast away the darker race for her own advancement.

In front of the church, at the corner of Castro and Fourteenth Streets, Lisbeth paused. The women looked as if they wished to cry, but none let their tears spill over.

Lisbeth said in a quiet voice, "I'm so ashamed. I do not know what to say."

Jordan replied, "There is nothing to be said. Her sentiments are the truth of this world. Our people are trampled and then blamed for lying on the ground."

Lisbeth wiped at the corner of her eye with a finger. Jordan looked at Sadie, at May, and then finally at Naomi. Her heart softened.

"We will be all right," Jordan reassured . . . Lisbeth, Naomi, herself? She did not know. "Despite the insults and abuse, perhaps because of them, we will find the strength to believe in a better tomorrow. It may take one hundred years, but someday we will have equal treatment and equal respect. I can't say when it will happen, sometimes I fear it never will, but I have to believe it is possible, for without a vision a people will perish."

She looked at the despondent faces around her. She wanted to give her daughter hope with her words, as her mother had done for her so often. Jordan reached into her pocket and fingered the shell that had journeyed so far.

"I am the fruit of my grandmother's labor . . . she never met me, but she dreamed of what I could be. I can do no less for my grandchildren." Jordan patted May's back. "For all our children we must plant the seeds of a liberty tree that they may eat the fruit of justice we will never taste."

She kissed the top of May's sweet head, and passed her back to Sadie.

Jordan swallowed her sorrow and forced a poignant smile. "I guess I have more of my mama in me than I realized."

"Yes." Lisbeth looked right at Jordan and replied with a tender, moist-eyed smile. "You do."

And then they parted ways.

EPILOGUE

SADIE

Oakland
July 1895

I had never seen my mother look so defeated. Not after Poppa's death. Not after Mattie's last breath. Her spirit seemed to fly away from her body with Miss Anthony's words.

"I should not have come," she forced through a tight voice. "I do not want to know that the world is still this cruel."

I tried to reassure her. "Jordan seemed to understand the need for this strategy."

Momma replied, "Are you so willing to throw away one kind of people to advantage another?"

"No," I replied, feeling the sting of her challenge.

Teary, Momma said, "I desperately want to believe that the ugliness of the past is behind us. That we have moved past doubting we can be one nation with liberties equally given."

"We may not be entirely unified in that understanding, but we are making great strides," I argued, feeling it deep in my soul. As if convincing my momma would make my argument true.

Momma replied, "If a woman as strong and great as Susan

B. Anthony cannot hold fast to the dream, how can I?"

Hugging May close, I felt the weight and the possibility of her precious life. I wished I had a certain answer to my momma's question, but I was only able to muster, "For her sake, how can we not?"

AUTHOR'S NOTE

I knew I wanted to continue with the story of these families. Even when I wrote *Mustard Seed*, I thought they would all end up in Oakland. In that novel I put Sadie's uncle, Matthew's brother, in California.

I'd heard of the Pullman Strike, but knew very few details about it. And I knew the Pullman porters led to the large black middle class in Oakland. I read details about the Pullman Strike from newspapers in that time period. They led me to Ida B. Wells and her anti-lynching campaign, the suffrage movement in California, and the anti-miscegenation laws. All good material for these families to wrestle with.

Most of the details in the novel are historically accurate. Despite the Southern strategy that left black women out of the movement, Ida B. Wells speaks of her admiration of Susan B. Anthony in her autobiography. Miss Anthony's dialogue in the end is fiction.

ACKNOWLEDGMENTS

My gratitude is overflowing for all that has conspired to allow me to bring the stories of my heart and soul into being.

I'm deeply indebted to the readers who have reviewed, purchased, and spread the word about my novels.

Thank you to

- Σ the early readers whose kind and honest feedback made this story better—Rinda Bartley, Gogi Hodder, Sheri Prud'homme, Liz Ford, Kayla Haun, Hannah Franco-Isaacs, Margie Biblin, Darlanne Mulmat, Charlotte Dickson, Cathy Cade, Jacqueline Duhart, Sherry Weston-Vigil, and Kathy Post.

- Σ all the wonderful people at Amazon Publishing, Lake Union, and Amazon Crossing that bless me with their hard work and devotion to bring these stories to readers around the world: Jodi Warshaw, Gabriella Dumpit, Tiffany Yates Martin, Danielle Marshall, Jeffrey Belle, Mikyla Bruder, Hai-Yen Mura, Alex Levenberg, Nicole Pomeroy, Erin C., Laura Barrett, and all of you whose names I don't know (extra shout-out to marketing!!).

- Σ Terry Goodman—always!

- Σ my agent—Annelise Robey of Jane Rotrosen Agency.

- Σ my family in its many forms.

RESOURCES

These resources were invaluable in making the historical details more accurate:

Visions Toward Tomorrow: The History of the East Bay Afro-American Community, 1852–1977, by Lawrence P. Crouchett, Lonnie G. Bunch III, and Martha Kendall Winnacker

Black Chicago: The Making of a Negro Ghetto, 1890–1920, by Allan H. Spear

Rising from the Rails: Pullman Porters and the Making of the Black Middle Class, by Larry Tye

Lives of the Dead at Oakland's Mountain View Cemetery, by Michael Colbruno and Dennis Evanosky

Railroads in the African American Experience, by Theodore Kornweibel Jr.

Crusade for Justice: The Autobiography of Ida B. Wells, by Ida B. Wells; edited by Alfreda M. Duster

The Reason Why the Colored American Is Not in the World's Columbian Exposition, by Ida B. Wells, Frederick Douglass, Irvine Garland Penn, and Ferdinand L. Barnett; edited by Robert W. Rydell

"Beyond Boundaries: Controversies, Frontiers, and Growth in Unitarian Universalism," convocation speech by Tisa Wenger

Iola Leroy, or Shadows Uplifted, by Frances Ellen Watkins Harper

African American Women in the Struggle for the Vote, 1850–1920, by Rosalyn Terborg-Penn

Southern Horrors: Lynch Law in All Its Phases, by Ida B. Wells

From Labor to Reward: Black Church Beginnings in San Francisco, Oakland, Berkeley, and Richmond, 1849–1972, by Martha C. Taylor

Child Labor in America: A History, by Chaim M. Rosenberg

A City for Children: Women, Architecture, and the Charitable Landscapes of Oakland, 1850–1950, by Marta Gutman

How We Won the Vote in California, by Selina Solomons

The Women of the Suffrage Movement: Autobiographies & Biographies of the Most Influential Suffragettes, by Elizabeth Cady Stanton, Emmeline Pankhurst, Anna Howard Shaw, Millicent Garrett Fawcett, Jane Addams, Alice Stone Blackwell, Ida Husted Harper

History of Woman Suffrage, Volume I, edited by Susan B. Anthony, Elizabeth Cady Stanton, Matilda Joslyn Gage

The History of Woman Suffrage, Volume IV, edited by Ida Husted Harper and Susan B. Anthony

Becoming Citizens: The Emergence and Development of the California Women's Movement, 1880–1911, by Gayle Gullett

The Negro Trail Blazers of California, by Delilah Leontium Beasley

"Lydia Flood Jackson" (web page), Black Past: www. blackpast.org/aaw/jackson-lydia-flood-1862-1963

"Truth-Telling: Frances Willard and Ida B. Wells" (documentation of the verbal conflict between Ida B. Wells and Frances Willard), Scalar: http://scalar.usc.edu/ works/willard-and-wells/introduction?path=index

"Perez v. Sharp," (California Civil Code outlawing interracial marriage), Wikipedia: https://en.wikipedia.org/wiki/ Perez_v._Sharp

Historical editions of the *Chicago Inter Ocean*, *Chicago Tribune*, *Oakland Tribune*, and the *San Francisco Call* accessed at Newspapers.com

BOOK DISCUSSION

1. How do you believe Jordan's personal losses led to her despondency about the state of the world?

2. Why did Sadie make so many excuses for Heinrich's behavior?

3. Willie was prepared to keep his personal life private for a financial advantage. Do you believe he was wise to do so? Have you, or anyone in your family, chosen to hide a part of yourself to be more successful in the world?

4. Heinrich attributes his behavior to being German. Do you believe his excuse? Have you heard a characterization of any other culture to explain abuse?

5. What made Jordan come to peace with Naomi's decision to marry Willie?

6. Given what you know about the world, do you believe it was brave or foolish for Naomi and Willie to marry each other?

7. At the end of the novel, Lisbeth says, "I do not want to know that the world is still this cruel." Have you ever read something or seen something that caused you to feel similarly?

8. This novel is set in the Gilded Age during the industrial revolution. How are the effects of the digital revolution similar and different to the Gilded Age?

9. How does Susan B. Anthony's strategy for getting the

vote for women strike you? Is it good to take a partial win for a civil right?

10. Were there any historical details that were surprising or entirely unknown to you?

11. Who was your favorite character and why?

12. At the end of the novel, is Jordan speaking to comfort Lisbeth, Naomi, or herself? Does she believe her own words?

13. Do you believe these two families will continue to be close now that Mattie, the matriarch, has died?

ABOUT THE AUTHOR

Photo © 2014 by Roots and Shoots Photography

Laila Ibrahim spent much of her career as a preschool director, a birth doula, and a religious educator. That work, coupled with her education in developmental psychology and attachment theory, provided ample fodder for the story lines of her bestselling novels: *Paper Wife*, *Mustard Seed*, and *Yellow Crocus*.

She's a devout Unitarian Universalist, determined to do her part to add a little more love and justice to our beautiful and painful world. She lives with her wonderful wife, Rinda, and two other families in a small cohousing community in Berkeley, California. Her young adult children are her pride and joy.

Laila is blessed to be working full-time as a novelist. When she isn't writing, she likes to take walks with friends, do jigsaw puzzles, play games, work in the garden, travel, cook, and eat all kinds of delicious food. Visit the author at www.lailaibrahim.com or on Facebook at www.facebook.com/lailaibrahim.author.